ALSO BY ALJEAN HARMETZ

The Making of *The Wizard of Oz*: Movie Magic and Studio Power in the Prime of MGM—and the Miracle of Production #1060

Rolling Breaks and Other Movie Business

On the Road to Tara: The Making of *Gone With the Wind*

Round Up the Usual Suspects: The Making of *Casablanca*—Bogart, Bergman, and World War II

OFF THE FACE OF THE EARTH

ALJEAN HARMETZ

SCRIBNER

S

SCRIBNER
1230 Avenue of the Americas
New York, NY 10020

SCRIBNER and design are trademarks of Simon & Schuster Inc.

DESIGNED BY ERICH HOBBING

Set in Bembo

Manufactured in the United States of America

10   9   8   7   6   5   4   3   2   1

Library of Congress Cataloging-in-Publication Data

Harmetz, Aljean
Off the face of the earth/Aljean Harmetz.
p.   cm.
I. Title.
PS3558.A6242955048   1997
813'.54—dc 21   96–40345
                              CIP

ISBN 0-684-83617-3

To
Rose Meltzer Martell and Anthony, Daniel, and Elizabeth Harmetz
who form the bookends of my life

OFF
THE
FACE
OF
THE
EARTH

CHAPTER 1

No one had reported that David Greene was missing because no one had missed him yet. Two hours ago, with the bravura that always unnerved his third grade teacher—she had been speechless last week when he brought a box of snails to weigh and measure for his science project—David had sat in the kitchen and called his brother a "suckdick" in a deliberately loud voice.

As he had planned, he was sent to solitary confinement a minute later. "Inappropriate language," as his mother phrased it, was one of a dozen things punished by at least an hour of contemplating the walls of his bedroom. They were garish walls, since Drew Greene had celebrated her divorce by allowing both boys to redecorate their rooms. Kiley, who was five, had been talked into pale blue walls with his choice of Disney characters on the curtains. David, who was eight and too angry to be talked into anything nowadays, had alternated navy blue paint with stripes of red across a white ceiling, leaving the impression that he lived inside an American flag.

As soon as he had closed—slammed, for emphasis—the door

of his room, David had pulled his knapsack from the pile of books and Nintendo games under his bed and started to pack. He was an untidy but surprisingly well-organized child; the shoe boxes of baseball cards that filled two shelves of his bookcase were sorted by team, batting averages, and—when he was bored with those configurations—alphabetically by position. David had run away twice before, and the anticipation had been considerably more pleasurable than the event. So this Saturday afternoon, he packed thoughtfully, tossing a sweater and flashlight on top of the comic books, Hershey bar, baseball mitt, colored markers, polished rocks, magnetic Scrabble Jr., and snack packs of peanut butter and crackers. It was a warm afternoon but, last time, his mother had not found him until after dark.

When he pushed open his window screen and slid on to the sill, David pricked his knee on a nail. He slapped at his leg and dropped into a bed of drought-resistant rosemary that his mother had planted midway through the six-year California drought. The Greenes were—had been—that kind of family: earnest, knowledgable, environmentally sound. For a second, the smell of crushed rosemary jolted the air. Then David was gone, leaving behind one oblong drop of blood.

"Tell David he can come out now." Drew Greene nudged Kiley. "You tell him."

"Tell him we can go for pizza."

It was a double bribe. Although Kiley knew that his mother hoped the offer of pizza would put David in a good mood, he was unaware that he was being bribed to act as messenger. He ran down the hall to his brother's bedroom, unconscious of the fact that his mother was using him as a shield. He would deflect or at least delay the dragonrage of her older son.

"Mommy!"

Drew knew, even before Kiley announced his brother's absence.

"David's not there."

Drew's first reaction was anger. Her second, so close to the first that there was hardly time to take a breath between them, was guilt. The blood on the sill had dried, but the screen hung open and the signature of tennis shoes still imprinted the soft ground. For a second she imagined tracking her son by the smell that had to linger on his legs and socks. "There's rosemary; that's for remembrance." She had been an English major at Stanford, and tag ends of great literature were stored on open shelves inside her brain. Automatically, she closed and locked the screen, and guilt flicked back into anger, like the switch on a rearview mirror being popped back and forth between day vision and night vision.

"Can we still have pizza?" Kiley asked. But his tone said, "Without David, we won't go anywhere," and Drew—too angry now to feel guilty about her older son—was suffused with guilt for the younger one, who was doomed by order of birth to forever tag along.

She bent down and kissed his forehead, her lips brushing sand-colored hair.

"Please, Mommy," Kiley said.

Drew hesitated.

"Please."

"All right," she said. David was probably hiding at Danny's house, like the last time. Making him wait an extra half hour to be rescued might be good for him. "We'll go for pizza. Just the two of us. As soon as I make a few telephone calls."

Drew made three phone calls and reached three answering machines.

The first two calls were similar in content although different in tone.

"Hi, Laura. My escape artist has done it again. Maybe I should invest in handcuffs. Listen, I'm sure he'll end up with Danny again, so please feed him something and keep him for me. I promised Kiley pizza. It won't take long, and we'll swing by your house afterward." The last time, David had hid for an hour in the lower branches of Danny Matranga's avocado tree.

"Emily? It's Drew Greene. I wonder if David might have come over to play with Josh. If you see him, I'd appreciate your giving me a call."

The third phone call was to her ex-husband. Her fingers dialed the number efficiently, despite the efforts her brain made to disconnect. Drew was efficient even when she preferred not to be. What Drew dreaded was hearing Chuck's casual machine words: "Tiffani and I aren't in right now. Leave your number and we'll call you back as soon as possible." The fact that Chuck had left her for another woman was understandable. That he had left her for twenty-two-year-old Tiffani—spelled with an i—infuriated her.

Drew tried to make her voice bland, but neutrality had never been her strong suit. Her voice and her face usually gave her away. "Chuck, it's Drew." She always left her name, as though the divorce that had cancelled nine years of marriage had also erased his recognition of sounds. "David has run away again. It's after five o'clock now, and Kiley and I are going to get some pizza. Then I'll cruise the neighborhood. But he might call you to be picked up before it gets dark."

David Greene had already called his father, from the old-fashioned, wall-hung pay phone in the food court at the Sherwood Galleria. The handicapped pay phone, at a suitable height for wheelchairs and children, was out of order. The other phone was too high for David, and it had taken him three tries to put his dimes in the right slot and to punch the proper area code. He had learned a lot of things in the eighteen months since his parents had separated. There are skills involved in being a child of divorce.

Like his mother, David listened to his father's voice on the answering machine, but he didn't leave a message. He wanted to frighten his father. The answering machine would not be afraid or impressed that he had crossed two boulevards he was not allowed to cross and was now standing on the fourth floor of the Sherwood Galleria where he was never to go without an adult.

David fished for his dimes. His father would probably just have had his mother pick him up anyway. Maybe he'd wander around the mall for a couple of hours, buy some baseball cards. There was no one to stop him. Had they missed him yet? He'd call his mother after she'd had a chance to get really worried. Maybe they could stop for pizza on the way home.

He was wearing, as his mother would later tell the police, tan shorts, his favorite Ace Ventura T-shirt, nondescript twenty-dollar tennis shoes because she had refused to buy him seventy-dollar Air Nikes, and a stained blue backpack purchased for his first week at day camp two summers earlier. Dozens of people must have seen David Greene, but no one noticed him as he slipped into the jet stream of the crowd. The parents were far above his eye level, and the children were too self-absorbed. He vanished on a warm Saturday afternoon in May from a mock art deco mall in a pleasant city surrounded by but not yet totally contaminated by Los Angeles. The Sherwood Galleria had never had a carjacking or a rape. The weekend's graffiti was painted over every Monday, and there was rarely more than one BMW or Ford Bronco stolen from the parking garage each month. It was, on the relative scale of Southern California in the 1990s, a safe place.

Almost the last person to admit to seeing David Greene was a sixteen-year-old boy who was making fruit shakes at The Yogurt Garden about twenty yards from the pay phone. What had caught his eye, he told a policeman on Tuesday, was how patiently the boy kept starting over. It must have taken him ten minutes to make his call.

That was seventy-two hours later. By then, three snapshots of David Greene had been slipped out of the most recent family album, leaving rectangular blank spaces among the seductively smiling images. With a picture of David in his head, the policeman closed his eyes and imagined the boy standing on tiptoe in dirty white shoes. Detective Sergeant Angus West was good at imagining things, too good, although that was not the reason he had buried himself in the Sherwood Police Department. He froze for a second, as though smelling the air for some trace of the lost boy. But the trail was cold. The storage lockers and storerooms would have to be searched, but he knew that the boy would not be found here. Whether David Greene was alive or dead, he was no longer in the Sherwood Galleria.

CHAPTER 2

At the moment when her life changed forever, Drew Greene was holding the remains of a large cheese pizza. It would have been pepperoni if David had been along, but Kiley was still in the bland, white stage of early childhood, filled with macaroni, mashed potatoes, and vanilla ice cream. Kiley had rightly understood that the huge cheese pizza this evening was his reward for being more malleable than David. He usually had to eat around the greasy spots that were left after his mother removed the pepperoni from his slice.

Most days are imitations of what came before and what will follow. It is not just that the same amount of coffee is measured into the same white filters or that the sheets are changed each Wednesday. It is that these acts draw out the same emotions, so that living becomes as rote as multiplication tables, until it is broken by a crisis at work, a wedding, a funeral, a straight-A report card, or a car accident. From the vantage point of year's end or graduation, one can look back at hills and valleys, but most of the walking seems to be over level ground.

For Drew Greene, the panic started when she returned home a few

15

minutes after 8 P.M. The Matrangas's backyard had been searched twice, and Danny had been pushed to the edge of tears before the adults believed that he really hadn't seen David and didn't know where his friend might be hiding. From the telephone in the Matranga kitchen, while the children built a Lego castle on the floor, Drew made a dozen calls. No one had seen David. And Chuck's answering machine still repeated the same bloodless message.

Laura handed Drew a cup of coffee. "He won't get lost. He's a competent kid."

"I know."

The boys were still covered by Chuck's health plan. The first time David ran away—three months earlier—they had sent him for the allowed two visits with a psychologist at Chuck's HMO. David was, Dr. Rosen had assured them, a perfectly normal little boy with a great deal of anger and a deep level of disappointment in his parents—par for the course after a divorce. It would be best to give him as much love as he would tolerate, but continue to make him set the table and put his dirty clothes in the hamper. The Greenes were also advised to forget about tampering with David's psyche unless absolutely necessary. David was, soothed the doctor, too intelligent to put himself in real danger.

"Where's David?"

Kiley pulled at the sleeve of his mother's sweatshirt as they drove in circles through the familiar streets. He had been half asleep for the last twenty minutes, lulled by the car's geometric ballet. Up this block and down the next and around the corner and up this block in the long, lazy twilight, until the sun was suddenly extinguished in the Pacific Ocean.

Drew tried to say, "He's probably home by now," but couldn't. The Greenes were never parents who told their children that vaccinations didn't hurt and life was fair. "I hope he's home by now," she said. But that cautious hope turned to terror when she opened the door of the dark house, holding Kiley with one hand and the lukewarm pizza with the other.

"And there was darkness over Camelot." As usual, Drew's brain autonomously deflected life with literature. But this time

16

she could not replace the malfunctioning emotional battery with the nine-volt intellectual one. She felt as though she had swallowed a spoonful of molten steel. David hated the dark. Odd that her younger boy had slept without a night-light since infancy, while David needed night-light, hall light, and a blanket to cover his stuffed animals so that no vampires or werewolves could find them while he slept. What genes made one child slide out of the womb content with the change of scenery while the other was a testy traveler from the moment the journey began? Kiley embraced the days and slept soundly at night. David hated to be alone in the dark and would never deliberately hide in it.

Drew called the police immediately. The number was pasted to the bottom of the kitchen phone, along with the numbers for the fire department and the Los Angeles poison control center. She had dutifully taped the numbers to the phone when they were sent home by David's nursery school four years ago, but she had never dialed any of them before. She was thirty-three years old and she had never been burglarized or mugged, never had a kitchen fire that she couldn't smother with salt, never had her well-watched children climb into the high, locked cabinets where she kept the silver polish and Draino. When Drew turned the telephone over, she saw that, instead of writing "Greene" in the name space, she had written, "I am David's mother," and she remembered the pride she had felt in the fact of those words.

"Sherwood police."

Beneath the panic Drew was surprised to feel self-conscious, as though she were taking part in some bizarre, under-rehearsed play.

"My son is missing."

The drama of the statement had no effect on the neutral voice at the other end of the phone. Routed through another neutral voice that was waiting for the usual Saturday night car thefts and drunk drivers—intensified because this was Memorial Day weekend—she was handed off to a Sergeant Townsend, who seemed to be in charge of odds and ends.

"How old is he, ma'am?"

"Eight."

The sergeant, who was reaching into the box of doughnuts that would sustain him through this night shift, pulled his hand back. "Tell me what happened. How long has he been missing?" Sergeant Townsend, who lived in a tract house in Carson, was contemptuous of the sloppily permissive parents of Sherwood. His own six children had pulled weeds and walked the neighbors' dogs to earn their spending money, while Sherwood's video arcade and pizza parlors were full of sixth graders with ten-dollar allowances in the pockets of their name-brand jeans. Still, eight year olds were rarely sent off with a ten-dollar bill and orders to stay out of their parents' hair until midnight.

"I sent him to his room around two o'clock."

"Someone broke into your house?"

"No. David ran away. But . . ."

"Has he run away before?"

"Twice. But . . ."

Sergeant Townsend was no longer listening. He was already concentrating on his next doughnut and made the choice of a glazed maple twist. Before morning, he would eat half a dozen doughnuts as he did every night. He weighed two hundred and forty pounds, and his only exercise was walking from his desk to the coffeepot. He would retire in six months if he didn't have a fatal heart attack first.

"He's probably trying to scare you," the sergeant said with a soothe-the-little-lady heartiness. "Have you called his friends?"

Drew tried to regain his attention by shouting. "I've been look-ing for him since four. David would never stay out alone after dark. Something's happened—" She had started to say, "Some-thing's happened to him," but the words seemed too final, and she choked them off.

Her barely controlled anger had some effect. "Why did the boy run away?"

"We had a fight," she said. "We were playing a game, and David got angry." They had been playing Clue, and Kiley had confused the lead pipe with the wrench and insisted he didn't have the con-servatory when he did. And David had thrown his cards down and shoved the board and asked why things couldn't be the way they used to be, with his father playing instead of Kiley. Drew had suggested that he pack the game when he went to visit his father the next time. "Tiffani's as lame as Kiley," David had said.

"I'd give it another hour or two," the sergeant said. "Maybe you and your husband can check . . ."

"I'm divorced," Drew said curtly. "And I can't get in touch with my ex-husband. I've been trying for hours."

"Do you have custody, ma'am?" The sergeant's voice had changed, although Drew didn't know why.

"Yes," she said.

"Maybe your husband wanted the boy."

Drew understood that "wanted the boy" was the sergeant's euphemism for "stole the boy." "Chuck would never steal David," she said.

The sergeant plowed comfortably on. Now the field was well rutted. For every homicidal maniac snatching children, there were dozens of angry fathers eager to get a little revenge on their ex-wives. "Where does your ex-husband live?"

"Chuck would never steal David," Drew said again.

"Maybe the boy wanted your husband," the sergeant said.

Drew gave a description of David and the address of Charles Greene's apartment in Encino. Later, when Kiley had been read three chapters of *Rabbit Hill* and had fallen asleep across the foot of her bed, Drew emptied the dishwasher, swept the floor and sorted toys, the mechanical routine deflecting thought until she sat cross-legged on the floor picking up Clue and discovered that David had taken the solution cards—murderer, weapon, and place where the murder was committed—with him. No one could complete a game of Clue until he returned. She rocked back and forth, her brown hair falling in her eyes as she hugged the game.

Around 10:30, the LAPD did the Sherwood police a favor and cruised the apartment building where Chuck Greene lived. Since it was one of those old-fashioned two-story garden courts with eight apartments encircling a small, kidney-shaped swimming pool, no breaking and entering was required. The police knocked politely on the door, got no answer, and left.

At 3 A.M. another patrol car stopped. This time the police pounded more emphatically. There was still no answer, and one half of the double parking space for apartment four was still empty.

Drew was asleep by then, her feet resting against Kiley's ribs, subliminally taking comfort in the warmth of his body against her toes. She had not expected to fall asleep. She had gone from room to room turning on all the lights—even the closet lights—so that the house had become a giant beacon to welcome David home. Flooded with light, she had sat on her bed keeping a vigil. But, sometime after 2 A.M., she had been overthrown by sleep, and she slept until dawn. When she woke, her first thought was that she had failed some kind of test. Methodically she switched off the lights. Then she brushed her teeth and called the police.

A new voice—Sergeant Townsend had walked out of Drew's life several hours earlier—told her that an APB had been issued for Chuck's 1992 Toyota Corolla. If he were still in California, the Highway Patrol would probably spot his car.

"If he's still in California? He has to teach tomorrow." Chuck Greene taught American history to eleventh graders at Sherwood High School.

"Tomorrow's a holiday," said the voice.

"Tuesday then. He has to teach on Tuesday."

"In these cases," said the voice, "lots of times they head for the state line."

"And if David isn't with Chuck?" "If"—conjunction meaning "supposing that." Horrified by her own words, Drew realized that she had allowed the possibility that David was with Chuck, that her ex-husband who was so inept at the routine of taking care of children—from changing diapers to finding the soccer practice field—had inexplicably kidnapped their son. "You have to look for my son," she said. "I'll bring pictures."

"I want David," Kiley said. He was wearing David's hand-me-down pajamas, the *Teenage Mutant Ninja Turtles II* design marking the year of purchase as accurately as fossils are dated by the rocks which hold them. The T-rex from *Jurassic Park* that stampeded across Kiley's other pajamas would always shriek 1993. "Where's David? I want David."

They were sitting at the kitchen table, looking at each other across bowls of untouched cereal. "I want David, too," Drew said. But she was incapable of leaving it at that. She went through life educating, lecturing, questioning, teaching. Did David know that the Norse gods Odin, Thor, and Frigg gave their names to the days of the week? Did Kiley want to follow the garbage truck back to the dump? When Kiley was born, the baby nurse that they had hired for a week overheard Drew explaining something to David and told Chuck, "She's talking to that boy in a way he won't understand until he's twelve years old." Stoned on the high of being a real family—they were both only children—at last, Drew and Chuck had mocked the nurse in whispers. But Drew, who amused herself by doing cryptograms in her head, did have an endless need to analyze, synthesize, and, most of all, to ask questions. Even for the children, it was embarrassing to sit in a restaurant and listen to their mother questioning the waitress about the components of every dish on the menu. For Chuck, it was torture.

"I have to go to the police station. They have computers that can do all sorts of things . . ." Drew realized she was giving Kiley too much information and started over. "I'm going to try to find David. I'll see if you can play with Sam while I'm gone."

Kiley shook his head.

Sam, almost ten months older, was the kid all the other kindergarten boys wanted to sit next to, but Kiley shook his head again. "No. I want to stay with you."

She pulled him on to her lap. "You can't, pumpkin. But I'll come back soon."

His shoulder dug into her breast as he burrowed into her chest, too big now for the special game they had invented when he was two. "Then I want to stay with Daddy."

"Daddy's gone away for a little while."

"Did he take David with him?"

Drew was struck, for perhaps the thousandth time, by the things her children knew without knowing that they knew them. When David was four, he had warned her against the man who put new soles and heels on her shoes. "He's a bad man," David had said. "I'm like a dog, and I can smell bad things." She had switched to a different shoe repair shop, and a few months later the man whom David had scented was arrested for forging checks. Now she was reminded again how sharp smell and touch and instinct are before they are blunted by reason.

Kiley kicked at the table. "I want you. I want Daddy. I want Grandma."

Comfort food, Drew thought. Mommy, daddy, grandma. As she dialed her mother's phone number, she tried it out in her head. "I want my mommy." But she didn't.

Ruth Miller had betrayed Drew in the same way Drew had betrayed David. Was divorce a multigenerational bonding? Her father had vanished when she was three, leaving in Drew's mind a single memory, of having her hands slapped when she reached for something—she couldn't remember what—that belonged to him.

"Hello." Ruth talked as briskly as she moved. "Hello. Damn it, Brisket, get off the cord."

"Mom?"

"Drew?"

There was always something tentative in their greeting, as though Ruth had a dozen other daughters and Drew hadn't quite picked a mother yet.

"Mom, could you stay with Kiley this afternoon?"

The only answer was passionate barking followed by a number of yelps and an angry, "Pasha, that's Brisket's biscuit."

"Mom, I hate to ask you to drive in, but Kiley wants you."

"The boys and I have tracking practice this afternoon. I'll come tomorrow."

The boys were three golden retrievers, each bigger and more boyish than the last. They were Drew's younger brothers, the children of Ruth's menopause, bathed once a week in Pro-coat to put a shine in their fur, flea-combed every day, taken to agility lessons on Monday mornings and tracking practise on the weekends when there were no obedience trials. Their trophies filled a bookcase, and the rosettes they had won decorated the living room walls. Ruth had been easily aroused to passion by half a dozen lovers and by both of her husbands before the marriages went sour. But no time previously spent in bedrooms had satisfied her as thoroughly as falling asleep in a tangle of paws and silky fur.

"David's missing." Drew had not intended to say it that way. She bit her lip to keep from crying. The last time she had let her mother see her cry she was twelve years old.

It took Ruth Miller almost an hour to drive down to Los Angeles from Oxnard. For Drew, it was excruciating to let sixty minutes tick away. "Had we but world enough and time." For the moment, the world was Kiley running into his brother's bedroom and climbing back into Drew's lap and running into David's room again as though, if he ran fast enough, he could surprise his brother stealing home.

"Grandma." Kiley ran to get his stuffed animals and dropped bears, rabbits, and unicorn at his grandmother's feet. "Be Dr. Toothy-Noothy."

"Who has a toothache?" asked Ruth, ignoring her daughter.

"They all do," Kiley shouted triumphantly.

At thirty, Ruth Aronson had followed the dictates of society. The rules were hardly those of the nineteenth century, but they required that she wear a dress to the supermarket, cook meat and potatoes for her husband, and encase her fat fanny in a girdle before going to work or a movie. At sixty, Ruth Miller followed few dictates except her own. As pear-shaped as ever, she wore nothing but shorts. She ate most of her meals from the vegetable bins of her refrigerator. Her second husband had been an insomniac. To protect his sleep, the lights in the bedroom were turned off at exactly 11 P.M., the windows shut against external noise, the miniblinds closed against the dawn. Now she slept in a chaos of light and noise, moonlight streaming through the curtainless, open windows, her bed a futon on the floor, her bedtime the moment when the open book dropped from her hand.

When Drew left for the police station, her mother was sitting on the floor examining imaginary teeth.

Policemen and doctors share a rule of thumb, although only doctors verbalize it: "If you hear hoofbeats outside the window, don't go looking for zebras." The Sherwood Police Department already had its horse—Charles Greene, thirty-four years old, five feet, nine inches tall, brown eyes, light brown hair, and a star-shaped scar on his left palm where he had fallen on a broken pickle jar when he was four years old.

Drew watched the pictures of her husband and her son being scanned into a computer. It was the Sherwood PD's one piece of high-tech equipment, bought with special federal grant money, and the department tended to show it off whenever possible. The police had asked Drew to bring one photograph of the entire family, and she held the picture of the four of them in her hand—the glossy, intact, smiling family of memory. The Sherwood police station seemed more like an insurance office than like the cluttered, overemotional rooms so familiar from television. It was carpeted in beige, and the unscarred desks were separated by panels of dark brown corkboard on which the clerks had thumbtacked photographs of their own smiling families. The policewoman who did the scanning could have been an insurance agent, too, pleasant and helpful with disinterested eyes. Drew wasn't to worry. Everything would be for the best was the unspoken message. The photographs would be sent electronically, magically, to people who could help, would help.

"What if you find Chuck and David's not with him?" Drew asked. "What do you do then?"

The policewoman examined her little finger—the polish was

beginning to chip—and chirped reassurance on breath laced with peppermint Breath Savers.

Drew responded by throwing a tantrum full of "Damn you . . ." and "Why don't you do something?" Aware that her rage was earning her nothing but the anger of the people on whom she had to depend for help, she still couldn't stop. Sobbing "Damn you all," she was as out of control as David knocking over the game board. Had he inherited his rage from her? If so, it didn't come in mother's milk. Kiley was even-keeled, steady in all but the worst winds, while David and his mother were often blown off course. Skilled at undermining love with anger, the similar spikes of their emotional temperatures made it easy for them to understand each other and difficult for them to live together.

In ten minutes the squall had blown itself out. Embarrassed into passivity, Drew accepted a paper cup of water and a murmur of "I understand how difficult it must be," and "We'll get in touch as soon as we hear anything." Then she left, walking aimlessly into the brick courtyard with its tiled wishing well, where a plaque labeled the single-story stucco building an heirloom from Sherwood's early days. In Southern California such historical markers are the only way to be sure a building will outlast the people who build it.

A police station, even one as deliberately benign as this one, sops up emotion as though the walls are layered with paper towels. But Drew's anger had made the policewoman uncomfortable. She was young and bored, but she was neither naive nor dumb. And there was that case in Riverside where the mother and stepfather had killed a four-year-old girl and then reported her missing. She looked through her drawers for the address of the Los Angeles County Department of Children's Services. She filled out a form asking the department to look into the Greene family for possible child abuse.

CHAPTER 3

It was noon on Monday when the Santa Maria police spotted Chuck Greene's car in front of the Jasmine Cottage Bed 'n Breakfast where it had been parked all weekend. Eyes closed, Chuck was floating on his back in a wooden spa one hundred sixty-eight miles north of Los Angeles, a dead man's float they used to call it.

"Are you Charles Greene?"

He opened his eyes and was blinded by the glare from two gold badges. Made slow and dull by the hot water, he saw the uniforms without comprehending them.

"We'll have to ask you to come out of there."

It took a minute before Chuck was standing up, half out of water now, and the force of gravity pushing his brain back into place. "What's happened? What's wrong?"

The officers were young and rural with new badges and blond cowlicks and no sense of what to say to a dripping suspect in a yellow bathing suit. "Wouldn't you like to get dry, sir?" one asked.

Chuck didn't want to get dry, but he wanted his glasses. He

dressed himself in wire rims while water trickled down his legs. "What's happened? What's wrong?"

"We're looking for an eight-year-old boy. We think he's with you."

Alert and frightened, Chuck said, "David? What's happened to David?"

"Will you show us your room, please?"

Up a dark cherrywood staircase, there were three guest rooms in Jasmine Cottage. In the Lilac Room, Tiffani was sleeping under a patchwork quilt on a bed piled with pillows of lace and chintz. Mrs. Corey, who had sewn the pillows and made the quilt, had already told the police that she didn't allow children under the age of ten and that none of her guests had brought children at all this weekend. Now, she ignored the officers and concentrated on blotting Chuck's wet footprints from the stairs.

When it was obvious that David was not in the bedroom, the police tried the trunk of the Toyota. It was filled with term papers Chuck had collected before leaving school on Friday. Chuck's honors class had been asked to compare Charles Francis Adams, Abraham Lincoln's secretary of state during the Civil War, with John Quincy Adams who served as secretary of state for Presidents Monroe and Madison. In each of his regular classes, students had been given a book to analyze, from Robert E. Sherwood's *Roosevelt and Hopkins* to John Kenneth Galbraith's *Ambassador's Journal*. Chuck matched the books as much as possible to their backgrounds and interests. He was a kind man and a gifted teacher.

The trunk slammed shut. Having ripped a hole in Chuck's world, the two policemen backed away.

It was Tiffani who packed the suitcases, while Chuck stood on a rag rug, weighted down by the questions he had been too slow to ask. Tiffani was blonde, with generous hips and a heart-shaped face that would have sat more symmetrically above smaller breasts. She had been working as a clerk at Sherwood High School for two years. On her first day there, while unpacking a box of textbooks, she had found Chuck Greene's auditorium keys which had been missing for a week. Her name wasn't her fault. Tiffani with an i was typed on her birth certificate.

When Tiffani ran her hands through Chuck's hair, droplets of water splattered her shirt. She kissed his neck. "Call your wife," she said.

"My ex-wife," Chuck said automatically, without moving toward the phone. He was still in his bathing suit.

Tiffani pulled the phone from the bedside table and handed it to Chuck. "You need to call her."

Tiffani had met Drew several times, most often when Chuck had left a set of papers at home and Drew had brought them to the office, once when Chuck sat on his glasses in the lunchroom and Drew had brought his extra pair. Until Chuck walked out, Drew had been aware of Tiffani only as a pleasant young girl with a pleasant smile.

On Sunday night, after she sent Ruth home to her dogs, Drew had worked her way through her address book, calling everyone who might know where Chuck had gone. She had called again on Monday morning, but Chuck had told no one that he was leaving town.

Now when the telephone rang, Drew—with the everyday telepathy that is as common as salt—reached for the phone and said, "Chuck?" The where and how and when of what she knew about David's disappearance took such a short time to tell that Drew's body ached when she hung up the phone. Years earlier, she had felt the same heaviness on days when one of her babies was teething and refused to suck at her swollen breasts.

"Daddy will be here by bedtime," she told Kiley, who had taken permanent possession of her lap. Hour by hour, the buoyant five-year-old of Saturday morning had regressed, like one of those television nature documentaries in reverse, with the flower bud closing rather than opening. She held him tighter. "Want some ice cream?"

Kiley shook his head. "Is David with Daddy?"

"No."

"Where is David?"

It was the unanswerable question.

Somewhere between Santa Barbara and Carpinteria, the California Highway Patrol spotted Chuck's car. This time, both of the officers had the wariness that comes with experience. The one who had played linebacker for a semipro football team had been shot in the wrist at a traffic stop three years earlier, and his arm still ached often enough to keep the memory from fading. He had his gun in his hand when he asked Chuck to step out of the car and lean facedown against the hood of the Toyota.

Each time Chuck tried to speak, he was shoved harder until his nose was squashed against the red paint, and he could only breathe in shallow pants, like a dog left too long without water on a hot day. So he lay still. He was a pudgy man, with rounded contours that Drew had always found comforting in bed. On cold nights, it was like sleeping with an extra blanket. But he was a soft man in other ways, too, with no sense of direction and no skill in sports. And the coils and hoses and engine under the hood against which his nose was pressed were a foreign country to him.

Chuck was handcuffed and sitting in the backseat of the patrol car before he was allowed to explain that he had been contacted by the Santa Maria police and that he was driving home to join whatever search had started for his son.

"I'm his father." He said it more than once, masculine shorthand for things he couldn't afford to say—that he was outraged and mortified at having his trunk searched once again and that he loved his son.

"Yeah," said the man who had handcuffed him.

When the handcuffs were taken off, Chuck rubbed his wrists with a gesture made familiar by a lifetime of watching B movies and bad television. There was no apology this time either, although one of the officers said something that sounded like, "We have to be careful." They were getting into their car when Tiffani stopped them.

"Can you give us something? In case we're stopped again."

"It should be all right in the computer now."

She smiled her best smile, the one that worked at the Department of Motor Vehicles and the Department of Water and Power. "Just in case it isn't all right," she said.

The ex-linebacker wrote and signed a note—not guaranteed to provide safe passage through Ventura and Thousand Oaks, but better than nothing. He was rubbing his wrist as he drove away.

Chuck was alone when he parked in front of the small stucco house that had been his home for four years. He had dropped Tiffani and her suitcase at the apartment without turning off his motor and had gunned the car south onto the 405 Freeway as though he were a reckless seventeen again. His own suitcase was still on the backseat.

The house belonged to his ex-mother-in-law. It was, in fact, the house in which Drew had grown up. When Kiley was born and their apartment was immediately too small for the four Greenes, Ruth Miller had offered them the house at half the rent she could get from real tenants. Ruth had been shrewd enough to buy two other small, nondescript houses during one of Southern California's real estate troughs, and the rents kept the dogs in Nature's Recipe biscuits. By the time Chuck got married, decent Los Angeles real estate was out of the reach of high school teachers, no matter how shrewd or far-sighted they were. The perfectly ordinary house out of which Chuck had moved eighteen months earlier was worth more than three hundred thousand dollars.

The front door key was still on Chuck's key ring. The rules, mostly unspoken, by which Drew and Chuck now regulated their relationship said firmly that the key was for emergencies only. It could be used, for example, if Chuck and the boys returned from a movie while Drew was still at the market. Otherwise, the house was Drew's space, and Chuck, like any other guest, was expected to wait until he was invited in.

Chuck put his key in the lock and opened the door.

Kiley, a wounded bird, had to be coaxed from his mother's lap.

Then he clung equally tightly to his father. The three of them sat at the kitchen table. The formal dining room with its vaguely Moorish arches had no space for eating. But it was used every day as a terminus for things entering or leaving the house. The table was stacked with library books, magazines that Drew had not gotten around to reading yet, mail, spelling workbooks, unpaid bills, and half a dozen cans of tuna that David was to take to school on Tuesday as a donation to less fortunate children. The tuna sat next to a thousand-piece jigsaw puzzle with half the pieces still in the box. At the bottom edge of the puzzle, the Hobbit Frodo and the wizard Gandalf had started on a journey they would never complete until David returned home. The dining room also held two bookcases, the computer which had replaced the family typewriter four years earlier, and the spinet Ruth Miller had bought when Drew was seven and demanded piano lessons. Until Chuck moved out, the dining room had been chaos. Now it was merely messy.

"Coffee?"

Chuck nodded and reached in the wrong cupboard for a cup. He had lived in the house for four years without ever having more than a vague idea where pots, pans, mugs, or tea bags were kept. When he was asked to hand Drew a jar of applesauce or Kiley's Peter Rabbit bowl, he would cautiously fumble, much like those chimpanzees in science textbooks who use trial and error to fetch an out-of-reach banana. Toward the end of their marriage, Drew found it was more trouble to direct Chuck than it was to get the things herself.

"To the right," she said now. "On the bottom shelf."

"What do we do?" he asked when they were sitting opposite each other at the white stone table which had been bought, like most of their furniture, secondhand from fancy houses in Beverly Hills whose owners were replacing sleek Swedish with overstuffed Mediterranean. Rigorous frugality combined with decent taste had made the house an eclectic stew of what used to be called modern furniture. Drew sat on a wire Eames chair with a seat of electric blue vinyl, Chuck on a twenty-two-dollar chair from Ikea.

Instead of answering, Drew told the story again: How she had sent David to his room, how he had disappeared, how she had searched and called the police and waited and searched and gone to the police station. Even as she told her tale, she realized that, in the telling, she was distancing herself from having to think about the future. The frightening, unimaginable future.

"The police, I guess," she said. "The police will do something now. They thought it was you."

"Fuck the police," Chuck said, suddenly burning with the anger he had not allowed himself to feel when his cheek was pressed against the hood of his car. "Fuck the fucking police."

His father's anger was such an unusual event that Kiley, startled, reached for the protection of his mother's arms. Drew's anger was so routine—she was always damning a zipper that wouldn't zip, a plunger that wasn't strong enough to clear the mess in the toilet, a bank that had closed too early—that it washed over Kiley. And he was rarely caught in the undertow, since Drew's anger was almost never directed at him. In fact, although Kiley could never have articulated it, he felt safe within the protective circle of his mother's rage. So he was horrified when his mother, without warning, began to cry. "No, no, no, no, no," he said, pushing his hands against her eyes to hold back the tears.

Then Kiley was crying, too, and Chuck, across the table from his wife and son, was left to hold the fort of reason with its shattered windows and broken doors. "Don't cry," he said helplessly. "Don't cry."

CHAPTER 4

$\mathbf{B}$atter Up was one of a cluster of small shops on the third level of the Sherwood Galleria, flanked on the left by Four Eyes Only and on the right by Sweet Dreams. Most of the stores on the third level had clever names. There was definitely an overdose of cleverness in the semicircle between the Body in the Bathtub bookstore and Running Room. The mall's two anchor department stores and the upscale national chains, from The Limited to The Gap, spread across the first and second floors. The odd shops that sold baseball cards, detective novels, or sequined socks were stuck in a corner of the third floor below the food court.

Denver had arrived at the Sherwood Galleria before noon on Saturday, and he had been waiting near Batter Up for more than two hours. His name wasn't really Denver. The last time, he had been Dallas and the time before that, Cheyenne. Whatever his real name was, he hadn't used it for years. If he had been accused of hiding his identity, he would have managed a slow grin, suitable to the character he was currently inventing, and he would have stared in genuine puzzlement out of guileless blue-gray eyes. Denver was hiding nothing. He was recreating himself—yesterday as a pickled-in-sand Texan, today as a cowboy ambling along under the blue sky, The Big Sky. America was a huge country, and he had grazed over most of the map.

Clean-shaven and dressed in the Southern California uniform of jeans and flashy T-shirt, he was exquisitely ordinary. Even so, anywhere else he might have been noticed. But malls are temples to the self. Slouched on a bench, with an empty Slurpee cup lightly resting on his chest, he was as motionless as a lizard in the sun. And of as little interest to the people carrying plastic keys to the treasures within the semicircle of shops.

Anyone watching Denver carefully might have seen his tongue flick out and touch his upper lip. His half-closed eyes were following a seven-year-old boy in a baseball uniform. Sometimes, when he was not quite empty and not quite sated, Denver would walk past the wire fence of an elementary school at recess and amuse himself by predicting which boy would come willingly with him. If the boys were playing close enough, within thirty feet of the fence, his predictions were accurate. He had tested them twice, once sharing twists of cherry licorice and a two-block walk before he sent the boy home.

Although Denver was an inch or more under six feet and thick from waist to shoulders, he gave the impression of uncoiling his body from the bench. He was ready when the boy left Batter Up with both of the packs of cards he had bought already torn open. The boy had gone into Batter Up alone and he came out alone, but Denver waited five heartbeats to see if anyone would claim him.

"What league you play in?" Denver asked from a proper distance. If the boy was frightened by a question from a stranger, Denver could move a step away and the space between them would be solid as a wall. "My little brother plays in Culver City."

"North Sherwood." But, through a glob of bubble gum, the words were slurred into Norse Urwoud.

The question didn't matter. It was merely a way of slowing the boy down, braking him so that Denver could move casually into position at his side. But the chubby boy in New York Yan-kees pinstripes was not at all frightened. "I'm in five pitch. I get to go into real Little League next year. Is your brother in the minors?"

"The majors," said Denver. His voice was surprisingly light, mismatched to his size. His accent had a flat sound that could have been bred in any of the flat states that fill the center of a United States map. "Third baseman."

One of Denver's advantages in conversations like this was his ability to convince himself that what he was inventing was real, that he did have a younger brother who played third base and had a tendency to swing late and pull his hits to right field. It was barely a moment before the fish was well hooked, and Denver began to reel him in. He motioned toward the baseball cards in the boy's hand. "Want to trade?"

"Sure. Who you got?"

Denver handed over half a dozen cards and made a trade of utility infielder for journeyman outfielder. Then he leaned against a pillar and motioned down a long corridor to the exit. "I got better trading stuff in my car."

"Can I see?" The fish was eager for the gaff.

"Sure," said Denver. "If you want to."

But luck and a 3 P.M. baseball game dictated what happened next. "Randy! For God's sake, what are you doing?" The mother had not been absent, merely shopping. Her words preceded her by a hundred feet, and before the echoing "Randy, d, d, d" had died, Denver was gone, through the men's room door and into a stall. He had chosen this particular corridor with care.

"You'll be late for the game. I told you to wait in front of Batter Up. Honestly, I don't think your head is screwed on right." She had already grabbed the boy and was pulling him toward the esca-lator, too engrossed in her monolog to have noticed Denver as more than brown hair and a T-shirt advertising some violent movie. It wasn't until hours later when they were driving home from the game that she asked where her son had been going.

"Nowhere," he said sulkily. He had let two balls slide through his legs, the other team had won, and only sullenness held back tears. "It wasn't my fault," he whined. "I was just unlucky."

Before Denver came out of the men's room, he changed into a white shirt advertising Adidas shoes and stuffed into his small gym bag the *Lethal Weapon 3* shirt he had worn all morning. The bag held, among other things, two more shirts. For only an instant had Denver's equilibrium been challenged. But such sudden challenges to balance were part of the game, sometimes the best part. He drifted down the escalator and back up again, this time to the food court. He wasn't thirsty or hungry, but a plastic cup was protective coloration. On dozens of varnished wood benches, people ate and drank and waited. Denver picked a bench on the other side of Batter Up and slouched down, his large Coke sweating through the cardboard container.

More than a dozen boys went in and out of the baseball shop without causing Denver to do more than blink and stir the ice with his straw. The ice was long melted, and he had stood up to leave when David Greene jumped off the down escalator.

David knew exactly what he wanted, Stadium Club Extreme. The only question was whether to buy one pack and have enough money left over for a hamburger or to buy two packs of Score as well and eat peanut butter and crackers until his mother rescued him. He was too pleased with himself to be angry now. Able to cross wide boulevards in a single bound. David the daring. Greene the great. If he bought two packs of cards instead of three, he'd have enough money for a cherry Icee.

When David left Batter Up twenty minutes later, the two packs of cards were still unopened. He always waited as long as he could, running his fingers across the slick foil and willing the best cards to be inside. Sometimes he was able to wait until he got home. And sometimes it worked. David the magician. He decided to buy an Icee and then see what his five dollars had bought. If there were any duplicates, he'd trade them to Kiley.

"You like Stadium Club better than Ultra?" David was almost at the escalator when Denver caught up with him. There was no one within fifty feet of them. The Galleria wouldn't close for another two hours, but the afternoon shoppers, surfeited, had tossed their plastic bags onto the rear seats of their Blazers and were driving home to dinner.

For a moment it seemed that David was not going to answer. "I buy Ultra, too," he said finally. "And Upper Deck."

"Want to trade?"

"Where?"

Denver pointed to a corner out of reach of the sun that spilled through the skylight. "There's a bench."

David took one step into the shadows and then backed away.

Denver had a dozen or more cards in his hands now and was slowly shuffling them. His hands were small, at odds with his thick neck. "How about over here?" He laid three cards out on a broad railing, their gold letters and red backgrounds catching fire in the late afternoon sunlight. Still, David didn't move until Denver had casually stepped backward and was leaning against a mock alabaster pillar. No fish eager for the baited hook this time. "Hey, we don't have to trade," Denver said. "I gotta get home soon anyway." He scratched his cheek and yawned.

David picked a card off the railing. "Trade you Bryan Harvey for Mike Piazza."

It was a sucker's trade.

"Hell, no," Denver said, still keeping his distance. "Trade you Jack McDowell for Harvey though."

David relaxed. "Deal," he said.

Denver smiled. There was always a languor, a lack of urgency, in these opening moves. He looked. He needed. But his need was reined in, bridled. He often said that he was raised on horseback—another lie. But he had ridden often enough to know the feeling of being in control, of pressing the reins against the huge damp neck and sensing the animal begin to turn. The boy was beginning to turn now, although the leather had barely touched his neck. There was no urgency. The urgency would come later.

"I got better trading stuff in my car," Denver said.

David had been digging through his backpack for a 1995 Bryan Harvey among the pile of cards he had tossed in at the last moment. He didn't intend to end up at Danny Matranga's house this time. But, just in case, he had wanted to have something to trade. "You get them," he said. "I'll sort mine."

Denver took half a dozen steps, then turned. "Want to come?"

David shook his head. "What's your name?"

"Denver."

"How old are you?"

Denver shaved off as many years as he could. "Twenty-six." He had left thirty behind and was climbing.

Politeness was not a virtue in the Greene family. "Why are you still trading baseball cards then?"

"It's what I do," said Denver. "I've got me a shop. In San Diego."

"Like Batter Up?"

"I sell other stuff, too. Batman shirts. Old movie stuff." He reached into his gym bag and tossed the boy a rubber banded pack of *Star Trek* trading cards. For a second, their heads were close together, and the coarse hair of boy and man blended, although the boy's long hair was the color of darkened honey and the man's as brown as river mud. Ears, nose, mouth were the legacy of different gene pools, but they both had square faces and blue-gray eyes, and the boy, too, was chunky, thick around the chest. A stranger might have thought they were related. Not father and son. There was nothing paternal in Denver's voice or manner. But brothers perhaps. Or cousins.

Denver moved toward the exit sign. Out of sight, he pulled two dozen cards from his gym bag, waited a few moments, and walked back. In the minute or so of Denver's absence, David had become shy. In addition, he was being abandoned by the light. Dusk poured through the skylight now, and the railing where Denver's plastic images had danced was shadowed.

"I have to go home," David said. "I have to call my mother."

Denver reached into his pocket and handed David two quarters. "There's a phone over there," he said.

Once more, David relaxed.

He let the phone ring six times, until he heard his own voice

40

announcing that the Greenes weren't in but they sincerely hoped the caller would leave a message. Then he dialed his father. By the time he returned to Denver, he was angry again.

Denver read David's face. "Gone out and left you," he said. "Want a ride home?"

The answer was automatic. There had been five or six conversations about automobiles and strangers.

"Guess you'll have to stay around here then," Denver said. "And wait 'til your mother gets home."

The lights were thin and artificial, and the mall was empty. Denver started down the exit corridor, then turned back. "Maybe I could drop you at a friend's house," Denver said. "Then your mother'd have to wait for you."

"His name's Danny," said David, as they walked through the door to the parking garage. "I'll show you the way."

CHAPTER 5

The Sherwood Police Department had dumped David Greene's disappearance into the lap of Angus West. Actually, Angus had spilled the file from the corner of his desk into his own lap on Tuesday morning. He had spent the weekend self-administering his preferred anesthesia. But since the weekend included an extra day, the pile of beer cans in his recycle bin was taller than usual, and he came to work with a headache that was bad enough to make him clumsy.

He stared for a long time at the picture of the four Greenes before he started to read the file. So far this year, the Sherwood PD had opened fourteen files on missing children. Six of the kids had returned home within an hour or two of their parents' first frantic phone call to the police department. Another four, enraged by or raging at their parents, had gone to ground at a friend's house and were dragged home within forty-eight hours. Divorced fathers had taken two boys, and the other two—teenage girls—had run away to the pleasures and dangers of Hollywood Boulevard. All present and accounted for.

Angus read the file twice before carrying it into Lieutenant Zane's office. "Trouble," he said.

"The kid ran away before," Zane answered.

"Doesn't matter. This is trouble."

Zane was a slight, sandy-haired man in his mid-thirties, a born follower whose manner constantly apologized for the necessity of leading. Standing, he shifted from foot to foot like a second grader on his way to the bathroom. Seated, as now, and shielded by his desk, he could relax comfortably into his office management skills. Angus outweighed him by fifty pounds.

Zane handed the file back. "You'll handle it," he said.

Angus shook his head. "It goes to Howell."

"He's getting that knee arthoscoped. He'll be on crutches for three weeks. There's no one else." Zane could make a statement sound like a plea.

"Give it to Townsend, then. He logged it in." It was an absurd suggestion, and both men knew it. Zane had no particular gift for police work, but he did have a B.A. in business administration and a talent for flow charts and resource allocation. Each year, the Sherwood Police Department was praised by the City Council for its fiscal responsibility, and Chief Zarelli rewarded Martin Zane with promotions that made him nervous.

"There's no one else."

Beverly Hills had one hundred thirty-two sworn officers and seventy secretaries, clerks, and dispatchers to patrol and control its six square miles and 32,000 people. Sherwood—smaller, less affluent, and closer to the ocean—had eighty-nine policemen and twenty civilians. They dealt with two murders a year, and one was usually a spillover from a Los Angeles drug deal gone sour. So most of the policemen worked burglaries, aggravated assaults, and traffic problems and spent their days off moonlighting as security guards at the Galleria. Zane was one of three lieutenants, Angus one of three detective sergeants. If an instinct for crime were a prerequisite for promotion, their positions would have been reversed.

"Is the kid dead, West?"

"Good chance," Angus said. "Or some creepy crawler has him." IIis voice was layered like an onion, unreadable. "Whoever's taking Howell's place in Juve better get over to see the mother. She's called in twice already this morning."

"Call and tell her you're coming," Zane said.

"The hell I will." Detective Sergeant Angus West was too good for Sherwood and he knew it, wasted on shoplifters and grafitti. A forty-one-year-old big fish who had chosen to intimidate a small pond. By tacit agreement with Zane, he picked his own assignments, and they never involved children. In the ten years since he had left the Los Angeles Police Department for the neat lawns and well-trimmed bougainvilleas of this suburb, he had investigated all of Sherwood's murders, mayhem, and armed robberies at the 7-Eleven; but the missing children had been found without his help.

Now Zane surprised him. "The hell you have to. Unless we're lucky, this is the day Sherwood hits the five o'clock news. Zarelli told me to assign you. Angus West, ace detective, will make sure our chief doesn't look stupid in front of the cameras." Zane was trying to make a joke, but the words came out envious and bitter.

Chuck Greene had gone to work, allegiance to one hundred sixty-five children outweighing loyalty to one. Drew had tried to work and failed. She was a freelance script reader for two small movie studios. No automatic weekly paycheck, no benefits. But, now that Chuck had moved out, Drew's mother let her live in the house rent free. If she covered eight scripts a week, she made an almost decent living, and one thing Hollywood didn't lack was new screenplays every week. About 50,000 screenplays were registered with the Writers Guild each year, and most of them were bad. Unreadable scripts made Drew's job easy. Summing them up was like reproducing form letters. "Production values: Low. Recommendation: No. Writer recommended: No." "This bleak mood piece falls short of the mark in several areas." "This comedy is seriously flawed." "This well-intentioned script is, ultimately, just another story about an ex-con trying to go straight."

Drew was staring at a blank computer screen when the doorbell rang.

"Detective Sergeant Angus West," he said, with a perceptible emphasis on the first syllable of Angus. He must have been five when he was called Gus for the first time. He walked away, and by the time he was twelve, the world had learned to call him Angus or, more often, West. Even then, he was tall and broad. There was only one blemish on eight generations of Anglo Saxon forebearers. His great-grandfather, also named Angus, had lain for a season with an Apache woman. When the woman died, six months after childbirth, he had given the baby a sugar teat, strapped it to his horse, and ridden off. Angus's half-Indian grandfather had married white and died before Angus was born, but he held the boy's imagination permanently captive. With his size, fair skin, and yellow hair, Angus should have led the cavalry charges, but he always chose the role of Indian chief.

Surprised by West's size and expecting a sympathy in his eyes that was not there, Drew cleared a space at the dining room table by making a wobbly stack of scripts and library books on the floor next to the computer. Unasked, she brought West a cup of coffee. Then Drew and the detective sat uncomfortably in the dining room while she answered all the obvious questions and asked one of her own.

"Do you have children?"

The question bounced off his impenetrable face and fell to the floor unanswered and, perhaps, unheard.

In telling about David, Drew veered between pride and anger. David had already read the first two volumes of the Tolkien trilogy, *The Lord of the Rings,* struggling with the unfamiliar language but refusing to give up. He was awkward at sports, but he loved baseball. After his five-pitch coach said he wasn't good enough for Little League, he had spent an hour every day throwing a ball at chalk circles on the garage door. He didn't get along easily with other children the way Kiley did, but he always had one best friend. When she was late picking him up from practice, he would have a tantrum and accuse her of not loving him.

Angus put his notebook back in his pocket, pushed aside his untouched cup of coffee, and asked to see David's room. Drew led him there reluctantly. Once the door was opened, there could not be even the pretense of safety.

Drew's house, like many in Sherwood, was more than fifty years old, and over the years, it had settled unevenly. It was hard to keep Kiley's door closed while David's door always stuck. When Drew shoved the door open, her shoulder brushed the NO BROTHERS ALLOWED sign David had defiantly printed with his marking pens. The surface of the room was warm in the midday sun, but the chill of David's anger was still there beneath the warmth, and Drew was aware that the sergeant felt it, too. Both of them stood too stiffly, the way people stand in a hospital room while they try to keep specks of mortality from staining their clothes.

"What's missing?" was West's first question.

"I told the police, two days ago, what he was wearing . . ."

West's voice brushed her aside. "Don't tell me what you think. What did he take? Look."

Drew had spent two days looking inward, tracing the guilt as it moved through her veins and charting each "If I had only . . ." in her head. Now she was overpowered by what she had tried to avoid. The smell of David—colored markers, dirty socks, airplane glue, fruit punch bubble gum—was overwhelming. Half a dozen packs of gum were piled in his Easter basket. Every Easter Drew made each of the boys a separate hunt with a chocolate rabbit as the prize at the end. To a family in which religion was irrelevant, there was a need for such rituals. David had paper clipped the dozen rhyming clues Drew had written for this year's hunt and had stored them in the grass of his basket. That her son had so carefully kept the treasure hunt she had created for him undid Drew. She stood helplessly at the foot of the unmade bed.

West was brusque and impatient, his voice sandpaper. "Look on his shelves. Look under the bed. If we know what he took, we might know where he intended to go."

She knelt. Her hands buried in David's blue carpet, her mind still buried in dreamtime, Drew looked under the bed without seeing. "Look," West said again, and his fingers pinched her shoulder.

It took only a fragment of real time. "His blue backpack. It's not in his closet. It's not under the bed. And his school books are on the floor."

Item by item the backpack was filled. Flashlight, sweater, a pack of marking pens. Baseball and mitt. Magnetic Scrabble. But Drew missed the comic books and the agates. "He took the Clue cards, too," she said. "Colonel Mustard. The rope. And the billiard room. Clue was what we fought about." That was when it came to her. "Cards. Baseball cards."

West responded to the excitement in her voice. "You know where he went?"

"To that baseball store at the Galleria."

When David was two years old, Drew's mother had shocked her by noting that all the things that disturbed Drew about her son—the way he hoarded private thoughts behind opaque eyes, his stubbornness, and his attacking anger—were "just like you." Drew had looked quickly at her mother, expecting vindictiveness, but Ruth appeared only to be stating a fact. Drew knew what Kiley was thinking because he willingly told her. She could guess the thoughts David was hiding because she thought them, too. The first time David ran away, Drew had found him in less than an hour. She had known—although she could never say how she knew—that he would be hiding in the wood fort at the playground.

"He's not allowed to cross Seaview," she said to West.

West was ahead of her. "He wanted to show you?"

Both of them were supple now, leaping surefootedly from conclusion to conclusion. "David gets reckless when he's really angry. And he had saved more than six dollars."

West had been a block of ice carved into roughly human form. The heat from this verbal game melted him. "How long before David would have phoned you?"

"He would have called his father first."

"There was no message on Mr. Greene's answering machine."

"If Chuck weren't home, David wouldn't have left a message. And he would have called me before it got dark."

Experience had taught West the skill of reading faces, but his ability to hear nuances was inborn. Often, he would stand in an interrogation room with his eyes closed and listen to a suspect being questioned. With his eyes closed, he could guess more accurately about guilt and innocence. "Isn't he a little old to be afraid of the dark?" West asked.

"He isn't a timid kid," Drew answered defensively. "In daylight, he's fearless."

When there was nothing more to be said, West left. Drew followed him outside. "Are you going to the Galleria now?"

West nodded.

"Can I come with you?" Drew asked. She could hear the begging tone in her voice. For an instant, she was ten years old again and left behind on some important outing because she was too young.

Angus shook his head, the molecules of ice reforming. He gave a speech about police department policy and assured her that she would be notified as soon as they knew anything. Then he gave her his card and told her to call him directly if she thought of anything else.

Helplessly, Drew tagged along to his car and planted her palms against the warm glass of the passenger window. She kept them there until the unmarked police car slid out from under her hands.

CHAPTER 6

David had been kneeling on the toilet seat, with his head in the motel washbasin, for forty minutes. Denver had told him to keep his eyes closed, but he had blinked them open a dozen times. All he could see was black hair dye obliterating Ace Ventura.

Denver's rubber-gloved hands poured cups of cold water over his head. David squirmed, but he had already learned not to complain. Denver had only hit him once, hours ago, but his cheek still ached.

"I hate kids who cry," Denver had said.

The cold edge of a pair of scissors sheared the lamb. Then something sticky trickled down David's forehead, as Denver's fingers made circles on his scalp. Shampoo.

"Can you wash your hair?" Denver asked.

His eyes still closed, David nodded, and the gesture sent globs of foam into the air. The man seemed amused. "You're lathered like a colt," he said, and wiped David's eyes. The towel had the cardboard stiffness of cheap towels that have been washed too many times, but the gesture was surprisingly gentle.

Denver handed David the plastic bottle of shampoo. The boy took it without touching the man's fingers.

"Rinse your hair and wash it again. And throw your shirt in the sink." Denver reached over David to turn on the shower; he kept his hand under the tap until the water was warm.

Denver didn't leave the bathroom, so David stepped into the rusted bathtub in his underpants. Through the brittle shower curtain, he watched the man use his favorite T-shirt to wipe the sink and his socks to scrub black spots from the floor. Then Denver threw socks, shirt, and towel into a plastic bag and put the stained rubber gloves on top. Whatever color and texture the shower curtain had been when new, it was now the hue and consistency of clotted varnish. The man on the other side was a silhouette in a shadow play. David closed his eyes against the sting of the shampoo. When he opened them again, the silhouette had disappeared.

The wall of hot water was a shield. David hid in the shower until the water turned cold and forced him out.

"You been in there so long you must think you're a fish," Denver said from the motel room and laughed at his joke. He was lying on one of the twin beds, throwing and catching and throwing David's baseball.

"That's mine," David said before he could stop himself.

"Hey, buddy, we share," Denver said, sitting up and tossing the ball to David. "From now on, we share everything."

Denver's mildness made David bold. Standing in wet underpants and cradling the ball against his chest, he said, "I want to go home." When they had left the Galleria and Denver turned the wrong way on Seaview, David hadn't been frightened. "That way," he had said, pulling at Denver's arm. But the moment he touched the rigid forearm, he knew. "Take me home," he had demanded. "Take me home now. I want to go home." Denver had taken his right hand off the steering wheel and swung his arm, the elbow knocking David against the door and the open hand lashing David's cheek. David had reached for the door handle, and Denver had jammed his fingers into the dashboard. David had screamed from pain and fear, and Denver had covered the boy's nose and mouth with his hand. "Shut up," Denver had said. "Don't be a sissy." When Denver took his hand away, David swallowed air in cup-size gulps and cried silently while the car went down strange and stranger streets. They drove for an hour in what seemed to be circles. If Denver was trying to confuse the boy, it was unnecessary. David knew many of the alleys and all the bike paths of Sherwood. But he was too young for his homing instinct to be fully formed. Every doughnut shop and concrete block warehouse on the underbelly streets of Los Angeles looked the same through eyes blurred by tears.

They had stopped once, at the drive-through window of a Burger King, for Cokes, fries, and double cheeseburgers. During the two minutes it took to pick up the food, Denver squeezed David's fingers together. It seemed more a warning than a punishment. When they drove away, he had said, "Eat what you want," and had dropped the bags on the boy's lap. For a moment David felt comforted by the warmth against his chest. Then he rubbed his fingers and pushed the food away.

Denver ate exuberantly. By the time he left the lighted streets and pulled into a dark space at the rear of a motel in Gardena, he was mellow with success and french fries. "You don't know what you missed, kid," he had said, as he crushed the bags into a ball and made an exaggerated hook shot into a trash can. Then he had picked up David's backpack, unlocked the door to Cottage 12 with its DO NOT DISTURB sign on the door, and called the boy. "Come on. We're home."

Now, at midnight, David stood out of reach and asked, "When will you let me go?" For eight years, David had given orders. Sovereignty was the prerogative of the firstborn. From his screams demanding mother's milk to yesterday's battle with Kiley, he had yelled, "Give it to me," and the world had usually obliged. But in the last six hours he had been shorn of entitlements. "Please let me go," he begged. "Why won't you let me go?"

Denver was still unruffled. "You'll go in a while," he said, his breath stale with grease. "We'll have some fun first. You ever been to a Dodgers game?"

Denver's good humor did not make him careless. David watched as the man bolted the door's top and bottom locks, turned a key in the deadbolt, and tied his belt around a chair he had wedged under the doorknob. Then he threw David's baseball mitt on to the other bed. "Your mitt's kind of stiff," he said. "Better rubber band the ball inside. We'll get us some oil tomorrow."

There is a sleep too deep for dreaming, a blackness of exhaustion where even the involuntary muscles fail to twitch. David had crawled between rough sheets and cradled the mitt as, when younger, he had hugged his yellow rabbit. He cried automatically and soundlessly, but he was asleep almost before the pillowcase smothered his tears. His heart pumped blood, his lungs exhaled air, and his autonomic nervous system ran his body in all the necessary ways. But his mind lay drowned in long oblivion, as though the tap water he had brought to his mouth in cupped fingers had been piped to the Royal Motel from the River Lethe.

David woke first on Sunday morning, handed back to consciousness by the alien feel of the bed. All the soft things of his previous life—fabric softener in the washing machine and 200 thread-count percale sheets and a down comforter of blue and purple—were in a house a world away. Throbbing with the need to pee but too homesick for any other thought, David sat up and saw Denver face down in the other bed. The man's closed eyes and even breathing were snares set for an unsuspecting rabbit. By the time David pulled away the chair and unhooked the hand-tooled cowboy belt from the doorknob, Denver was standing next to him. With the ease of someone who has some skill in martial arts, Denver kicked at David's leg. As the boy was falling, he kicked the other thigh. There was neither malice nor anger in the two quick kicks. Again, the boy was being warned.

As he rolled over, David began to pee. He told his body to stop, and still the urine spurted out. Shamed beyond words, he lay in the yellow puddle until Denver took his hand and pulled him up.

"Throw your pants on the floor," Denver said. "And go back to bed."

Denver had put the plastic bag of David's clothes next to the door. Even the new brown sweater was trash for the Dumpster. Now he took a switchblade knife and cut the straps of David's backpack and threw them in the bag. Then he emptied the backpack on to his bed and cut out David's name and address, printed in laundry marking pen on faded blue fabric, and put the folded square in his pocket. David watched the knife slash down the backpack and up again, until the other pieces were small enough to fit inside the trash bag.

"Mine, mine, mine." The word stormed in his mind but didn't reach his lips. Naked under thin blankets, he couldn't take his eyes off the discarded things that used to clothe him. "Me, me, me."

Whistling a country western tune about abandonment and cheating hearts, Denver closed the bag with a rubber band. David's tan shorts and wet underpants still lay on the floor. Denver opened his gym bag and took out a sheet of thin plastic that might have been a leftover bag from the cleaners. He put the shorts and soggy underpants on the plastic and, still whistling, opened the knife again and walked over to David's bed. "Close your eyes," he said. And David did.

More carefully than he had slashed the backpack, Denver cut David's left arm and, holding the plastic like a cup, let the blood drip onto the shorts and underpants. Then he wiped David's arm on the fabric. In a minute or two the arm had stopped bleeding, and Denver crisscrossed Band-Aids over the cut.

"Brave boy," he said. "I like brave boys."

Denver sealed the shorts and underpants in the plastic and took both bags to the car, not bothering to lock the door behind him. When he came back, David hadn't moved.

This time Denver said, "Good boy." He took from his pocket a pair of handcuffs and deftly cuffed David's arm to the metal frame of the bed. Then he reached into the pile that had spilled from the backpack and handed David half a dozen comic books and the peanut butter crackers. "You don't move until I get back," he said. Then he was gone, keys turning in three locks. A car engine coughed and caught, and there was the heavy sound of a car pulling away.

At the edge of the vacant lot that ringed the motel, Denver waited and listened. When he walked back ten minutes later and looked through the one small window, David was still lying on his back, the comic books untouched on the blanket. Denver rapped gently on the window. "Good boy," he said again. "You wait right there."

"Hey, Andy," Denver said.

Not asleep but barely awake, suspended like a fly caught in cobweb, David smelled Denver rather than saw him. An antic Santa Claus, Denver dropped a box of fried chicken into David's arms. It was almost twenty-four hours since David had eaten. One minute he was too disoriented to be hungry. The next— made ravenous by the remembered smell—he was tearing the box apart and cramming his mouth with chicken breast and mashed potatoes. He ate single-mindedly, everything else forgotten, until only the bones were left.

When David looked up, Denver was sitting on the other bed, licking honey from a plastic tub. "Hell, that was good," he said. "We didn't leave nothing but bones for the dog." David started to say that chicken bones weren't good for dogs, then awkwardly swallowed the words. He had not had much practice at censoring himself. His parents and two years at a nursery school founded by psychologists had encouraged free expression. "How do you feel about that?" was as common at the dinner table as "Pass the milk." Now he did not dare say how he felt.

Denver stood up, again with that sinuous grace so at odds with his wrestler's torso. Panicked as Denver raised his arms, David closed his eyes and curled himself into a ball.

He was pelted by half a dozen packages.

"Hey, open your presents, Andy," Denver said.

There were stiff new blue jeans, three pairs of off-brand jockey shorts, two thin souvenir T-shirts with "Welcome to L.A." and palm trees, half a dozen white athletic socks with different colored stripes around the ankle, and a secondhand blue jacket. David lay under the rain of his new identity until Denver pushed a pair of socks into his hand and said, "You might as well get dressed."

"My name is David Greene," the boy had said at the Galleria. But Denver had never used his name, choosing to define him as Kid, Buddy, and Pal. The boy in tan shorts, with honey-colored hair and a stained backpack, was David Greene. This boy, sent to look at himself in the bathroom mirror, had black hair cut short with blunt scissors; he was wearing coarse jeans that rubbed against a bruise on his thigh that was the size and shape of a cantaloupe.

"There's more stuff," Denver said. "Come see."

He had bought David a green toothbrush.

"Here, Andy," he said as he handed it to the boy.

"My name's David. Why can't I be David?" He knew enough to ask the question softly, the words just brushing his lips.

It wasn't soft enough. As Denver twisted the boy's wrist, the cellophane-wrapped toothbrush fell from David's hand. Denver picked it up and pushed it back into the boy's hand. "This belongs to Andy," he said.

David's toothbrush—safe in the ceramic dinosaur holder he shared with Kiley—was red.

Denver leaned forward, his square face so close that his hair grazed David's forehead. "What's your name?" he asked.

"David," the boy said with terrifying bravery. "David." For the last time.

Denver hit him across the mouth, forcing him to swallow the word. "There isn't any David," he said as he hit the boy a second time. "What's your name?"

Blood trickled onto David's tongue as he whispered, "Andy."

Denver sat back and put exaggerated fingers to his ear. "I can't hear you."

"My name is Andy," David said.

CHAPTER 7

In her dreams, Drew was three years old again. She ran from room to room in a strange, windowless house, groping for something she had lost. Just before the dream ended, she reached the thing—she was never certain of its shape or size—that had eluded her. She grabbed with both hands, but it slipped from her fingers and floated away.

There were other dreams, remembered mostly in fragments. It seemed to Drew that she dreamed incessantly, and when she woke her legs were stiff and her throat ached as though she had run screaming through the night from real and not phantom danger. The dreams added to the weight of helplessness that she dragged through the days. Awake, she was never less than half asleep, as though imperfectly paralyzed by the bite of one of the dream spiders that pursued her through the night. Asleep, she was alert, listening for David's footsteps.

Instead of West returning to Drew's house on Tuesday afternoon, there had been a call asking Drew and Chuck to come to the police station. This time they were led beyond the stage set with its unstained beige carpet and its prominent color photographs of the Sherwood Rangers, the Little League team sponsored by the SPD. Behind the front room where the citizens of Sherwood came to complain about neighbors with wind chimes or too many barking dogs—the city code allowed a maximum of three dogs per house—was a group of small, dark offices and interrogation rooms with scarred tables and scuffed floors.

Drew and Chuck had barely spoken in the car, and their hands did not touch as they sat across from West and waited for him to tell them what had happened to their son. Chuck, passive by nature, played strong and silent. During their marriage, Drew had responded to Chuck's passivity by talking loudly and being twice as forceful as necessity demanded. Now she was silent, too, but with no pretense that silence was strength. Unexpectedly, the anger that fueled her had been extinguished, suffocated by the cloak of helplessness she wore even in her dreams. She found it an effort to breathe.

As coldly and concisely as a surgeon, Angus West stitched together what was known about the disappearance of David Greene. The finished pattern made only partial sense. David had been seen at the Galleria sometime after five o'clock by a teenage employee of the mall's yogurt shop. There was a short stop at the mall's toy store. About half an hour later he had entered Batter Up. He had asked half a dozen questions and then spent twenty minutes looking at old baseball cards before buying a pack of Stadium Club and one of Score. He had left the store and vanished. The Galleria had been searched. There was no trace of David.

West looked over Drew's head and continued in an expressionless voice: "Because of the holiday, the Dumpsters weren't emptied yesterday. When we sifted through them today, we found nothing. No baseball cards, no backpack, none of the clothes the boy was wearing."

At almost the same moment, Chuck and Drew realized West was telling them that there was no evidence their son was dead.

"What do you . . . ?" Chuck started.

"Can you guess . . . ?" Drew began.

They disentangled their words. "What do you think happened?" asked Chuck. "Can you guess how David might have left the mall?" Drew asked.

"We think he went with someone. He probably left willingly. The mall was almost empty, but someone would have noticed a boy struggling. It's also possible that he left by himself and got a ride from someone right outside. We've shown David's picture to the people who live on the streets near the Galleria. A few of them remember seeing him walking toward the mall. No one saw him in the evening."

"Where is he now?" Drew would have liked West to answer with a street address and telephone number. But she was asking for reassurance, for the detective to say that he thought David was alive.

West understood the unasked question. "We've had no unidentified . . ." He fished for the least hurtful word—corpse, body, cadaver, mortal remains— ". . . no unidentified body of a Caucasian child David's age anywhere in the county. We've checked Orange and San Diego counties, too."

West sat rigidly upright on his straightbacked brown chair. Neither his face nor his voice gave a hint of how desperately he wanted to be rid of these desperate strangers, of how much he wanted a drink. Vodka was his weekday medicine, one or two slugs at bedtime. He had discovered years ago that vodka kept the dreams away. He floated through the weekends on television and beer, but hard work and a shot of cheap vodka neatly deflected memory Monday through Friday. But not always. Not now. His own pain made him cruel.

"But the boy might be out of the state by now," he said. "Or . . ." There was no need to finish the sentence.

Too exhausted for denial, Drew and Chuck allowed themselves to be led into a room with a mahogany desk and walls decorated with expensively framed pictures of Sherwood Police Chief Frank Zarelli shaking hands with two dozen California politicians, divided equally between Democrats and Republicans. On the wall just above his desk, Zarelli had hung a blowup of a

Los Angeles Times article that compared the success rates of Southern California cities in solving crimes. Sherwood was number two on the list.

Zarelli had the jowls of a bulldog and small, watchful eyes. He combined the skills of a linebacker with those of an undertaker. It was a combination that allowed him, with equal dexterity, to blindside adversaries and soothe blameless Sherwood citizens.

West stood near the door and watched the chief's performance. He had been contemptuous of Zarelli for too long to waste energy disguising it. He had stopped trying to hide his contempt when the chief had refused to ask the city council for money to buy new patrol cars even after the radiator on one car had blown up during a chase and another car's mechanical problems had ruined a stakeout.

Since the SPD had decided it was unlikely that Drew and Chuck Greene had killed their son, Zarelli stood up and smiled sadly. So good of them to come. This was terrible, but everything that could be done would be done. Everything was already being done. Half a dozen policemen had been assigned to David's disappearance. Sergeant West was diligently following every lead.

That was West's cue to nod and stride diligently forward. Blank-faced, he didn't move.

Zarelli lost his rhythm for a moment and then continued. David would be found. Nobody vanished off the face of the earth. As Sergeant West had told them, so far the trail ended at the Galleria. It was time to ask the newspapers and local television stations to circulate David's picture. Very likely, someone had seen him during the last three days. The Greenes wouldn't have to talk to reporters, of course.

Like people setting sail on a voyage into serious illness, Chuck and Drew handed their lives to the professionals. If they had options, they were not aware of them. There was no debate over whether a kidnapper seeing color pictures of his victim on the evening news might decide to rid himself of the evidence of his crime. Afraid that even the mildest questions would endanger their son, they signed on the psychic dotted line.

During the ride home—although it was now only Drew's place, Chuck still thought of it as home—they might have been on separate continents. Chuck, who was driving, stared at the road ahead. Drew massaged the back of her neck and rubbed her eyes. If they had spoken, it would have been to accuse each other. "If you had been a better father . . ." "If you hadn't forced me to leave . . ." "If you hadn't walked out and made David angry . . ." "If you hadn't paid too much attention to the kids and not enough to me . . ."

But it had been years since their conversations had been more than the exchange of laundry lists. "Chuck, be sure to pick up Kiley at gym class by noon, and remember to go to the side gate." Or, "Drew, Kiley forgot his jacket; I'll give it to him next week-end." Drew's requests usually included the word *remember,* because although Chuck remembered bits and pieces of a task, he rarely remembered everything. Even before they separated, Chuck had responded by snarling or sulking. Yet he had usually settled comfortably beneath the wing of his wife's competence, asking her for help in finding his keys or searching for his glasses or sewing on a button he had just discovered was missing from the shirt he was wearing.

Since they would not talk, even to accuse each other, they sent their secret guilts, heat-seeking missiles, deep inside. The jacaranda trees were in bloom, lavender blossoms framing the white stucco houses and carpeting the streets of Sherwood, making the city into a tropical paradise this spring, as always.

"It's my fault," Chuck thought. "If I had stayed, this never would have happened."

"It's my fault," Drew thought. "If only I hadn't driven him away."

CHAPTER 8

"What's your name?"

"Andy Ellis."

"Why aren't you in school today?"

"My school's over."

"It's too early for school to be over."

"We start in August."

"What school?"

"Iowa. I go to school in Iowa."

"This is a long way from Iowa. What are you doing in California?"

"I came with my . . . with my . . ." The word clogged David's throat. He strangled on it.

Denver slapped the boy across the face, then repeated the question.

"I came with my daddy. He's going to take me to Disneyland."

"Where's your mother?"

"She's . . ." This word was broken glass, stabbing his tongue. His eyes on Denver's hand, David stammered, ". . . d-dead. My mother's dead."

They had been playing this game since Sunday morning. Denver would be shaving or buckling his belt or reading one of David's comic books, and he would ask with sudden ferocity, "What's your birthday?" or "What's the name of your dog?"

Sometimes, instead of asking David questions, Denver would tell him about Andy. Andy lived in a white farmhouse surrounded by fields of corn. In front of the house there was a tire tied to a tree. "You got a dog named Scooter," Denver would say, and David would have to remember that Scooter was a big brown dog with a long tail.

On any measurable scale, the boy was smarter than the man, and he was clever at the game. The Stanford-Binet intelligence test, given when David was in first grade, had scored his IQ as 168. But, in this motel room, power was height, weight, car keys, and money in the pocket.

"What's your name?"

"Andy Ellis."

"What's your birthday?"

"December eighteenth." That was the hardest thing, remembering the new birthday. David had been born in October.

Each time Denver left, he made David lie faceup on the bed. Then he would handcuff the boy's arm to the bed frame. The fabric covering the box springs had long since frayed. "Don't move 'til I come back," Denver would say, as much a mantra as a command. And David would lie motionless and remember how, in the last game of Clue he had won, the weapon had been the knife, like Denver's knife. Holding the picture of a knife in his hands had been a warning. But he hadn't listened. If only he had heard the warning, he could have stayed home and changed everything.

He created other omens out of the ordinariness of that Saturday morning. He had gone biking with Danny Matranga, and Mrs. Butler's black cat had run across the street in front of him. The cat had been between Danny's bike and his bike, so the magic hadn't hurt Danny. And he had deliberately ridden over the sidewalk cracks, even turning the wheel to make sure he didn't miss any.

There were cracks on the ceiling of the motel room. David would stare at the cracks until they moved toward each other, long-tongued monsters. Then he would close his eyes and rub his handcuffed arm until the skin was red and his mind was blank to everything but the feel of his fingers making circles on his arm. Denver always came back with junk food and a present. Once, it was a pair of cheap glasses with round rims. "Get used to wearing these," he said.

David no longer dared to wonder when he was going home. "When can I take a walk?" he would say, or "When are we going outside?"

"Soon," Denver might answer soothingly. But if he turned quickly and whispered, "When I say so," David closed his eyes and lay rigidly, not breathing until Denver turned away. There was no telephone in the room, no clock radio, and the television was broken. David told time by his bruises. The big one on his thigh was yellow and green now. His wrist, where Denver had twisted it, was purple.

"Do you know where I went just now?" Denver asked on Monday afternoon, handing David a slice of pepperoni pizza. "I went to see her. "That woman who used to be your mother. She says she doesn't want you anymore. She says you were bad to run away, and she has that other boy. She says he's a nicer boy, and she only needs one."

Denver's voice was flat, the words spread as evenly as butter, unaccented, as though they came from a dimly remembered lesson.

David threw the pizza down, the cheese making a new, triangular greasy stain on the stained bedspread. "You never saw my mother. My mother never said that." But his words curled up at the end, turned themselves into questions. Whenever he hit Kiley, his mother always pulled him off and sent him to his room. If he looked back as he was walking down the hall, he could see her rocking his brother.

67

Denver pulled the faded denim with David's carefully printed address from his pocket. "I went there. You have trees with purple leaves, and the woman has long brown hair. The other boy is smaller than you, and the woman was hugging him all the time. She said I could have you."

"No, no, no, no, no." David had had a few boxing lessons at day camp the previous summer, and he pounded at Denver's chest with both hands. Denver didn't retaliate, except with words. "Yes," he said. "She said I could have you."

Now David had his hands over his ears, pushing his palms against them until all he could hear was the roaring in his head. After a while, Denver pulled David's hands away. "What's your name?" he asked.

"Andy Ellis," David said tonelessly.

David painted Denver's Norman Rockwell portrait again and again, and then again. Denver never seemed to get tired of hearing how Andy lived in the two-story white house and ran through the fields with his dog and came home at suppertime to a mother in a green apron holding a fresh cherry pie.

"Tell me where you live, Andy."

"On a farm. I have my own bedroom. The house is painted white. I have a big brown dog. His name is Scooter."

Did he? He could close his eyes and see Scooter lying under the tire in the shade of the big tree. Suddenly, almost like a stab of hunger, David was curious. "Why is he named Scooter?" he asked Denver.

"You named him. You tell me."

"I didn't," David said. "You told me his name."

"Andy named him. You tell me why," Denver said, this time with the emphasis on "tell," and swung himself off the bed.

"Maybe because he likes to scoot along on his rear," David said quickly, before Denver's feet could reach the floor. One of David's grandmother's dogs, Pasha, did that.

Denver grinned. "That's exactly it," he said. "Scooter sure likes to scoot."

Denver believed in all his inventions. By Tuesday morning,

David teetered on the edge of belief, too. By then, Denver was calling him "my boy, Andy" with what seemed like embarrassed pride. He would stare at the raised bronze bronco on his belt buckle, tracing the outline with his fingers, and say, "My boy Andy can hit a baseball hard enough to break your hand if you try and catch it. Can't you, Andy?" And David would look into Denver's calm gray eyes and nod. When David hesitated or sobbed, Denver would hunch his shoulders and punch a fist into the palm of his other hand, and David could see the anger in his eyes. So David always nodded—and began to believe.

Denver was gone a long time on Tuesday afternoon. David thought it was Tuesday, but he wasn't really sure. He had learned to be coffin quiet when Denver was gone, but it was almost dark now. The corpses stacked up in the globe that surrounded the overhead light—burned moth bodies and bits of wings—were no longer visible. Lying on his back in the bed, he rocked from side to side, trying to pull his hand free. An uncoiled spring stabbed his palm. Darkness was an ocean that would crash over him, and he was chained in its path and would drown.

He screamed for his mother and hated her for not coming. He shouted and pounded at the bed, and the noise was swallowed by the spongy dark and by the brown dirt clods and dying grass that ringed the nearly empty motel. "I want to go home, I want to go home, I want to go home, I want to go home." The words ran together, a downhill torrent. Then Denver's hands were around his neck.

"Shut up, you ungrateful brat."

Hiccoughing and hysterical, David had an instant to realize that the voice was wrong. He was pulled up and flung back on the pillow and pulled up again, and he could hear his own wrong voice crying, "You're back. You're back. I was afraid you wouldn't come back."

Then the lights were on, the dark dismantled, and Denver was rubbing salve on the bracelet of raw flesh on David's wrist. "Daddy always comes back," he said. He reached into a greasy wax bag and gently pressed a french fry against David's lips. David opened his mouth and swallowed. His head tilted back, he could have been some huge baby bird. His mouth opened again and again, and the ketchup-dipped fries warmed his tongue and slid into the void beyond.

"Daddy won't let anyone hurt you," Denver said, cradling the boy's head against his chest.

David remembered another daddy, but faintly.

"You believe that, don't you?"

"Yes," David said.

CHAPTER 9

Since David Greene was unimportant and there was nothing particularly bizarre about his disappearance, his vanishing was reported halfheartedly by the media. One local television station flashed a picture of the boy on Tuesday night and asked viewers to contact the Sherwood Police Department if they had any information. On Wednesday morning, the *Los Angeles Times* gave the story two paragraphs in its daily roundup of grotesque events on page five of the Metro section—just below a sheriff's deputy indicted for sexually abusing his stepchildren, and just above a drive-by shooting that caused the death of a four-year-old girl. The shooters had been aiming at her nineteen-year-old uncle, a known gang member. Most of the misery and corruption that had floated to the surface in Los Angeles the day before never made the paper at all. A subeditor had found room for David Greene because he was white.

It is odd how quickly the abnormal becomes normal. Kiley was at school, gummy dinosaurs and a peanut butter sandwich in his lunchbox and his teacher warned. Although her sons' teachers and the principal at Sherwood Elementary School seemed genuine in their sorrow, Drew could hear a greed for details in their sympathy. Most of all, she could feel their relief that they had escaped once more, that their own children were safe. And she knew that she would have felt the same relief.

When Drew was Kiley's age, she had walked the eight blocks to Sherwood Elementary School carrying her peanut butter sandwich in a *Gilligan's Island* lunchbox. Now, both the lunchboxes and the streets were full of monsters. By the time they graduated from nursery school, Sherwood's children could distinguish between the bag ladies and the crazies who shared the streets of the city. Kiley, like all the younger children, was in a carpool. Today, to make the separation from home less painful, Drew and Kiley had walked. Going home, Drew's feet automatically turned left at Maple and right at Durand as they had day after day twenty-five years earlier. She found that she was jumping over the squares of pavement that were imprinted with the developer's name. When she was a child, it had been a bad omen to step on the concrete stamped with the round "Janss Investment Company" symbol.

In Southern California, May is the kindest month—mild days cooled at both ends, by early morning and late afternoon fog. And the kindness lingers until the days turn hot in mid-June. Spring in California, to people who live elsewhere, is a banquet for the eyes—glossy magazine photographs of beaches and surf, Rollerbladers in fluorescent spandex and movie stars in shades standing beneath swaying palm trees. For those who live there, it is a feast for the nose. Along the quiet streets of Sherwood, the air was dense with roses; and the smell of jasmine, honeysuckle, and gardenias mingled with the scent of orange blossoms. The two orange trees in the Greenes's backyard were overachievers. Although their branches were still weighed down by ripe fruit, they were already forming a new crop. On Saturday morning, David had picked and cut half a dozen oranges and made orange juice for himself, his mother, and his brother.

The pavement beneath Drew's feet seemed solid, but she was not deceived. All her life Drew had tried to live safely—always wearing a seat belt, never driving more than nine miles over the speed limit, marrying the most decent of the men with whom she had gotten involved. She had deliberately spent thirty-three years not taking chances; and Chaos had rewarded her by staying beyond the garden gate. Yet she had always known that one day the abyss beneath her feet would open up and swallow her. Until now she had kept the chasm papered over with the long lists she wrote each day of errands to be run and tasks to be accomplished. She had kept it closed with luck and with anger. David's disappearance had irrevocably torn her paper-thin pretense of safety.

While Drew was walking home, an unidentified boy with a John Doe tag secured to his toe by a rubber band was being shoved into a stainless-steel box in the top tier of metal boxes in the Cedars-Sinai morgue. The boy had been alive when paramedics brought him to the hospital at 8 A.M., but he had never made it out of the emergency room. Since he appeared to have been beaten to death, the boy would eventually become the property of the Los Angeles County Coroner's Office. But, for the moment, he was Cedars's problem. It was an unusual problem for the upscale hospital where Hollywood stars could order gourmet food after their Cesarean sections and plastic surgery. But the boy, obviously dying, had been found lying in the middle of a street less than a mile away.

Cedars put the body in cold storage and waited. There was a large room with three empty autopsy tables but, without identification, Cedars didn't dare to touch the body. Nothing was the way it had been in the old days. Now the family's permission was needed for almost anything a hospital wanted to do. Otherwise, there was always a lawyer determined to drag the hospital into court. So Public Information went to work, and bulletins were sent to police departments as far north as Santa Barbara.

When the bulletin was handed to Angus West, he said, "Shit. Fucking shit."

"Not my fault," said the clerk who had handed it to him.

West drank two cups of coffee to the bitter grounds before he called Drew. During the best of times, the sexiest thing about Drew was her voice. It was expectant, slightly breathless, deeper on the phone than in person. What her voice seemed to expect, it was hard to say—perhaps a winning lottery ticket. But this was not the best of times. Her voice was frayed and wary.

With one quick thrust, West cut the fraying sinews that bound the various sections of Drew Greene together. "There's an unidentified boy at Cedars."

"In the hospital?" Drew asked.

"No."

"He's dead?"

"Yes."

"It's David?"

West relented. "It might not be. There's not much description. The fax says a white boy between seven and ten years old."

"What do you want?"

What West wanted was to be a million miles from Sherwood. "It might be David," he said. "Someone should try to identify him."

It didn't occur to Drew to call Chuck who was fighting World War II two miles away. Brilliant at explaining the fine points of Germany's collapse, Chuck was dull normal at the details of real life. Sent to the market for half a dozen items, he would return with four or return with none because he had lost the list. Getting emergency supplies from the supermarket had become easier since Chuck moved out. David went to the market on his bike. Even when he was angry at being sent, David never forgot what he was supposed to buy or brought home the wrong size.

"I'll have to be the one," Drew said. "I'll do it."

It was a twenty minute drive to the hospital. The policeman didn't try to comfort Drew, and Drew's exhaustion kept her quiet. West drove crisply. His big hands flicked the wheel with delicacy; he had an unexpectedly dainty touch.

The morgue at Cedars was in the basement. They had to thread their way down a hall that was lined with cardboard filing cabinets. In two or three places, West's size defeated his attempt to avoid the cabinets, and he buckled the cardboard with his knee. The drawers were filled with specimens—muscle tissue, bone, and bits of other things—fixed in wax. There was no place else to put them.

Drew and West waited in a too bright, too cold room with generic prints on the dirty cream walls. Neither of them sat down. Morgues are always bright and cold. Flesh decomposes when the temperature rises.

Standing beneath a poster advertising Los Angeles's triumphant 1984 Olympics—a sprinter in the starting blocks—West stood solidly, carved from oak. Fight or flight. West's choice would have been flight. He had been avoiding a moment like this for thirteen years. Drew was, by instinct, a fighter. But there was no fight in her now. She was as paralyzed by this cold place as a rabbit is by the headlights of the car that will end its life.

"Don't let it be David. Don't let it be David. Don't let it be David. Don't let it be David." Drew closed her eyes and cracked the whip of her mind at Chaos. "Don't let it be David. Don't let it be David. Don't let it be . . ."

West was pulling at her arm. "You didn't hear me. I said they're ready for us."

The room where the bodies were stored was unlocked by a broad-shouldered Japanese college student. He had been spending his summer vacations at the morgue for three years, long enough to save considerable money for medical school, long enough to decide he didn't want to be a doctor after all. He matched John Doe Jr.'s identification number with a sticker on a vault and pulled out the stainless-steel drawer.

The body was naked, wrapped in a clear plastic shell. The torso was blue with bruises, and one leg flopped at a strange angle, as if it were rag rather than bone. The face was purple and distorted, like a sculpture by a surrealist painter who had stumbled into the wrong medium. It was floating under the plastic as though under a layer of ice. Before she looked at the boy's face, Drew knew that it wasn't David. The boy's feet were too small, his chest too delicate. He lacked David's sturdiness.

"It's someone else's son." She never understood why she used those words. Then Drew's will relaxed and let her body react to the forty-eight-degree temperature and the stink of diluted formaldehyde. Suddenly cold, she started to shiver and retch.

The body slid away on oiled rollers, but West continued to stare at the place where it had been. Whatever he was seeing, it was more real than Drew's voice. Now it was her turn to pull at his arm.

In the same moment that she knew the dead boy was not David, Drew knew that she would never let it be David wrapped in plastic and stored on a steel slab. Her anger, she discovered with a sudden rush that felt like a mixture of joy and drunkenness, had not been quenched. The embers had been there all along. Now it burned again, consuming her helplessness and exhaustion.

On the ride home, Drew poured out ideas: Posters with David's picture stapled to the trees of Sherwood, a canvas of all the baseball card shops in Los Angeles, a reward. "One of my mother's dogs is a good tracker," she said. "Maybe we could take him to the baseball shop at the Galleria."

West's face was blank. Like all big men, he could give the impression of being impassive and impassable. But the car skidded when he made a right turn onto Olympic Boulevard, and his fingers trembled.

Drew attacked, trying to scorch his impassivity. "You've written David off. You think he's dead."

West said nothing.

"You don't care. If it were your son, it'd be different. Because it's my son, you don't care."

When he dropped her off, she slammed the door and shouted after him, "I'll find David. Even if you don't help, I'll find him."

CHAPTER 10

It was Wednesday morning. Early risers who were also careful readers of the *Los Angeles Times* had already digested "Sherwood Boy Missing" along with their orange juice and coffee. In the hills, where the rich people lived, the day was still zippered. Down in the flats, the freeways were already clogged, although it was not yet seven o'clock. "Flatlanders are all right," the old joke went. "But would you want your daughter to marry one?" The Royal Motel, on a flat and barren street, was surrounded by freeways, and David woke to a roar that might have been the ocean but was only the anger of automobiles not free to retaliate.

"I know where you used to live," Denver had said when he tucked David into bed the night before. "I know where to find you. I know where to find her." He had only used the word *mother* once. After that, when his tongue had circled back to the house with jacaranda trees, the woman with brown hair had been indistinct, turned into the dim "that woman" and, finally, "her."

Once Denver's hand had jerked—almost hitting David— when he said "her," but he had shoved his fist into the pillow.

Denver spoke too quickly, as though he were trying to outrun his own words. "We won't talk about her anymore. She isn't anyone. But I know where to find her and the little boy, and I'll know where to find you, if you ever go back there." Then he had gently pulled the sheet to David's shoulders and tucked him in. David no longer evaded Denver's hands. Andy Ellis was comforted by Denver's touch.

"We won't ever think about her again," Denver said as he turned off the light.

Waking, David looked quickly at Denver's bed. The man was sprawled facedown, entangled in the sheets as though he had fought a war with them during the night. When Denver was awake, the space inside David's head that belonged to David kept shrinking, like one of those plastic toys you bake until they are less than a quarter of their original size. Because Denver was still asleep, David could explore the space, the way he had probed the bloody holes with his tongue after his baby teeth had fallen out.

Denver awoke almost as soon as David glanced at him, awoke with that cat-quick alertness that had ruined David three days earlier when he had tried to bolt. A year ago, the boy had tested off the top of the chart in analytical reasoning. But the man was crafty, with animal instincts and animal skills. When Denver stretched and scratched the tufts of dark hair on his chest, David let himself be pushed aside by Andy. David shriveled, melted, plunged down the rabbit hole into blackness.

Breakfast was Coca-Cola and potato chips. David sipped the lukewarm Coke, while Denver crushed the last fragments of chips on to yesterday's pizza. Afterward, they sat on Denver's bed and traded baseball cards. David demanded six cards from Denver in return for two 1992 Upper Deck Home Run Heroes, Barry Bonds and José Canseco. His throat had a collar of blue bruises where Denver had choked him, and he could barely whisper, so he found his colored markers and printed the trade he wanted to make on a piece of toilet paper.

Denver wrapped a wet towel around David's neck. "Does that feel better, Andy?"

"Yes," David wrote. "Yes, Daddy."

If Denver had been kind or cruel, one thing or the other, it would have been easier for David to keep his balance. But the boy was trying to stay atop a log that rolled in one direction and then twisted suddenly the other way. And each hour was full of unexpected storms. It was better not to fight to stay atop or afloat, better to fall, to drown.

A little while later—or was it a long while, since a listless David drifted down a slow-moving river of time—Denver said, "Hey, Andy, let's go to a ball game."

Denver, the patient hunter, had stalked and caught David. Now, four days later, prey in hand, he had traded tenacity for spontaneity. "Hey, Andy, let's play catch," he would say and push the lamp out of the way. Or, "Let's trade cards," and he would clear his bed by sweeping comic books and blankets to the floor. Once, a sleepy David had said, "I'm tired." Denver had thrown the baseball and hit him hard on the leg. So now David, a puppy desperate to please its capricious master, nodded and smiled, even before he understood what Denver was saying.

"Out? We're going out, Daddy?"

The words gurgled, all soft, runny vowels, and Denver had to put his ear close to David's mouth to understand them.

Denver soaked the towel in the washbasin and wrapped it around David's neck again. "Gotta go out sometime," he said.

The Dodgers were in Philadelphia. The Angels were playing the New York Yankees in Anaheim Stadium, two freeways away. Denver zipped David's blue jacket and held his hand. The bruises were a secret world, under the jacket, under the blue jeans. What was visible was a man and his eight-year-old son, walking hand in hand, hidden among 19,246 baseball fans.

Chuck had never taken David to a ball game. Drew had taken him once, a field trip she found not nearly as interesting as the Page Museum with its saber-tooth tigers and dire wolves. Denver was as excited as the boy. It was a giveaway day, free baseballs, and David threw his ball into the air between innings, sending it higher and higher.

"You'll be a pro some day, Andy," Denver said, and David—Andy—believed him.

If David could have spoken as David, he would not have, so deeply was he buried in Andy Ellis. The ice cream with which Denver lavishly supplied him cooled the hot patches in his throat. Denver's pockets bulged with bags of peanuts, and he spit the shells in rhythm with each pitch.

The Angels pitcher was effective, and the game was won almost before it began. In the first inning, Rex Hudler sent a bloop double to left, stole third base, and scored on Tim Salmon's sacrifice fly. It was all the Angels needed, but they added a run in the second inning and two more in the third when the Yankees walked Chili Davis to load the bases, and then J. T. Snow slapped the 0-2 pitch into center field. Denver and David were on their feet, crushing the peanut shells, cheering as the American pastime aroused primitive feelings. A man in an Angels jacket on David's right lost his balance and sloshed beer on the boy. A father himself, he automatically reached over to help David out of the soaking jacket.

"Sorry," he said. "Let me help you take that off."

"It's okay," David tried to say as Denver pulled him close. But the words were mush.

"Something wrong with your boy?" the man asked sharply.

"He's got a sore throat," Denver said. Grinning, he garnished the truth with lies, making them credible because he could always hypnotize himself into believing that his lies were true. "Andy got thrown by his bicycle, handlebars made an awful mess of his throat. Didn't they, Andy?"

David nodded as Denver unzipped the jacket and pulled David's arms out of the sleeves and in the same motion draped his windbreaker over the boy's head. "Some bucking bronco, that bike," he said, as he threw the sopping jacket onto the bench. But the man was no longer paying attention.

Asleep in the car, with his head on Denver's shoulder, David dreamed of green ears of corn with silken tassels. At first it was Andy's corn, planted in David's head by Denver but growing so huge that the ears blocked out the sun. Then he was running through the rows, lost and alone, and the corn was dripping with blood. He had seen *Children of the Corn* on television one night when Drew was out and the baby-sitter had spent the evening on the telephone. His mother had come home fifteen minutes before the movie ended and turned off the TV, so he was left with people running and dying in terrible ways. In his sleep, he clung to Denver's arm.

He was aware of Denver carrying him into the motel room. He staggered into the bathroom to pee. "Thank you, Daddy," he said, as Denver tucked him in.

"Give Daddy a hug," Denver said. And Andy stretched out his arms and was comforted.

David still slept with his baseball mitt. The second day Denver had brought glove oil, and together they had rubbed it into the mitt. David lay on his side, hugging the glove and looking at the small pile of things he owned. They were stacked on the night-stand, the polished rocks brightened by moonlight.

"Good night, Andy," Denver said.

"Good night, Daddy," David answered.

He could feel himself slipping into Andy, the David space hardly the size of a dime. It was easier not to struggle, easier to close his eyes and allow himself to be submerged.

The current was carrying him more quickly now, carrying him out of reach of David Greene. But Denver had made a mistake letting David keep the mitt and the agates, the small pocket Scrabble and the comic books. These things did not belong to Andy Ellis. With a less stubborn child it might have made no difference. In the past it had made no difference. But Andy's white house and brown dog—Andy's brush-stroke memories—buckled against the metallic edges of the pocket game and were blunted against the polished rocks.

David slipped his hand into the mitt and made one last attempt to reach the surface. "My name is David Greene," he said in his head and then waited, terrified, for Denver to hear the thought. When nothing happened, he thought the words again. And again. "My name is David Greene."

CHAPTER 11

Jesús García worked in Sherwood each Tuesday and Wednesday. The rest of the week, he cut grass and clipped hedges in Santa Monica. García was paid considerably more by the owners of the big houses in Santa Monica, but he trimmed just as diligently for Violet Flynn and his other Sherwood clients.

Mrs. Flynn lived at 2026 Kelvin Avenue in one of the small houses across the street from the back wall of the Sherwood Galleria. A retired teacher, she had lived in the house for thirty-seven years and had planted and replanted every inch of her neat front yard. In recent years, she had had to replant more often. Some of the homeless men who begged in front of the Galleria during the day found solace in the oleanders and iceplants of Kelvin Avenue at night.

It was about 1 P.M. on Wednesday afternoon, while Mrs. Flynn trimmed dianthus and watched Jesús cut the dead iris, that she noticed the bundle of clothes stuck into the boxwood hedge that separated her property from 2028 Kelvin. The ball of tan shorts and white underwear was hard to miss.

Jesús had sliced enough fingers on scythes and bougainvillea thorns to guess that the brown stains on the underpants were dried blood. But he said nothing when he pulled the clothes out of the hedge and handed them to Mrs. Flynn who prodded the stiff lump. During spring vacation, David had gone to an Indian Guides overnight camp, and the waistband of his underwear was clearly marked D. Greene.

The police had come to Mrs. Flynn's door the day before to show her the picture of a missing child and to ask if she had seen anything unusual on Saturday. She had not heard or seen anything out of the ordinary, she had told the young officer. Now she went inside to phone him.

Like most small police departments in Los Angeles County, Sherwood paid the LA Sheriff's Department Crime Lab to do its fancy work. David's shorts and underpants were slipped into a bag and sent downtown. David's blood type—O—had been recorded at birth, along with a tiny footprint. The hospital had had a pilot program then—discontinued a few years later as too expensive.

Lieutenant Zane was waiting when Angus returned from the hospital morgue. "It was the Greene boy?"

West shook his head. He had made a detour on the way back, and his breath was sour. It had taken him less than fifteen minutes to medicate himself with three bottles of beer. It was the first time in years that he had broken his major rule of behavior—no alcohol until his gun was stored in his dresser drawer and the doors of his small house were locked against the world.

"Anyway, the boy's most likely dead," Zane said. "A lady who lives across from the mall found his bloody shorts. I'll send Rich and Gomez to work that street again tonight." Zane turned from side to side in his chair. "A kid. A kid last seen at the Sherwood Galleria. That's a hell of a public relations problem."

"Yeah," West agreed. "It's a shame he wasn't killed at the Century City mall."

With the discovery of David Greene's shorts, a missing child had turned into a probable dead child. When he investigated an armed robbery, West could leaf through the files in his head and match the style and bravado of former robberies to the current crime. But he had worn blinders when it came to crimes against children. He had seen no evil—not brutal parents, not the pervert who lived down the block and paid six-year-old girls with chocolate bars. When it came to little boys who might have been murdered, the files in his head were blank.

So he turned the pages of the manila folders that he had had two clerks pull from the file room. He wiped the dust from all of Sherwood's crimes involving children, 1986 to 1996, and comforted himself with work. Within an hour, dozens of discarded files—drunken fathers too free with their fists, eleven year olds roughed up for their lunch money by thirteen year olds, high school sophomores who had had the misfortune to buy their marijuana from undercover officers—were piled on a chair next to him. He had scanned the files and rejected those he considered impossible. He had placed the files that were left in two stacks. He pushed the stack of crimes against girls to the far corner of his desk. Beyond was the empty desk of Sergeant Ron Howell. This was, should have been, Howell's case.

When West called, Ron Howell was lying on the couch, watching some ancient basketball game on cable television. He had forgotten to take the portable phone to the couch with him, so he had to grab for his crutches and swing his bandaged knee into the perilous air. The phone rang a dozen times before he reached it.

"You doing okay?" West asked.

"I'd be nuts without ESPN," Howell said. "I'm almost nuts with it."

"We've got a missing kid who may be dead," West said, and outlined everything that was known about David Greene and his disappearance. "You got any ideas?"

"I've been waiting for Trout to kill a kid" was Howell's answer.

When he hung up the phone, West had five names. Two were registered sex offenders with a penchant for boys under the age of ten. One was a piano teacher who had been acquitted of lewdly touching the young boys who sat next to him on the piano bench. The jury had believed the handsome young man who swore he was innocent, but Howell thought he was guilty. The fourth was John Scherdsky who had worked in Sherwood's upscale toy store until he had held a box cutter to the throat of a nine year old who was attempting to steal a Nintendo game. The fifth was Trout, who split his time between the streets of Sherwood and Los Angeles County's mental hospitals.

West looked through his stack for the five names and put those files in his wire basket without opening them. Then he spent two hours reading through the rest of the files, opening each folder without prejudging what he would find inside. When he was through, there were two more cases in his wire basket. In 1994, a nineteen year old who lived on Kelvin Avenue had beaten his eight-year-old brother and fractured the boy's left arm and three ribs. This year, during the month of February, a man—described by the boys as "creepy"—had stood outside the fence of the boys' athletic field at Sherwood's middle school during 10 A.M. P.E. He had come every morning for two weeks until the school's principal had asked the police to send him away. The man had been charged with no crime, but the police had taken his name.

West read through each of the seven cases twice and then dropped the files on Todd Carter's desk.

"More?" said Carter. He wanted to say, "Shit," but he had only been a detective for four months. West had already asked Carter to put together a list of children killed in Los Angeles County since 1990, with special emphasis on cases where the children had not been slaughtered in the crossfire between two rival gangs. Since few police departments in Southern California were computerized and several hundred children were killed each year, Carter had been on the phone for hours.

"Find out where each of these men is," said West. "Current jobs and addresses. And see if they've had any recent arrests. Get Alameda to help you. And get word to Rich and Gomez that if they see Trout they should pick him up."

An hour later, West was standing in the Sheriff's Crime Lab, holding the preliminary serology results. The underwear and tan shorts had both been swabbed. The presumption of blood had turned out to be the reality of blood. Parts of each bloodstain had been cut out, and the blood typed. All of the stains were consistent. Type O. Of course, someone else with type O blood might have bled into David Greene's shorts. That could be ruled out by taking samples of the parents' blood and doing DNA testing. The results would not be available for six weeks.

West followed the shorts and the thin, young analyst who held them into another room. The girl put on a pair of goggles and handed a pair to the policeman. Then she switched off the light. She moved a laser light wand deftly across the surface of the clothes. Nothing happened. She tried again, touching the wand to every fold and crease in the underpants.

"No fourth of July," she said, as she turned on the light. "No fireworks."

"What?"

She tossed her ponytail at the policeman. "No semen. Semen stains floresce. You get lots of fireworks."

West signed the evidence out in triplicate. It would be necessary for Drew Greene to identify, in a formal fashion, her son's clothes, just as she had been asked to identify her son's—but it was not her son's—body. Bureaucracy left no space on its forms for grief.

On some streets, rush hour in Los Angeles lasts all day. When West retrieved his car from the parking lot, he was an hour's drive from Sherwood. He drove slowly west on Beverly Boulevard. He was not even tempted to block the road jockeys who moved from lane to lane in a frantic effort to arrive wherever they were going a hundred and twenty seconds sooner. West could remember when the wide boulevards were clear runs east to west, downtown to the ocean. It had been twenty minutes from Hollywood to the beach with four teenage boys punching one another in the backseat of a '67 Mustang convertible and a bottle or two of beer rolled in each of their towels. When he was in high school, it hadn't mattered what beach you went to. From Zuma to the Santa Monica pier and south from there, the sand was white and the water clean. Most places, the sand was still white, but there were beaches where nobody in his right mind went near the water.

When the car in front of West turned right on Vermont, a Honda Accord and a dented Chevrolet raced for the hole. The Chevrolet won and was immediately stopped by a red light. Taking the freeway might have been quicker, but heading toward the ocean at 6 P.M. was a barrel of molasses, no matter which street or which route you chose. And West was patient. If he had been asked what made him a good policeman, he would have shrugged, but he knew the answer—intuition and patience. He could outwait the traffic just as he had, on a hunch, waited all night outside the Cozy Corner Cafe for one of Sherwood's homegrown, acne-faced desperados to make a raid on the cash register, just as he had waited motionless, lying on his stomach in a vacant lot, in long ago games of cowboys and Indians.

Drew sat at the kitchen table next to Laura Matranga who was holding up a snapshot of David. "Should we put *Reward* at the top of the poster or put David's name first?" Laura asked.

"*Reward,*" Drew said. "Always give the people what they want." It wasn't a good joke, but it was the first time Drew had even tried to joke since Saturday night. "Put David's name under the picture and make it the same size."

The joy and the rush of relief had vanished, but Drew's determination was even stronger than it had been when she had looked at the dead boy and made David a promise. Kiley, who sat on the floor at Drew's feet, was warming himself in the heat of her tenacity. Kiley and Danny Matranga were making their own signs. "Find my brother," Kiley had printed, with Danny's help. "My friend is missing," Danny wrote.

Chuck had come and gone. His daily routine had expanded quite easily to accommodate his son's disappearance. He was at the house by four each afternoon, and he went home to Tiffani at six. Mostly, he watched cartoons with Kiley. In less than two weeks the semester would be over. The students would be cut loose for the summer, as would Chuck, although he usually spent a month of his vacation teaching summer school.

"I'll take this to Copymat in the morning," Laura said, holding up the finished poster.

"Get a thousand of each size," Drew said. "We'll want eight-by-tens to leave at all the stores."

"Mine, too." Kiley pushed his poster into his mother's hands. Kiley had written, "Find my brother. I love him." and signed his name and phone number.

"Yours, too," Drew said as the doorbell rang.

West held his package behind him, like an awkward teenager with a gift of flowers.

"No," Drew said. Kiley had wrapped himself around her leg, and she pulled him closer as she looked at the policeman. The two of them—mother and son—filled the doorway, blocked the entrance of the policeman and the devastation he held behind his back. "These fragments I have shored against my ruin," Drew thought.

"I'd like to speak to you alone," West said.

She left him standing on the cement path surrounded by pots of orange marigolds. Drew had never been much of an actress. Sending Laura and Danny and Kiley for ice cream fooled none of them. But not even Kiley protested.

Once again, Drew and Angus sat at the dining room table. The bloody shorts were on the table between them. Days after Denver cut David's arm and let the blood soak into the tan shorts, the stains could have been anything. David loved to let the sun turn chocolate into soup. He could have melted a chocolate bar on the dashboard and dripped the brown liquid on his shorts as he licked it off the paper.

"We'd like to get blood samples from you and Mr. Greene," West said. "To make sure the blood is David's." His words were rocks skimming the surface of a pond—uninflected, shallow.

"He's not dead," Drew said.

How many doors had West knocked on? How many doorbells

had he rung? "I'm sorry, ma'am, but there's been an accident." He was a twenty-two-year-old patrolman, and she was, maybe, forty, and he could still remember that she was wearing a pink bathrobe. While she was sleeping, a drunk driver had run a stop sign, and her husband wouldn't be coming home. "He's not dead," she had screamed. "He's bowling. On Thursdays, Mike always goes bowling."

"David's not dead," Drew said again. "I can't let David be dead." She wasn't screaming. In fact, she was surprised at how calm she felt until she realized that she believed the words she was saying. She had felt David's absence for five days, but it was the missing piece of a jigsaw puzzle, not a hole in the universe. She felt incomplete but not empty.

She knew that the detective didn't believe her. West was deliberately looking beyond her, at the wall filled with drawings by David and Kiley that Drew had mounted in drugstore frames. Drew reached up and pulled West's head down until his eyes were opposite hers. His face was narrower than she expected, and his yellow hair was so fine that it fell through her fingers. "I would know if David were dead," she said. She said the words twice before she allowed West to look away.

"We don't know for sure that David is dead," West said. He was staring at a crayon scrawl that Kiley had called a bird sitting on a lion's head. "There's always hope." But his tone said, "There's never hope."

Drew stood up and threw the bloodstained shorts at the detective. "Damn you," she said. "I don't care what you found. I don't care what you think. David's alive. I'm his mother. I'm still his mother. There's no empty place . . ." Then she was crying too hard to talk.

Half a quart of vodka didn't help. The dream leached through the barrier of alcohol. He was standing in a filthy apartment looking down at what had been a twelve-year-old girl. The cigarette burns on her half-formed breasts made a madman's game of connect the dots. The raw red circles spelled *Bitch.* The long brown hair which she had worn in cornrow braids had been sliced with a razor so close to her scalp that pieces of skin had come with it. The hair had been tied across her eyes so that she could not see what else her killer was doing to her.

West had kept the memory at bay for the last three years. Released, it ravaged him. He woke in a bed soaked with sweat and stumbled to the bathroom to vomit. The first few years, when the dream came once a week, his body had adjusted to it. Now he knelt at the edge of the toilet for fifteen minutes, and still the pain in his stomach didn't go away.

He had been an LAPD detective for twenty-eight months when it happened, and his promotion had come with a price. New detectives were assigned to rotting precincts in rotting ghettos. The woman who stopped at his desk that night was coffee-colored and frightened, and she smelled of cheap wine as she poured out a barely intelligible story about her daughter not coming home. West had seen the woman before. She had slept in the drunk tank half a dozen times. She was a raucous drunk for a day or two after her AFDC check arrived. He thought she had been picked up for prostitution, too. But she wasn't a pro, just a sad-eyed wino who needed a few extra bucks until the next check came.

West's sergeant had told the woman to go home and sleep it off. "The sergeant's right," West had told her. "You go home. Your daughter's probably home waiting for you right now."

He remembered that she had taken his hand then and refused to let go. "Please," she had said. "LaChandra's my baby."

When they did search, they had found the girl easily enough, stuffed into a closet in the building next to the one in which she lived. That was eighteen hours later, and LaChandra had only been dead an hour.

"You killed my baby," the mother had said in the hall outside the courtroom after West testified. "That man cut her, but you killed her, too."

The man who slashed LaChandra Johnston fifty-seven times had exhausted his appeals and been executed ten years later. West hadn't bothered to appeal. He continued to go through the motions of living. "To Protect and to Serve" was the motto stenciled on to the side of every LAPD patrol car. LaChandra had neither been served nor protected.

Eventually, West pulled on his pants and made himself a pot of coffee. His wife had left the automatic coffee maker behind. He had thought at first that she had overlooked it. About four years later, it had come to him that Ellen had left the coffee maker, the best bread knife, their one copper pot, and the two expensive Italian mugs as funeral offerings, to be buried with him. Thus she had avoided the fate of Egyptian dogs and wives who were slaughtered and left to spend eternity in the tomb of their master.

West sat drinking coffee until dawn.

CHAPTER 12

David locked the bathroom door. Denver was awake. Sometimes it seemed to David that Denver was always awake, that if he, David, woke at midnight or 3 A.M. or just before dawn Denver would always be there ahead of him. Even in the race to consciousness, he could not outrun Denver.

David had been dreaming about Superman. Superman had seen into the motel room with his X-ray eyes and cut through the wall with his steel body and lifted David out of bed. He had ridden home on Superman's back.

He watched the stream of urine splash against the dirty porcelain bowl. The Royal Motel was rented by the hour or by the month, no questions asked, no Clorox or cleanser or clean sheets. David tore off a piece of toilet paper and pulled out a lime green marker that he had hidden in the waistband of his pajamas. Denver had brought him the pajamas the day before yesterday or maybe the day before that. Time was measured differently now. He had had the pajamas for two sleeps. The marker came from before this new time.

He printed "David, David, David," so quickly and with such

panic that the words would have been unreadable to Denver if he had burst through the door and grabbed them from David's hand. Then David crumpled the paper and threw it into the bowl, the green disappearing under the yellow, and both vanishing in a whirlpool of rusty water.

David Greene had gone to sleep on Wednesday night with "David" in his head and David's toys in his hands; and the black panther that lay awake in the other bed had not sniffed out the treachery. Nor had Denver's X-ray eyes bored through the bathroom door just now. But maybe Denver was only waiting to pounce. David turned his head so that Denver could not see his face and forced himself to walk slowly back to his bed. Was Andy Ellis's face long instead of square? Were Andy's eyes brown instead of gray? Did Andy's voice sound different? Would Denver listen to David's voice and know he wasn't Andy?

"Hey, Andy," Denver said.

David could feel himself slipping away, but this time there was no bottomless pit. He was stuck, like the concrete elephants at the tar pits. He loved the tar pits, rolling down the grass to the wire fence that kept him from rolling in and drowning in tar the way all those saber-toothed tigers did ten thousand years ago. People were stupid when they said there were dinosaurs in the tar pits. Stegosaurus had died millions and millions and millions of years before the tar. Right now, inside his head, it was like part of David was stuck in the tar watching the Andy part, but the Andy part wasn't sucking him down anymore.

"Hey, Andy," Denver said more sharply.

David tried to say, "Yes, Daddy." But he had no words. Andy had the words—"Yes, Daddy," "I love you, Daddy"—but Andy was stuck in the tar next to him. And David watched Andy sinking. Andy's fingers were gone, then his elbows. David could no longer see Andy's neck. Andy's mouth was stuffed with tar, and his ears were black, and the tar had closed his eyes and covered his forehead. Then there was only the sticky shining surface that had deceived all those animals all those years ago. Inside his head, David was alone.

In a panic that Denver might shake the words out of him,

might turn him upside down and shake out the secret thoughts, David whirled and twisted and bumped against the furniture—a frantic human ball shot into a video pinball game. Sobbing, he held his throat and shook his head so violently that his tears cascaded down Denver's arms when the man put out his hands to stop him. Teardrops glittered in the hair of Denver's wrists as David grabbed the small pack of florescent marking pens that he had packed so carefully so long ago and spilled the pens on to the bed. "No words," he wrote in cosmic blue on the greasy side of a Chicken McNuggets box. And in galaxy red on the bag from some other dinner, "I can't talk."

Denver touched the necklace of bruises around the boy's neck and seemed to wince. "It's all right," he said, pulling the boy's face into his chest. "Don't cry. Andy's safe now."

David could feel his body betraying him with every heartbeat, but Denver didn't seem to hear the pounding sound of "David, David, David." Denver was humming—not a country western song this time. A baby song that his mother had sung to Kiley about a baby in a tree. Then Denver started rocking him. "Hush," he said, in a funny, high-pitched voice. "Andy's safe now."

Denver put the dime store glasses on David's eyes. For five days David had looked down, looked away, careful not to see too much. The cheap glasses hurt his eyes, but they magnified things, too. Denver had no suitcase. But the gym bag was too small for all of Denver's shirts. And where had his other pair of jeans come from? Maybe he kept his things in the car. Maybe in the trunk of the car.

Denver had secrets, too. David had known that from the beginning. It was what had made him start talking to Denver in the mall. He had wondered what Denver kept in his secret hiding places. David had three secret places. There was the paving stone near the back fence. He had pulled it up and dug a hole underneath and then put the stone back, and nobody knew, not even Danny. He had hidden his leftover Easter candy there but, when he came back, it was covered with sow bugs. Now he wrapped his Kit Kats in sandwich bags and hid them in the pittosporum tree about fifteen feet off the ground. He had nailed some wood for steps on the far side of the tree so he could climb up without his mother seeing. He was clumsy at ball games, but he loved to climb. He was never afraid to climb. Eating candy in the leaves at the top of the tree was the best secret of all. His other secret place, the one he shared, was in a brick wall a block away from his house. He had seen that one of the bricks was loose. Then he and Danny had taken kitchen knives and scraped until they could pull the brick out. They left messages for each other behind the brick.

He wished he could leave a message for Danny now, could tell Danny where he was. One of the towels in the bathroom said "Royal Motel," but he didn't know where the Royal Motel was. If only he had pebbles in his pockets. Hansel and Gretel found their way home because Hansel dropped pebbles when his daddy tried to lose him in the woods. But Denver had a car. It wouldn't do any good to throw pebbles out the window.

Denver took out his knife and flicked it open. Against his will, David yelped—a strangled, puppy sound—and put up his hands, knocking off the glasses. With lazy grace, Denver caught the glasses in one hand and put them back on David's nose. Then the hand with the knife reached up and cut a lock of hair from David's forehead—honey-colored hair that had escaped the black dye.

"Let's go eat," Denver said. "I want me a hamburger."

The real David, cunning, hid. If he were a Ninja warrior, if he were Leonardo, his favorite Ninja turtle, he could take his katana sword and chop and chop and then he could go home and no one would follow him. He knew his mother hadn't given him away. But maybe she *was* glad he was gone. Maybe she didn't want him back. Maybe she only wanted Kiley. For Mother's Day, three weeks earlier, David had made a special card for Drew: "To My Mean Mother on Mother's Day." He had crayoned pictures—of a heart, an eye, a mother—instead of writing the words. "My heart does not want U to have a very happy Mother's Day," he had written. "I hate U very much. I want U to have a very unhappy Mother's Day."

"You want a hamburger, Andy?"

David nodded. He had been sorting a stack of baseball cards, and he put them on the nightstand, next to the Clue cards he had taken so his mother couldn't play the game with Kiley even if she wanted to. He touched the painted coil of rope on one of the three cards. If it was a real rope, he could tie Denver up. If Colonel Mustard was real, the two of them could . . .

"Let's go, Andy," Denver said. He unzipped his gym bag and took out five or six twenty-dollar bills. Then he wiped his knife on his T-shirt and dropped it in his pocket before he opened the door.

It was lunchtime, but Jay's was too nondescript to be crowded. Denver was comfortable in nondescript, anonymous places. The Royal Motel was no more than twenty miles south of Sherwood, but no one who lived in Sherwood or West LA or Santa Monica would ever drive the graffiti-scarred streets that led to it. Denver had gone to ground where no one would look at David and wonder.

Like a wild thing examining the banks of a stream at half a dozen places before picking the safest place to drink, Denver had driven down a dozen streets before stopping at Jay's Eats—a counter, three tables with chipped Formica tops, and a fry cook in a dirty apron. As he crossed the sidewalk in front of the lunchroom, David made sure he didn't step on any of the cracks.

"Hamburgers for me and my boy," Denver said. "With plenty of french fries."

"What'da ya want to drink?"

"Two Cokes."

David could have reached out and touched the man's apron, but he didn't. He could have run to the two black men in moving van overalls eating lemon pie at the next table. But he didn't. He was only safe if Denver thought he was Andy. Denver liked Andy, but he didn't like David. There was a knife in Denver's pocket. If Denver found out that Andy was gone . . . David choked on his Coke.

"Take it easy, Andy," Denver said, pulling the glass away with the hands that had made purple circles on David's throat.

The hamburgers were slick with grease. What happened next was an accident of grease and distance perception. With the burger making his hands slippery and the glasses distorting what he saw, David missed his plate and squirted mustard onto the table. He looked from the yellow puddle to the man, afraid that Denver would be angry, unsure what ordinary things would make Denver angry.

"Butterfingers," Denver taunted. "Lucky you don't drop balls like that."

David—rigidly well behaved—started to blot at the mustard with his napkin. At McDonald's with Kiley and Drew, he would have been shouting and pulling his french fries through the mustard and pretending that they were yellow worms.

"Leave it," Denver said. "Let him clean it up."

His mouth full of burger, the fronds of the palm tree on his shirt stained yellow, David drew a wavy snake path along the edge of the mustard with his finger. For a moment, he thought of writing "Help" or signing his name, but Denver would read "David Greene" and know that Andy wasn't there.

Colonel Mustard was there. The thought was a balloon that got larger and larger until it filled David's mind and crowded everything else out. Between chewing and swallowing, he saw himself moving Colonel Mustard and Miss Scarlet and Professor Plum around the Clue board. He could leave clues that Denver wouldn't see— or wouldn't know were clues. He could leave his own trail of pebbles for someone to find. For his mother to find. This year, for the first time, he had made his mother an Easter egg hunt. "By my nature, I'm a pest. And of my kind, I'm the very best," was one of his clues. And his mother had guessed it was Kiley and had found the next clue, which David had hidden in Kiley's pocket.

"Let's go," Denver said.

When he reached the door, David looked back. The yellow lake was slowly spreading across the mottled black table.

CHAPTER 13

The Los Angeles County Department of Children's Services was at Drew's door before 8 A.M. on Thursday morning. The county had the power to give and take away. It was a power that many of the department's ill-paid employees cherished. To the polite but cynical black man in coat and tie who waited for Drew to open the door, child abuse was the norm, happy families the fantasy.

"Mrs. Greene?" He handed Drew his card. "I'd like to talk to you about your son."

Fred Jackson smiled with his mouth and checked the house with skeptical eyes. Whatever the cabinets might contain, there was no drug residue in sight. The lady in front of him didn't smell of alcohol, nor were her eyes glazed. The house was messy. He had to step around piles of books and newspapers on the floor. Carelessness should be noted, since careless might mean unreliable. But carelessness was not yet a crime. Offered a cup of coffee, Jackson nodded his head vigorously and followed Drew into the kitchen. He blew his nose equally vigorously and asked for a wastebasket. Drew pointed to the back porch. The basket held an abundance of paper, two ice-cream cartons, and the remains of Chinese takeout. No beer cans, no glassine envelopes, no smell of marijuana.

Jackson preferred his coffee black, but he asked for milk and stood where he could see into the refrigerator. Like the rest of the house, the refrigerator was untidy. It was also full of milk, fruit, cheese, and a two-pound jar of natural peanut butter. Jackson saw a lot of refrigerators that held nothing but ketchup, beer, and cola. Jackson saw a lot of refrigerators that made him wonder how the food stamp money was being spent. For the last six years, he had voted Republican.

An abundance of food didn't automatically rule out child abuse. More than twelve hundred children were killed by their parents every year. In about half the cases, the murderer was the mother. Jackson ran his thumb across his small, tidy mustache. The note from the Sherwood Police Department said that an eight-year-old boy had been reported missing, that the mother said the boy had run away, and that the mother got angry too easily. The parents were divorced, and there was another child, a five year old, who might be at risk.

Kiley sat at the kitchen table and spread peanut butter on his bran flakes. Jackson talked to Drew and watched Kiley. In a few minutes, he would excuse himself and ask for directions to the bathroom where he would check the medicine cabinet—partly to look for controlled substances and partly to look for evidence that a man was living in the house. Little boys were often battered by their mothers' boyfriends. So were little girls who cried too much, like the four year old in Riverside last year. Every social worker could tell stories about children who were left too long with their parents and ended up dead. There were matching stories about children who were taken away to spend the rest of their childhood in substandard foster homes. Jackson wasn't authorized to open medicine cabinets and empty wastepaper baskets. He did what he chose to do.

What Jackson chose to do when he returned from the bathroom was to make the woman angry. He sipped his coffee and used all the incendiary words. "A report of possible child abuse." "Concern for the welfare of the child left at home." "An obvious sign of trouble when a child runs away."

"David was angry," Drew said, her own anger loud in her throat. "He wasn't abused. We don't hit children."

"Some abuse leaves no marks," Jackson said and pushed his mug toward Drew to be refilled.

"Damn it," she said. "Nobody hurt David."

But we did, she thought. No parent can keep from hurting a child. Perfect love, unconditional love, is an illusion. Chuck and I hurt David. She spilled coffee on the table and mopped it up with a paper towel. Her anger spilled out but wasn't blotted. "I love my sons. What right do you have to say I don't?"

Feeling the force of Drew's anger, Jackson turned quickly toward Kiley. The boy had stopped eating, but he didn't move away from his mother. If he was afraid of her, it didn't show.

"You have a nasty temper," Jackson said, enjoying the chance to put his fingerprints on this woman's life. "You shouldn't let go like that."

Drew saw Jackson appraise Kiley. Frightened, she reached for her son. She was too sophisticated to think that good intentions are a shield. If you look at innocence from the wrong side of the prism, it seems bizarre. If only her love for David had been as uncomplicated as her love for this easier child.

Kiley squirmed away as Drew tried to hold him, and his hands left a streak of peanut butter on her face.

Jackson could take the boy aside and ask him questions. But the answers would be meaningless. No matter what the parents did to them, the children wanted to stay. He watched Kiley load Lego pieces into a dump truck and push the truck across the kitchen floor. Then he took out his neat black leather appointment book and made notes. He sat at the table and wrote ostentatiously, as though Kiley's fate depended on the swirls of his fine point pen. Actually, he had decided Kiley's immediate future several minutes earlier. The boy appeared to be in no danger, but it was always best to take precautions.

"It would be better," Jackson said, "if somebody stayed here with you for a while. Perhaps the boy's aunt or grandmother."

"I don't need . . ." said Drew and stopped. Once the system reached for you, you were caught fast, stuck in it like Brer Rabbit in tar.

"Until the police find out what happened to your older son, it would be better if you weren't alone," Jackson continued, as though Drew had said nothing at all. He held his pen expectantly above his pad for nearly twenty seconds before Drew conceded.

"I don't have a sister," Drew said. And then, "My mother can stay with me. I'll call her when you leave."

"Why don't you call her now?" Jackson said. He added, "I'd appreciate another cup of coffee. This time, I'll take it black."

Angus West had just finished shaving when Lieutenant Zane called. It was a little after 6 A.M. "We solved it," Zane said. "We fucking solved it." West could hear the strut in Zane's voice. "And we did it without any help from the LAPD." If the bantam-size lieutenant had been a rooster, he would have been standing atop the henhouse, crowing.

"You've found the boy?"

"We've found the man who killed him."

"You've found the boy's body?"

Zane barely hesitated. "Not yet. But we will."

A neighbor of Violet Flynn, a woman who hadn't been home when the street was canvased on Wednesday, remembered seeing one of the panhandlers pushing his shopping cart down Kelvin late on Saturday night. She had noticed that there was a large, awkwardly shaped package in the cart and that the man had hit the package several times, almost as if it were a drum.

Zane crowed again. "It was Trout. Rich found him around midnight and brought him in."

In Sherwood, as in the rest of Los Angeles, most of the homeless held out their hands to shoppers during the day and melted into shelters, doorways, or bushes during the night. The homeless problem, as it was antiseptically referred to in newspaper editorials, wasn't nearly as bad in Sherwood as in neighboring Santa Monica. The Sherwood city council had not made Santa Monica's mistake of inviting the homeless in and feeding them on the steps of city hall. A few local churches handed out free food but not free needles and not the keys to the city.

The Sherwood city council did offer a helping hand to the deserving poor who had toppled into homelessness after being hit by sudden bolts hurled by fate. It was considerably less helpful to the nutcases, crackheads, winos, and general losers who roamed its streets. Local ordinances against aggressive panhandling and against defecating on public property were enforced as robustly as civil liberties attorneys allowed.

Trout was a nutcase. Or, in the word favored by the older policemen, a fruitcake. He was also Sherwood's most dangerous schizophrenic. Tall and thin with bulging eyes and a narrow face that ended in pursed, thin lips, he had been given his nickname by the policeman who first booked him for disturbing the peace. His name was Robert Bumgartner, but he had been unwilling or unable to give it. In a boyhood spent outdoors, the policeman had hooked a dozen trout with similar faces. The nickname had stuck, even after Trout's brother provided his real name.

When he took his medication, Trout was almost too listless to ask for coins. When he threw his Haldol away, he draped his shopping cart with the carcasses of dead rats strung together like the bunches of garlic that decorate gourmet grocery stores. He wore a necklace of rat heads over a sweatshirt that had once been light blue but was now the color of night. Each time he was hospitalized, the rats were thrown away and the sweatshirt washed two or three times in carbolic soap.

He only attacked young boys. He pursued them with his shopping cart, the rat heads bobbing. When he knocked a boy down, he would laugh and shout, "Ten pin." Usually, the police took him to Santa Monica Hospital, and the hospital found a vacant psychiatric bed for him at Harbor, Olive View, County, or Norwalk on a seventy-two-hour observation hold. After seventy-two hours on Haldol or Thorazine—shaved, bathed, and clear-eyed—Trout went to court, promised to take his medication, and was released. About two months earlier, he had pinned a seven-year-old boy against a parking meter and crushed his arm. That time, he had been arrested and spent fourteen days in a locked ward at County USC Hospital.

"What proof do you have?" West asked.

Zane crowed again. "We've got his knife. And the guy's confessed."

The interrogation room was crowded. Trout's lawyer sat next to him. She was twenty-five years old, and her exhilaration at defending the downtrodden was beginning to wear off. That it had lasted through law school and for the next year was not a miracle. Abby Moore had grown up in a working class, strongly union family. Her father and two uncles had spent their lives putting doors on Chevrolets.

"You can't believe that," Abby said, putting down the paper on which Trout had scrawled "I saw him come out of the mall, and he laughed at me, and I hit him with my cart and hit him and hit him."

There was a more formal taped confession, full of grunts and screams as Trout fought his demons in the confined space of the small room. On the streets, Trout literally fought the demons that crawled around him, laughing at him. He ran at them, circled them, and shrieked to drive them away. He would never tell anyone why the demons were laughing, but he knew they thought the thing between his legs, his prick, was too small. He had taken a roll of toilet paper from the mall and stuffed most of it inside his pants to fool the demons.

Trout's brother paid Abby a hundred dollars each month. He wrote the check when he wrote checks for gas, electricity, and cable television. When calls came from the police or some hospital, he gave them Abby's number. Trout had always been the smart one in the family, the brother who got good grades, the brother who was going to go to college until the demons turned up one day when he was seventeen. Richard Bumgartner sold paint. He had not seen his brother since Trout made a pyramid on Richard's living room carpet of all the food in the freezer and then left with the television set. That was the twentieth time Trout had come into Richard's house to steal things or, once, to cut the couch cushions into squares and jam them into the toilet. After Richard Bumgartner cleaned the carpet, he changed the locks, put bars on his windows, and hired Abby Moore.

West stood in his usual corner. This interrogation was being led by Chief Zarelli himself. Zarelli had chosen to wear his uniform. He had his uniforms tailormade, but they still sagged and bulged in the wrong places, and his stomach pushed against the gold buttons.

"Where is the boy's body?" Zarelli asked.

"Don't answer," Abby said. She was sitting close enough to Trout to smell the rot that seeped from his breath, his clothes, and the body beneath his unwashed sweatsuit. She had become exhausted by Trout and his misery, but she was not tired now. A murder case changed everything.

"We have your knife," Zarelli said, moving closer. He was holding a plastic bag with a brown-handled kitchen knife. Each time Trout was hospitalized, they threw away the knife he used to decapitate the rats, but he always managed to buy or steal another one.

"Cut," Trout said.

"What did you do with the body?" Zarelli asked again, his beefy arms hanging in front of Trout's face.

Trout closed his eyes and covered them with crossed arms. "Cut," he said. "Cut, cut, cut." Then, "Buried. All buried." Then he hid his greasy head in Abby's lap and began twisting her sweater around his finger and making indecipherable sounds.

When a landscape architect had renovated the grounds of the Sherwood city hall earlier in the year, someone had put a hummingbird feeder in the tree outside the police department's windows. Todd Carter was watching a shimmering bird dip its beak in sugar water when West came out of the interrogation room.

"How many of them have you tracked down?" West asked.

Carter looked puzzled. "Rich said we got the guy."

West waited.

"So I haven't been . . . This morning, I mean. When I came in, Rich said . . ."

"Let's hear what you have."

What Carter had was addresses for four of seven names he had been given. West sat down, put his feet up on Carter's desk, and listened. West's huge feet in argyle socks and cordovan loafers were as brightly colored as the bird, and Carter stammered when he looked at them.

None of the four had had further trouble with the police, although one of the perverts had become an active member of a man-boy love society. The handsome piano teacher still gave lessons. The nineteen-year-old boy—now twenty-one—who had sent his brother to the hospital still lived at home on Kelvin Avenue. There was no current address for John Scherdsky who had lost his job after taking the knife he was using to slit cartons and placing it at the throat of a nine-year-old shoplifter. Trout's current address was the Sherwood jail. And the creepy man who had watched sixth grade boys play basketball hadn't been seen since. He had given a phony address, so he had probably given a phony name, too.

"See if you can get an address for Scherdsky from Motor Vehicles," West said.

"You don't think we have the right guy?"

"And get me a list of all children under the age of twelve who've been reported missing in the last five years where the cases are still open. From Ventura County south. Talk to the investigating officers. Get as much information as you can."

An hour later, West stuck pins in Zarelli's party balloons. When he knocked on the door of Zarelli's office, Zane had just handed the police chief a list of the television and radio stations that had agreed to bring their cameras or microphones to a news conference at 3 P.M. where Zarelli, in a newly pressed uniform, would announce that David Greene's bloodstained shorts had been found and that the SPD already had a suspect in custody.

West didn't wait for the police chief to ask him to sit down. Zarelli always made West stand. Zarelli was aware of West's contempt and, whenever possible, paid him back for it.

"I don't think Trout had anything to do with the kid's disappearance," West said.

West had come to Sherwood as a detective sergeant. As long as Zarelli was chief, he would stay a sergeant. Both men knew it. Neither had ever mentioned the subject, but there was a wordless acknowledgment. West did not ask to be promoted. Zarelli did not keep West from picking his own assignments. With three or four rapes, a few dozen armed robberies, more than two hundred burglaries and almost that many car thefts each year, there were a lot of assignments to choose from, and Zarelli was not a man to cut off his nose to spite his face. The newspaper blowup on the wall above Zarelli's head said that Sherwood had cleared twenty-nine percent of the crimes committed within the city's boundaries in 1995. Without Angus West, the percentage would have been considerably lower. But, to the chief's private pleasure, West had also been spectacularly wrong three or four times last year.

Zarelli brushed West aside. "We have a confession."

"A confession from a nutcase."

Zarelli was a clever, vain, ugly man. He had been Sherwood's police chief for nine years under three mayors. He was fifty-six years old and well versed in politics—the city council member who had suggested that he be hired was his wife's cousin—if not in murder. Previously, he had run a small security agency that provided private guards to warehouses and merchants. He looked up at the too tall, too fair, too confident sergeant standing in front of him, and his small eyes got even smaller. "You think the kid was killed by someone sane?"

"I think David Greene may not be dead," West said. He waited a second and added, "Yet." The word hung in the air for a moment, held up by its own insolence.

A team player, Zane bounded to the net to deflect the balls West was serving to the chief. "You heard Trout say he buried the boy's body."

"He probably buried something," West agreed. "I don't think it was the boy. I've got three or four leads. Don't stop looking for the boy."

West had gone this far before. A half dozen times, as now, his toes had touched the invisible barrier that protected Zarelli's vanity. He had always backed away. One more burglary unsolved, one less criminal in jail would make it no harder to get through the days. He had come closest to crossing the line when Zarelli refused to buy new police cars. "Damn the budget and the city council," West had demanded. In the end, though, the fight hadn't seemed worth the effort.

"We have the knife," Zarelli said.

"Rat blood," West said.

"The crime lab called five minutes ago. Rat blood." Zarelli's smile made his face even uglier. "And type O human blood."

West pushed Zarelli's triumph aside. "So Trout is type O like half the people in Los Angeles and he nicked himself with the knife. In six weeks you'll know the blood couldn't possibly be David Greene's, and in six weeks David Greene will probably be dead."

The smile was gone. "You haven't done a fucking thing in Juvenile for the last ten years," Zarelli exploded. "Howell says he's been afraid that Trout would end up killing a kid."

West tried to back away once again—and found he couldn't.

"If you stop looking for the boy, you're a fool," he said.

Zarelli's world was a grid in which each square was clearly marked—deference to the mayor and his wife's cousin, affable good humor toward Zane and other flatterers, and belligerence toward anyone who questioned his judgment. If Zarelli had been taller or West had been shorter, Zarelli could have crowded West to the wall, could have stuck his chest in West's face, and West would have had to step backward. If Lieutenant Zane had not been there, rocking on his toes as he brushed his sandy hair away from worried eyes, Zarelli might have roared and cursed and told West to stay out of his sight for an hour or two.

But Zane was watching, and West was tall and immovable.

"You're suspended for a week," Zarelli said. He snapped the words as though they were rubber bands. Then he waited for West to apologize or argue—to acknowledge by either response that he was outranked. A bow of the head, a word of submission, and Zarelli could send the sergeant back to work.

West turned and left the office.

CHAPTER 14

It was lunchtime when Ruth Miller parked her Plymouth Voyager in Drew's driveway. The driveway wasn't quite wide enough for the minivan, and the right front tire imprinted a neighbor's grass. When Drew was David's age and Ruth and her daughter lived together in this house, Ruth had owned a Volkswagen Beetle. Now she had a bigger family.

Flame and Pasha rode in wire crates. Brisket sat next to Ruth on the front seat. It had taken Ruth ten minutes to pack herself a few pairs of shorts, some socks and underwear, and a toothbrush. Then she had unzipped the bag and added one pair of slacks and a silk shirt, just in case. It had taken her half an hour to pack the dogs' suitcases—Linatone for their skin, vitamins, garlic and yeast wafers to defend against fleas, toenail clippers, cotton balls to clean their ears, Benadryl for bee stings, tea tree oil for cuts and scrapes, three different kinds of brushes. Ruth kept her own hair cut short. On summer mornings when she went swimming in the ocean with the three golden retrievers, she ran her fingers through her hair and shook herself dry.

Drew had cleared a space in Kiley's room, but Ruth led the three dogs farther down the hall.

"No," Drew said.

Pasha had already jumped on David's bed.

"You know we couldn't fit in there," Ruth said. Kiley's floor was a play city with two-inch wooden people delivering mail and tending parking garages full of miniature cars. "The dogs would break his city."

"Then I'll sleep with Kiley. You take my room."

But Drew was too late. When dealing with her mother, she was always too late. Ruth dropped the three vinyl bags she was carrying—one black, one green, one royal blue. Each dog had his own properly fitted dumbbell, chain collar, assortment of leashes, and tracking harness, as well as two or three special toys.

Flame licked Ruth's knees and then turned his tongue to Drew's elbow. Pasha made a nest for himself in David's comforter. "Down," Ruth said, and three dogs dropped like stones. "My sleeping in his room won't keep you from finding him," Ruth said.

"Mother . . ." Drew began, but it was decided, had been decided the minute Ruth opened the door to David's room.

"Help me with my stuff," Ruth commanded—not a guest but the owner of this house returning home. Drew carried in food dishes, water bowl, and dog biscuits. Ruth cradled a twenty-pound sack of lamb and rice kibble. She was strong and square. Her black hair looked as though a child had sprinkled silver glitter through it unevenly. Drew was three inches taller, with long legs and smaller breasts. David had inherited his grandmother's squareness, but Drew saw no mirror when she looked at her mother. Drew's muscles and bones had been sculpted by the father who disappeared from her life when she was three.

Ruth dropped the kibble in a corner of the kitchen and began to fill the water bowl. She was as heedlessly sloppy as her daughter.

"It doesn't look like you're watering enough" was the next thing Ruth said.

There were eight or ten old quarrels between them. Ruth

wanted Drew to take better care of the yard. Drew wanted Ruth to stop giving orders. Ruth more or less approved of the way Drew was raising her children but could never understand why her daughter had married Chuck in the first place. "I like Chuck," she would say unenthusiastically, or "Chuck's a nice man." The "but," spoken or unspoken, would follow. Their longest standing quarrel was over the way Drew was wasting her life. Neither Chuck—the divorce had removed that problem—nor Drew's job were worthy of her. "I sent you to Stanford," Ruth would say. "I couldn't afford it. I worked overtime six nights a week to send you to Stanford. You have a Phi Beta Kappa key, and you don't make enough money to pay the rent. You don't even have a real job." That argument had a formal pattern. Drew would answer, "I wanted to stay home with my kids," and Ruth would say, "I had to work hard to support you, and you turned out fine."

Now Drew said, "I watered yesterday."

"It doesn't look it," Ruth said and cleared a space in the cupboard for the dog biscuits.

"Kiley will be back in a few minutes," Drew said to her mother's back. "I'm going outside to wait for the carpool." Since David's vanishing, Drew had found it necessary to walk Kiley down the cement driveway to the kitchen door each day, as though otherwise Kiley, too, might vanish into the bed of rosemary.

"Grandma." Kiley threw his lunchbox on the floor and grabbed for Ruth's arms. "Is Flame here? Is Flame here?"

Kiley and Flame were the youngest children.

"You can give him a cookie," Ruth said and handed Kiley a dog biscuit. She pocketed biscuits for the other dogs and walked with Kiley to David's room.

Drew knew that her mother loved her children and was loved back. But Drew was not sure where her children fitted into the pack that Ruth led. David seemed to compete with Brisket for second dog, Kiley to be content with whatever space was made for him. Drew was even less sure who her mother would rescue if a car rushed madly toward dog and child. But that was a question she would never ask. The emotional connections that had bound together mother and child when Drew was David's age were warped and brittle now and carried few messages. When Ruth had asked on the phone how she was feeling, Drew had said she was "all right." It had been years since Drew had told her mother how or what she was feeling.

Drew held on to the doorknob for a fraction of a second too long before opening the door to David's room. Kiley and Flame were rolling on the bed, the boy's face curtained by butterscotch fur. Her mother sat on the floor, brushing patient Brisket.

"Laura and I and Jennifer's mother are going to put up the posters," Drew said. She reached for Kiley. "Do you want to come?"

Kiley couldn't choose.

"You and I could put some posters up later," Drew offered.

"On my street," Kiley said. "I want Grandma to see my poster. Yes, yes, yes." Pasha responded to the excitement in Kiley's voice by rolling across the boy's legs and knocking Flame off the bed. Ruth had opened the window. The smell of David was gone, overpowered by the scent of rosemary and the pungent, grassy odor of dog.

Before she left, Drew stood for a moment across the room from her mother and her son, envying Kiley's ability to discard grief and Ruth's skill at distancing herself from sorrow. "See you guys later then," Drew said and closed the door.

Half an hour after Drew left and half an hour before the press conference, someone at the Sherwood Police Department asked, "Has anyone notified the family?" A clerk was told to call and tell the Greenes that the SPD had arrested someone for the murder of their son.

When the phone call came, Drew was miles away, tying posters—HAVE YOU SEEN THIS BOY? REWARD FOR ANY INFORMA-TION—to lampposts and stapling them to magnolia trees with the stapler she had last used to create a navy blue, felt-covered bulletin board for David's wall. Drew, Laura, and Karen Sellars had met at the Galleria. Drew had taped posters in the parking garage even though she knew that the mall security guards would pull them down. No serpents were allowed in Sherwood's commercial Eden. Then Drew had gone south, Laura to the streets west of the mall, and Karen, north. More than once, Drew had stapled her sign next to a poster for some beloved cat—GRAY WITH WHITE PAWS, ANSWERS TO NAME OF DUSTY, CHILDREN HEARTSICK—lost months before and never found.

After an hour and a half, they had driven to the Copper Kettle for coffee.

"God, my arms ache," Karen said. Her daughter, Jennifer, and David had carpooled to nursery school. Despite being beyond playing with girls, David still played with Jennifer who could throw a baseball farther than he could. Crowded next to Karen, sitting across from her best friend, eating the pie that Laura had insisted on buying her, Drew felt, for one fragile moment, comforted. Sitting thigh to thigh on a burnt orange vinyl banquette, she was consoled by friendship; and the ache in her neck and shoulders was proof that she had done something to bring David back. "One Ring to bring them all and in the darkness bind them . . ." Comfort was a mirage as her mind finished the poem. ". . . in the Land of Mordor where the Shadows lie."

Drew drove home with posters and flyers stacked on the rear seat of her car. Tomorrow morning, Friday, Laura would take posters to supermarkets in Sherwood, Santa Monica, Culver City—as far south as the beach cities, north into the valley. Karen would drive the main boulevards and ask store managers to put flyers in their windows. Drew would go east—to Hollywood and the squalid streets where no one speaks English and illegal immigrants from Mexico and El Salvador buy their children sticks of fresh papaya from the street vendors who occupy every corner. Los Angeles was fifty miles wide, and David might not even be in the city now. Drew shook that thought from her head, and long strands of light brown hair fell across her eyes. On Saturday, they would go to the places David would choose to go—comic book stores, video arcades, pizza parlors, baseball card shops. Maybe he was with some nice person who would take him to arcades and buy him pizza. On Saturday, David would have been missing for seven days.

She parked in the driveway behind her mother's van, drawing up so many lists in her mind—dividing the city into segments for the three of them and a dozen other friends who had offered Drew their weekend—that she wasn't aware of the television reporter until she was blinded by the light of the minicam.

"Mrs. Greene, how do you feel about the homeless man who's been arrested for killing your son? What should we do to clear the streets of these people?"

The reporter was from a local channel, and he was hot for an interview with the weeping mother. "News at ten. Tragedy in Sherwood. Homeless man arrested for murder." He was young and fair, his face still acne-scarred, and he was too unpolished to do his job properly. News at 10 P.M. would show the grieving mother's startled face and catch a few rasping sounds before Drew turned away from the camera and ran into the house.

The networks—more careful if not more fastidious—had thought the story lacked strong photo opportunities. Without a body, there was nothing much to film, and so they had passed. And the local reporter was gone by the time Chuck arrived. In the five minutes it had taken to drive from Sherwood High School to his mother-in-law's house, Chuck had heard the news on KFWB—"If you'll give us twenty-two minutes, we'll give you the world." The world being full of weighty things, David Greene's demise was awarded twelve seconds.

This time Chuck reached for Drew, and she moved into the circle of his arms and laid her cheek on his shoulder. The best of Chuck, for Drew, had been his ability to envelop her. She was defended by his extra flesh. Nestled against the softness of his chest and stomach, she had been sheltered from a more angular world. For the first time in nearly two years, her long, sharp bones came home. Her sharpness and Chuck's softness had made David. Chuck had poured his passivity into the cup of her anger, and their genes had blended.

"How did they find this man?" "How do they know?" "Why didn't the police tell us?" "If they don't have David's body, how can they be sure?" Drew and Chuck asked questions of each other that neither could answer.

Nor could Ruth answer them. At 2:30 the police had called. When she said she was Mrs. Greene's mother, a woman had told her that a man had been arrested for the murder of her grandson and that more information would be available later. The briskness in Ruth's voice was gone. The subduing of her intensity bothered the dogs. Brisket paced in front of her. The other two lay submissively on the floor and licked at her ankles.

The telephone was ringing. There had already been messages from David's teacher, half a dozen neighbors, and two radio stations. Drew grabbed the phone.

"I'll be right over."

Drew's friendship with Laura went far below the surface, leagues below the politeness of "I'm so sorry." Being sorry was understood.

"Not right now. It's crazy here."

"I'll be over in an hour then. I'll bring the spaghetti Kiley likes. I can stay all night if you want."

"Thanks."

Drew was reaching for the phone to call the police when it rang again.

"Mrs. Greene?" The voice was female, energetic, and unfamiliar. It reeked of presumption.

"Yes."

"It's terrible about your loss. I'm really very sorry."

"Who is this?"

"I'm an assistant producer of *Talk Back with Bobbi Ann*. We're doing a show on parents whose children have been murdered, and we'd love to have you on the show. Your story could be such a help to other people who have suffered as you have."

"Fuck you," Drew said.

The booker had skin of sandpaper. For six months she had been rounding up guests for this second-rate syndicated talk show. Since *Bobbi Ann* was taped in Los Angeles and didn't have the budget of *Geraldo* or *Sally Jessy Raphael,* the booker combed Southern California for eccentrics, exhibitionists, and women who had experienced ectopic pregnancies. Agony was agony, no matter whether it was displayed on national networks or local stations. Because *Bobbi Ann* had neither a travel budget nor prestige, the booker's best weapon was getting there first. "We can pay you five hundred dollars," the booker said.

"Fuck you," Drew said again. She said it three or four more times before she hung up. Then she took Angus West's card out of her wallet and called his direct line. The phone rang half a dozen times before someone picked it up.

"Detective Carter here."

"I'm looking for Sergeant West."

A veil dropped over the voice. "Sergeant West isn't here."

"This is Mrs. Greene. Sergeant West was investigating the disappearance of my son. I need to talk to him."

"I'm sorry," the voice said. "Sergeant West is on vacation for a week."

"Can you get a message to him?"

"I think he may be out of town," the voice said hesitantly. "I don't think I can help you."

CHAPTER 15

"We need us a bat," Denver said.

They had played ball all Thursday afternoon in an empty park. The grass was yellow from lack of water, and there were darker yellow stains where dogs had squatted. In lieu of flowers, needles were embedded in the dirt, and tiny leftover fragments of crack rocks sparkled. In this park, no one would bother them until twilight.

Denver allowed David to take off his glasses when they played ball, but David had still dropped more balls than he caught. Denver had thrown dozens of high, soft flies and looping grounders. At first, David had been wary. He had waited tensely for Denver to taunt him when the ball went through his legs. But, instead of calling David butterfingers, Denver had said, "Hold the glove in front of you, Andy," or "Back. Run back." And, when David had unexpectedly caught a difficult ball, Denver had yelled, "Good catch."

When Denver had loped across the dead grass toward David, the boy instinctively shied away. But Denver only took David's glove and showed him how to bend his knees and block the ball with his body. Then he had stood next to David and said, "We'll make you a ballplayer yet," and showed him how to pull his arm back and straighten his elbow as he threw the baseball. All afternoon, Denver was smiling; and his hands were patient and comforting as he held David's arm and controlled the release of an imaginary ball.

When he was too tired to play anymore, David ran for a long, high fly and missed and chased the ball into a patch of greener grass accidentally watered by a broken drinking fountain. He threw himself stomach down on the grass, and Denver lay next to him, staring up at the cloudless sky, and said, "We need us a bat."

With his eyes closed, David remembered—or imagined—the balls falling from the sky into his mitt. When he was catching balls, even when he had to play by himself throwing tennis balls into the air, he never wanted the catching to stop. He was a difficult, dissatisfied little boy with too many secrets who was too smart for his own good, but he knew he could stand in the grass and catch balls forever and be happy. And he knew that catching balls and throwing balls made Denver happy, too. He moved closer to Denver until their shoulders were touching.

"I'll teach you to hit," Denver said sleepily. "Got to learn to protect the plate." His hair fell into half-closed eyes, and sunlight softened his face, coating its harshness with uncomplicated yellow paint. "No way you're much of a hitter yet. We'll get us an aluminum bat."

Even in five pitch, David rarely got a hit. Through a haze of imaginary home runs, another thought burrowed into his head. Maybe Denver didn't need Andy. Maybe he would teach David, show David how to swing the bat, cheer as David's home runs rose so high the outfielders could only stand and watch.

To hide the bruises on David's throat, Denver had stopped in Woolworth and bought a cheap gold turtleneck pullover. The shirt, made of some polyester blend, was thin, but the afternoon was too warm for thick clothing. Carefully, David moved close enough to place a gold arm on Denver's chest. Denver was wearing a T-shirt advertising a movie that David hadn't been allowed to see, and David lightly touched the warm black letters. Denver didn't push his hand away.

"I got anything to do with it, you'll be the best hitter in the league," Denver said, still lying motionless in the sun.

David sat up then and wriggled nearer, until he could put his head down on his arm and feel Denver's heart beating beneath him. He looked, lying there, like a puppy removed too early from its whelping box. The feel of Denver's heart, the puffs of breath from Denver's half-open mouth, were salve for his loneliness and for the sadness that lapped the shores of his mind.

Lulled by warmth and heartbeat, he let a more dangerous thought creep across the threshold: If he told Denver that he was David, maybe Denver wouldn't want Andy anymore. Maybe if he told Denver that he wanted him to be his daddy and to teach him baseball . . .

He sat up again and tried out the words. "I'm David, but I want you to be my daddy." The first time, soundless, they echoed in the empty park and lightened the darkness in his head. The second time—when he tried to speak—they came to the edge of his tongue and receded, like a river that stops short of overflowing its banks. He could make animal sounds, but words were beyond him. Stabbed by the need to talk, he ran to his discarded jacket and pulled a marker from the pocket. In the five-and-dime, Denver had bought him a pack of index cards so he could talk with his fingers.

"I'm David," he had printed before Denver grabbed the orange marker and threw it into the bushes, threw it with the same lazy grace with which he threw baseballs. Straight as an arrow, the marker rose and fell and pierced the ground.

"Talk, damn it," Denver said, using the hand that had thrown the marking pen to hit David across the mouth. "When are you going to start talking?"

The storm was brief, no longer than a cloud across the sun. Almost before Denver's palm had left David's face, the man turned mild again. He reached into his jeans pocket for a tissue and wiped the corner of David's mouth.

The sharp edges of the index card dug into David's fingers.

121

Terrified, he tried to crumple the stiff paper before Denver could reach for his hand to see what he had written. But the card wouldn't tear. Denver would see the words and know that David wasn't Andy.

"What'd you want to tell Daddy?" Denver asked.

David ran away and dropped to his knees in the mud next to the cracked fountain and, crying, buried the card in mud and tears.

Then Denver was standing behind him. "It ain't that bad, Andy," Denver said, pulling him up. "Let's go buy us a bat."

The sporting goods store had narrow aisles and Ping-Pong balls in dusty packages. Denver had driven past a superstore with mountain bikes and soccer balls in the windows and had chosen, instead, this small, dirty shop with a bored teenage clerk at the single cash register. Denver had insisted that David swing three different bats, and David had tried, but he found it hard to lift his hands. His mind was a wasteland—a colorless, dull landscape of nothingness.

"Hey, Andy, you're swinging like a girl," Denver said, and the words were gray dots lost in the wilderness.

"Hey, boy, you listen to your daddy. You hear me?" Denver pulled David to him and pinched his arm.

In the car, David had sat listlessly, knowing he should hide his face but incapable of the effort it would take to turn away. Betrayed by its own need to trust, his body was lead, sinking to the bottom of an ocean of loneliness.

Denver pinched David's arm again, and the pain dragged David to the surface. He clutched the rubber-covered handle, an aluminum life preserver, and, hating Denver, swung hard, the tip of the bat knocking dust from a rusted shelf.

"This is the one," Denver said, taking the bat out of David's hands. The clerk didn't bother to look up when he put Denver's change on the counter.

Stiffly, wearing leaden shoes, David followed Denver back to the car.

"Come on," Denver said impatiently. "Need a little help?" This time he stuck the bat into David's back and pushed him forward. Even before he threw the bat into the backseat, Denver turned on the radio. It was set at a cowboy station, heartbreak thick as corn syrup. A gravel-voiced lover had lost his darling and was drowning his sorrow in honky-tonk whiskey. When the song ended, there was a telegraphic stew of local news—a budget impasse in Sacramento, a fatal accident on the 405 Freeway, a suspect arrested for the murder of a missing Sherwood boy. For a moment, Denver rode the steering wheel as if it were a horse; and the car bucked beneath his hands, veering from lane to lane while Denver listened. As the radio slid back into plaints of abandonment and betrayal, Denver reached over and touched the boy's cheek. "Everything's all right, Andy," he said. "You're mine for sure now. Nothing will ever take you away."

CHAPTER 16

Laura had left at midnight. Chuck had fallen asleep on the blue Dux couch that had been a secondhand windfall during the happiest days of his marriage. Drew had been pregnant with David when they bought the couch from a television producer whose new decorator was throwing out all his old furniture. In those days, before they had children, they had spent their Sunday afternoons wandering from Bel Air to the Hollywood hills with newspaper advertisements as their guide. The producer had seemed reluctant to hand over the last of the cushions, so Drew—in her thrusting way—had asked why he was selling something he loved. Chuck, who preferred disguises, had flushed and turned away, but he had said nothing to Drew—not even that Drew and her mother were more alike than Drew imagined or wanted.

By 6:00 A.M. on Friday morning, everyone in the house was awake. Chuck was awakened by Kiley's weight on his ankles and a dog's hot breath against his face. Sometime during the night, Kiley had crawled onto the sofa, and, as soon as it was light, Flame had sought out Kiley. The restless dogs had woken Ruth. Drew had slept so near the surface of consciousness that she was not aware of waking up at all.

There was no reason to be awake. Kiley would not be going to school. And Chuck had offered to stay home. Those were the words he had used. "I'll stay home today." Home is where the heart is, or where the heart is missing.

"Aren't you giving finals?" Drew asked.

"I can call Tiffani and . . . call the office and ask to have Bob Guyer and Marv Schulman cover the morning. They have free periods. And I could go in for my honors classes this afternoon." His voice gave him away.

"You might as well go to school," Drew said. "No reason for you to just sit around here." With a different sort of death, there would be jobs for Chuck—a casket to be bought and flowers to be ordered and a cemetery to be selected. "Thanks, Chuck," she added.

They were formal with each other this morning, careful and polite. As though this were an ordinary day, Drew made a pot of coffee and put a bagel in the toaster. They had not touched. Instead of handing Chuck his coffee, Drew had placed the cup on the table in front of him.

Before dark the night before, they had learned all that the Sherwood Police Department was willing to tell. Chuck had tried to get information, failed, and handed the phone to Drew. She had kept both tears and anger in check, pushing her way through clerks and duty sergeants with a peremptory "Then give me someone who can," and "I'm sure you don't want me to tell the *LA Times* that you wouldn't let us have information about our son." At last she had reached a Lieutenant Zane who had given her details about the homeless man with a record of assaulting young boys who had been seen on the block where David's bloody underwear was found.

The press conference had not been the dramatic event Zarelli had planned. In the end, he had been prudent enough to scatter cautions, like tacks, across his announcement: "We won't have definitive proof until the DNA results are in," and "With his history of attacks on Sherwood boys, we consider Bumgartner a very viable suspect," and "He has confessed, but we have not yet recovered the boy's body." Zarelli hated Angus West for spoiling what should have been a half hour of triumph.

Drew put a carton of milk and boxes of cereal on the table and turned on the radio. The world had moved beyond David Greene during the night. All over Los Angeles, news editors had made judgment calls, and almost all of them had decided that the possible murder of a Sherwood boy didn't require a second-day story. There wasn't anything new to say. The police chief had been too cagey, and the details were too vague. If David Greene had disappeared from a small town in the Midwest, his disappearance would have been front page news in the local newspaper for weeks. There would have been candlelight marches to pray for his safe return and church bake sales to raise money for the search. But editors had only to dip their hands in the river of misery that flowed through Southern California to find fresher stories. Two girls on their way to church for their First Communions had been killed by a drunken driver. And, at 1:00 A.M., a security guard had found an abandoned baby in a shoebox inside the Fox Hills Mall. When someone stumbled over the boy's body, it would be different. That would be worth at least a minute of airtime. For today, however, the David Greene story was spiked.

The *Los Angeles Times,* lagging radio and TV, had given the story three hundred words on page three of the Metro section. The *Times* headline—"Homeless Man Suspect in Boy's Disappearance"—was not gaudy enough to stir the supermarket tabloids. So, for the moment as the Greenes sat at the breakfast table, they were left alone in their anguish.

"I wish . . ." Chuck said and did not finish the sentence.

Drew drank her coffee so hot that the roof of her mouth was scalded.

The body has its own demands. So does the day. Chuck took a shower, and Drew found him an unused disposable razor and some socks he had left behind. He would have to wear his shirt and jockey shorts a second day. She brought the socks into the bathroom while he was shaving. He had rubbed his palm across the steamed up mirror, and, looking unfinished without his glasses, was leaning forward while water dripped from his hair on to the razor. Drew buckled under the weight of a thousand similar mornings. Her body as well as her mind remembered sitting on the edge of the tub with Kiley in her arms and five-year-old David standing next to his father and pretending to shave.

"Why did this have to happen to David?" Chuck asked. "Why did David have to die?"

"We don't know that he's dead." It was Chuck's tone rather than his words that made Drew angry. He was already resigned to David's death. For Chuck, it was easier not to fight. When the dishwasher broke and it turned out that the machine had been installed wrong, Chuck had promised he would fill out the papers for small claims court; and then he had never gotten around to doing it, and he had been relieved to lose the money rather than make a fuss. That was before Drew started doing most things for herself.

"We can't give up," she said.

Chuck sat on the edge of the tub and started building an intellectual wall while he put on his socks. "It doesn't help to run away from the truth, Drew."

"I don't know what the truth is."

"It's never what we want it to be."

While Chuck dressed, Ruth sat on the living room floor with Kiley, building houses out of thick, brightly colored cardboard. When Chuck bent to kiss him, Kiley put his arms around Chuck's neck and held him down. "Stay, Daddy."

Chuck stood awkwardly bent over for a minute before disengaging Kiley's hands. "I have to go to school. I'll be back."

"Will you sleep in my room tonight?"

Chuck looked at Drew.

"Will you, Daddy?"

"Daddy can stay if you want him to," Drew said.

As Chuck reached the front door, Drew said automatically, "Do you have your glasses?" Chuck found his glasses on the coffee table. Then he was gone.

Kiley aimed his battery-powered dinosaur at the card houses. The Tyrannosaurus rex laid them waste. Kiley built the houses up again, three stories of educational graphics, and set the dinosaur loose to destroy. "Can we still put the posters up?" Kiley asked. "On our street?"

It was Ruth who answered. "Yes," she said.

When she was her daughter's age, Ruth had wept at the death of Kennedy and marched against the Vietnam War and worn around her neck the rectangular gold symbol proclaiming "Another Mother for Peace." She had been a good mother then— or so she thought. She was a better mother to the three dogs. Her love for them was unconditional. A decade ago she had retreated from trying to save the whales and get Democrats elected. She lived for herself now, a pure hedonist, although the pleasures she sought were almost spartan—chocolate and trophies. She avoided any pain that might unfreeze her heart.

"Can we go now?" Kiley asked.

There were hundreds of flyers on the backseat of Drew's car. She grabbed a stack and brought them into the house without looking at the picture of her son. Drew was defenseless against guilt and pain.

Ruth stood up, a square shape in khaki shorts and an "I Love Agility" T-shirt which had a cartoon of a beagle dangling across the tire, a doberman knocking down all the weave poles, and a frantic owner catching a poodle as it fell from the top of the A frame.

"Do you want to make fudge?" Ruth asked. The question was directed not at Kiley but at Drew.

"David isn't here so I get to lick the pan," Kiley said.

"I might not have enough sugar," said Drew.

When Drew was seven, it had rained for six days. After the second day, the streets were flooded. On the fourth day, half a dozen cars were swept into ditches and storm drains and the drivers drowned. The lawns looked like green lakes, and the towels that Ruth stuffed against the front door had to be wrung out every hour. Ruth and Drew had spent the fourth and fifth days making fudge. Drew knew they must have done something else, but all she could remember was stirring with both hands and watching the bubbles recede before the thickening chocolate liquid could overflow the pot. When the rain lessened on the sixth day and the water receded from the front porch, Drew and Ruth were bound together in a new way. Ever after, they could eat with each other even when they could not talk. Ever after, the smell of fudge would trigger love.

Neither Kiley's mother nor his grandmother reminded him why David was not there. "You can lick the spoon, too," Drew said.

By emptying the sugar bowl, Drew was less than a teaspoon short. Ruth poured milk and corn syrup. Drew handed her mother two squares of chocolate. Kiley stood on a chair and watched the separate solid things blend and blur. Cook over a slow fire, the cookbook said, until a few drops poured into cold water will hold together when rolled between the fingers. The cookbook, which was missing its spine and back cover, had belonged to Ruth's mother. Some of the chocolate smears on page 508 were fifty years old.

Fudge was a poor substitute for God, but it was the best the Greenes could do.

"I can't," Drew said.

Kiley had pushed a dozen posters into his mother's hands. He was carrying a hammer, string, and a box of thumbtacks. His eagerness was more than Drew could handle. What Kiley looked forward to as a great adventure was, to Drew, the act of sailing paper airplanes into the void. David's face beneath her fingers was too hot to touch.

"Come on," Kiley said, tugging at Drew's arm. "Let's go."

Ruth took the posters from Drew. "Let your mother rest," Ruth said. "We'll put up the posters. Pasha can come with us."

"Bring Flame," Kiley said.

Ruth shook her head. "Poor Pasha never gets to go. His leash is in the green bag."

Kiley ran to David's room to find the leash. "Thank you," Drew said to her mother and remembered, suddenly, being twelve, with the hamster dead in his cage and herself unable to touch the cold, curled body. Her mother had reached in and taken the hamster and wrapped it in colored tissue paper and put it in the box the checks had come in; and they had buried it in the garden. It was still there somewhere, but the stone Drew had painted with Hammy Hamster to mark the grave had long since disappeared. With the thought of the hamster's unmarked grave, she found that she was crying.

Drew stayed in her bedroom until her mother and Kiley left, but she was still crying when the doorbell rang.

Angus West stood between the pots of marigolds, his face flushed from anger and lack of sleep.

"They told me you were on vacation," Drew said.

He moved past her into the house. "I don't think your son's dead," he said.

West had known he was going to do this from the moment he stuffed Carter's report in his pocket before he left the police department. "I need some coffee," he said. He had spent the night driving the freeways—riding the empty concrete south to Mission Viejo and back. Around 4:00 A.M., he had slept for a few hours by the side of the road. For the first few years after LaChandra Johnston's death, he had driven for an hour or two nearly every night. That was before his wife left and West discovered that vodka would put him to sleep.

This time they sat at the kitchen table. The room smelled of chocolate. Incongruously acting as hostess, Drew piled squares of fudge on a plate. The stubble on West's chin was as pale as hay.

"It's wrong," West said. "Too neat. Why leave the most incriminating clothes in a place where someone would almost surely find them but hide the rest of the boy's things? We went through every Dumpster in the mall and every trash can on Kelvin and Comross. No backpack, no sweater, nothing of the boy's."

"Nothing of David's." Drew's emotions had not yet begun to process what West was saying.

Until now West had stared down at his coffee. Now he looked at Drew. "I'm sure David was alive when the shorts were left in the hedge," he said.

"Why would someone . . . ?"

"I don't know. But there's another thing." He stopped.

"What?"

He didn't know how to tell her, so he told her bluntly. "Most of these crimes—when boys and girls are killed—are sex crimes. There was no semen on David's underwear."

Then Drew asked the only question that mattered. "How do we find my son?"

West had no answer.

CHAPTER 17

All night David dreamed of rescue. In one of the dreams, he summoned the genie from *Aladdin* and flew home in the genie's huge blue hand. In another, Superman came, and with him were all four Ninja Turtles. Saturday morning cartoon heroes handed him their stun guns and the controls of their superadvanced cars and planes. Even his grandmother's three dogs hurtled through one dream. When Brisket was learning how to track, David's grandmother had let him play hiding games with the dog, and now he dreamed that Brisket led the other dogs to this motel and they fell upon Denver and devoured him.

He woke sullen. The dream rescuers had deserted him. So had his mother. He woke with a terrible, sullen anger. His mother should have been here by now. His mother should have found him.

Across the room, Denver was almost dressed. He bent to unhook his belt from chair and doorknob and polished the bronze bronco on the buckle with his T-shirt before he pulled the shirt over his head. "Where do we go today, Andy?" he asked. Pleased with a decision he had already made, Denver did not wait for an answer. "You ever seen an elephant? I didn't see an elephant 'til I was grown. Except on TV."

David found his index cards and wrote, "I've seen lots of elephants."

For the moment, Denver seemed to find David's sulkiness amusing. "Doesn't matter if you've seen a hundred elephants," he said. "We're going to the zoo."

David made no move to get up. With an exaggerated gesture that was almost a dance, Denver leaned over David's bed and pulled off the blankets. Since Wednesday when they had gone to the baseball game, Denver seemed abnormally eager to take David places and to buy him things. He had bought, in addition to the bat, a Bugs Bunny T-shirt, a Dodgers baseball cap, a paperback *Star Trek* novel and—to replace the backpack—a black nylon gym bag. Except for the clothes, the gym bag was empty. The treasures David Greene had brought with him were still carefully stacked on the table next to his pillow.

The boy reluctantly got out of bed. He spent a long time brushing his teeth, moving the green toothbrush up and down and behind each tooth. He had become, in the last six days, fastidious in ways that he had been careless before. He behaved as he had never behaved at home. He picked doughnut boxes off the floor and crushed them into the wastebaskets. He folded his pajamas. He hung his towel back on the bar. And he brushed his teeth until his gums hurt.

"Take your cards," Denver said. "We'll trade."

Without enthusiasm, David picked up eighteen or twenty baseball cards and stuck them in the pocket of his jeans. He put some index cards and a marker in the other pocket.

"Hot dog," Denver said. "This'll be a fuckin' good day."

When David spilled mustard at breakfast, the waitress wiped it up almost immediately. Then she took the yellow plastic squeeze bottle away. David already knew that it wouldn't work, that a thousand yellow lakes on a thousand tables wouldn't mean any-thing to anybody, maybe not even to his mother. And why would she come here anyway, miles and miles from home?

"What's the name of your dog?" Denver asked suddenly. He was looking at David with cold eyes.

David forced himself to see the tire and the white farmhouse and the fields of corn. He put down his jelly doughnut and wrote with sticky fingers, "Scooter."

Denver stared at David uncertainly as the boy pushed the card into his hand. It was hard to tell whether Denver was disturbed by the absence of something he expected or the presence of some-thing he did not expect. Panicked, David closed Denver's fingers around the cardboard.

Denver threw the index card away. "You should talk," he said. "Andy talks to his daddy."

The bruises on David's throat were almost gone now. He tried to please Denver and say "Scooter," but the words were still trapped inside, and he could only grunt. "Scooter," he wrote on another card. "Please, Daddy." Denver's eyes focused on the pur-ple letters. He finished his chocolate doughnut and rubbed his mouth. "Good boy, Andy," he said and stroked David's hair. "Tomorrow, you'll talk to Daddy."

In that moment of relief, David no longer hated his mother. The night angers faded, invisible in the brightness of present dan-ger. He couldn't let Denver miss Andy. And he had to leave his mother better clues.

On the ride to the zoo, David lived Andy's life. He ran through the cornfields with the big brown dog at his side and came home to a woman cutting a newly baked cherry pie. He wandered through the rooms of the white farmhouse. Except for him and the woman in the kitchen, the house was empty. David opened the front door and let his mother in. She sat on the floor with Andy, putting together a jigsaw puzzle, showing him how to fit the outside edges together first. When Denver turned into the parking lot, David made his mother vanish. The half-completed jigsaw puzzle vanished, too.

The elephants were alone, forlorn on their artificial veldt. On a Friday morning in early June, there was no one to admire them. Huge and gray, they flicked flies from enormous ears with wrinkled trunks.

"Next stop, tigers," Denver said. The man was an antic tour guide, pulling the boy from beast to beast, passing by gazelle and giraffe with barely a glance, heading always down the blacktop paths in search of predators.

"There," he said. "That's something."

Smooth skinned, the tiger walked its artificial lair. Denver walked with it. Fierceness faced fierceness across a moat, muscles quivering beneath black stripes and black T-shirt.

When the Greenes first started making Sunday trips to the Los Angeles Zoo—with a helium balloon bobbing from the top of Kiley's stroller, Chuck carrying the string cheese and cans of apple juice, and Drew lecturing too earnestly about endangered species—they let David choose the path. He always went across the bridge to the arctic pool where walrus and seal slid awkwardly into blue-tinted water and, freed from land, became different creatures. The day after he first watched the seals, David demanded swimming lessons. With two sets of lessons, he learned to swim moderately well that summer, but he was never able to discard his awkward limbs or silence the racing engine of his brain. He had expected that he would be transformed. The shame of remaining himself was one of the secrets he would never tell.

Denver had no interest in seals. His secrets were tied to the muscular flesh eaters who prowled concrete vaults at the far side of the zoo: Jaguar, ocelot, panther and tawny lion, the masters of hot continents, touched by sun and night, yellow blurring into black and black into gold. His fingers circling David's wrist like a handcuff, Denver pulled the boy from one to the other and back again. "I'm hungry," he said at last. "Let's get us some fried chicken."

They sat in the far corner of KFC, eating chicken and mashed potatoes from red-striped boxes. A shapeless place at the junction of two freeways, it was as empty as the zoo, and, like the elephants, the dark-skinned man behind the counter looked at the world with incurious eyes. Denver and the boy beside him—the chunky boy with short black hair and glasses—were captive to an indifferent world's presumptions. Father and son. In the absence of proof to the contrary, father and son. It is said that even the most famous movie stars can go unrecognized if they dull their strides and smiles and turn down the wattage of their personalities. Only once had Denver come close to being caught.

Denver wiped his fingers and took out a pack of baseball cards. Wriggling into Andy's skin, David imitated Denver's smile and dropped his own pack of cards on to the table. "Any three for any three," Denver said, first shuffling with his eyes closed and then turning a dozen cards faceup. It was a gambler's game, more exciting than merely trading; there was a chance to win—or lose—favorite cards. In the three days they had been playing this game, David had won and then lost a 1991 Upper Deck Nolan Ryan Hero. David dealt out the twelve cards on the top of his pack.

"Got you," Denver said gleefully and picked a 1992 Bret Boone rookie card.

The gamble, as always, excited David. His pretense of enthusiasm turned real. He took his glasses off and leaned eagerly over the table. But Denver's cards were uninteresting relics of previous games.

"No flies on me," Denver said and took a Mike Mussina that had come in the Stadium Club package David had bought six days earlier at the Galleria. Without enthusiasm, David picked up a 1993 Leaf David Hulse rookie card, worth .03 cents. At least it was a rookie card, a rookie who shared his name. He had a 1992 Upper Deck rookie card for David McCarty that was worth twenty cents. He had traded Danny Matranga for it.

The idea hit his stomach before it reached his brain. At first, he thought he was going to be sick. Last year, he had woken in the middle of the night with the same heavy feeling, and he had just had time to lean over the edge of the bed before he barfed his dinner on the carpet. But the Kentucky Strips—four strips of fried chicken for two dollars and eighty-nine cents—stayed down, and the idea climbed on chemical wings from neuron to synapse to neuron and burst into his head. He could leave his David cards behind.

He was still kneeling on the molded plastic seat and leaning over the cards spread across the gray Formica tabletop. Jolted by the thought, he jerked back. His arm knocked the remains of his chicken from the table.

"Butterfingers," Denver said. This time there was no good-will in his voice. "Pick it up."

David scrambled to the floor and pushed the mashed potatoes back into the box with his fingers. It was then he saw what he had seen without seeing before. Tucked into the corner of the box was a small tub of mustard with the colonel's face on its yellow top.

"Hurry up." It was the voice Denver used before he twisted David's arm or stuck his elbow in the boy's ribs.

David's fingers left shards of potato on his jeans as he dropped the mustard into his pocket. "About time," Denver said when the boy stood up. Denver was sweeping his cards together, and David saw a Dave Winfield on top. He reached past the mustard in his pocket for his marking pen. "I get two more," he wrote.

"Tough luck," Denver said. "Serves you right, butterfingers."

David pushed his empty box into the trash can. Then he slowly reached for the box in front of Denver. When the man didn't stop him, he carried that box to the trash can, too. When the lid swung back, there was another tub of mustard in the palm of David's hand.

CHAPTER 18

"Out of the night that covers me
Black as the Pit from pole to pole . . ."

Drew had memorized that poem when she was ten and working her way through *One Hundred and One Famous Poems* for a school contest. She had memorized nineteen or twenty of the poems. She had told her friends it was because of the prize—which she won. Actually, she loved the rhythms and the rhymes. At Stanford, she wrote her honors thesis on the British war poets from 1914 to 1918. Now she couldn't get "Invictus" out of her head: "Under the bludgeonings of chance, My head is bloody, but unbowed." Was David alive? And if he was, how did she find him?

Because Drew thought most clearly on paper, she had covered a yellow legal pad with questions and possible answers. She had a bold handwriting filled with defiant capital letters, but now her sentences grew frantic at the corners of the page.

"Why would someone want to convince us David is dead?" Drew asked the question aloud.

"Because the boy isn't dead," West said.

"So we would stop looking?"

"Maybe," West said. Except for his certainty that David was alive, almost all of West's answers began with "maybe" or "perhaps."

Drew's answers were fragile and incomplete. Babies were kidnapped from hospitals all the time because some childless woman wanted a child. Maybe someone wanted a son. Or maybe someone was doing terrible things to David. Maybe some cult was kidnapping and torturing children.

Ruth returned and drank the last of the coffee, and Drew made another pot. Somehow, the fudge had been eaten, too. Drew's fingers poured beans into the grinder and brushed the coarse brown grains into a white cone, while one part of her mind marvelled at the efficiency with which she made coffee and picked up lettuce and apples at the supermarket; the other part endlessly repeated "bludgeonings of chance, chance, chance." The three dogs joustled one another at the water bowl and then collapsed on the floor at Ruth's feet.

"We put up a million signs," Kiley said. "I nailed them. Grandma says we can put up more later." With the sureness of innocence, he added, "Someone will see them and bring David home."

West was too big for the kitchen. When he stood up, he could see the dust on top of the refrigerator. In David's room, on Tuesday, West and Drew had found a rhythm. Their minds had danced together in the Track David tango. Now, as they sat motionless, they were stumbling in the dark, hands in front of their faces, groping to touch the intangible.

West stared into his fifth—or was it his sixth—cup of coffee. Then he reached down and picked up one of the posters from the chair where Kiley had dropped it. His fingers brushed David's cheeks. "Somebody's seen him. Maybe dozens of people have seen him . . ."

"But nobody's noticed him," Drew said.

Once again, they were moving to the same beat.

West nodded.

"Even when they bump into something, people try not to see. How do we make them notice?"

"Put his face up," West said. "Everywhere."

This time it was Drew who read West's voice. "You don't think we have much time," she said, her chest so tight that the words came out in puffs, like smoke. However efficient Drew was and however tough she seemed, for eight years she had found her place in the world as David's mother. What she had not told her own mother—could never tell her brusque, efficient mother— was that she defined herself not as a summa cum laude graduate of Stanford University but as the mother of the right fielder on the Astros five-pitch team and as the Friday room mother in the Sherwood kindergarten. Without David and Kiley, her life would be as insubstantial as the house of cards Kiley built and destroyed and rebuilt. "Under the bludgeonings of chance . . ." Her mind shifted to the next stanza of the poem. "Beyond this place of wrath and tears, Looms but the horror of the shade."

West tried to put on his policeman's mask with its frozen eyes and immobile mouth, but it was too late. The mask sagged, held on with broken string. Drew silently begged her mother to take Kiley away. With unexpected tact, Ruth gave Flame an order to come to heel, and Kiley followed. "We'll go outside and practice," Ruth said. "You can throw his dumbbell."

Left behind, the other dogs lay with their eyes fixed on the kitchen door. Long minutes before Ruth returned—before she had even stored Flame's white dumbbell in the pocket of her shorts—the dogs would be up and waiting by the door. Once, West had avoided being smashed on the head with a motorcycle chain by jumping back when there was nothing to tell him not to move forward. He could not name the internal clues that had guided him then and were insisting now that David Greene was alive and in danger.

"They'll find out that they have the wrong man," Drew said of the police. The "they" was in opposition to "we," language making its own alliances.

"Yes." West was still holding the poster. "Eventually."

"But not soon enough?" Drew—who met everything head on—did not allow herself to sew a pretty costume on the truth.

West was silent.

"How much time do we have to find him?"

"I don't know."

Drew's eyes demanded an answer.

"Another week at most," West said. He tried to soften his answer with, "I think." But he was, by nature, no more devious than Drew, and the words had a rusty falseness.

Drew took the poster from West's hand. "Then I'd better start nailing these up," she said.

West didn't say good-bye. He touched the seven names and addresses in his pocket. Then he stood up and moved toward the kitchen door, leaving as abruptly as he had come.

Mitchell Poole and Collie Roston lived in similar one-bedroom apartments and had gotten into similar trouble with the law for being turned on by the rosebud penises of prepubescent boys. The street called men like Poole and Roston chicken hawks. The police had cruder names for them. Poole had served six months for exposing himself to an eight-year-old neighbor. Before and since, he had not even gotten a parking ticket.

"Honest . . ." he said. "Honest, I haven't done anything like that again. Never." He was short and slender. From the back, he could have passed for a boy himself. But he was forty-five years old with thinning hair and a mustache.

When West showed him David Greene's picture—honey-colored, longish hair falling into blue-gray eyes—Poole jerked his hand away. He refused to hold the photograph, as though he would compromise himself simply by touching the Kodak boy. "I've never seen him. Really." He sounded close to tears.

"Mind if I look around?" West asked.

There was no dust on the venetian blinds, no lint on the carpet, no hint of anything out of place. In the kitchen, every cabinet was neatly closed, and the luncheon soup bowl was already drying in the dish drainer. Poole inhabited this apartment without allowing himself the freedom to live here. West looked at the anxious man who watched him with spaniel eyes. West knew about self-paralysis as an antidote for anguish. For the last ten years, he had played the same game.

"Sorry to bother you," West said and left.

Collie Roston's apartment had a view of the ocean. "Not my type," Roston said, standing on his balcony and examining the photograph of David. "Too plump. I like them thin and very blond. I have a picture here if you'd like to see my type." He leaned closer to West and whispered, "A very provocative picture."

From the moment West arrived, Roston had baited him. Now he handed the detective a photograph of a naked marble youth. "A Greek kouros," he said. "Sixth century B.C. A civilized country where men were encouraged to fall in love with boys."

In America in 1996, Roston was working diligently to reestablish the Athenian status quo. "Would you like some literature?" he asked in mock earnest as he went to his desk and picked up two brochures from the National Association for Man-Boy Love which he offered to the policeman. West's hands remained at his sides.

"Oh, well," Roston said and dropped the brochures back on the desk.

"I would like to see the rest of the apartment," West said with careful politeness and headed for the bedroom door.

"Naughty, naughty." Roston barred his way. "Unless you have a search warrant, of course. Then I would be most happy to show you around."

Without touching Roston, West pinned him to the wall. Like some huge tame bear that has suddenly broken free of its chain and turned dripping jaws toward its tormentor, West moved closer. "You're going to invite me to look in your bedroom," he said. "An eight-year-old boy is missing, and I'm going to make sure he isn't here and has never been here. Wherever you store the pictures that can send you back to jail, we both know you're too clever to keep them here. But I can get a search warrant, and I can tear this apartment into bite-size pieces looking for them." He stepped back then. Whatever the threat in his voice, his face had never lost its chiseled blankness. Roston's face was as white as the marble in the photograph as he fumbled for the doorknob and pushed open his bedroom door.

Drew had started at Sunset Boulevard and worked her way south. With smiles and gestures and the remnants of high school Spanish—"El es mi hijo. Es perdido. Por favor, puede usted ponerlos en la ventana?"—she had taped posters in the windows of a hundred small groceries, panaderías, and shops that sold a jumble of cheap clothes and plastic radios. On Eighth Street, her way blocked by two ice-cream vendors and a man selling pineapple on a stick, she had offered the fruit vendor a dollar to let her tape a flyer to his cart. He had agreed, and then she had gone to the vendors on Seventh Street and MacArthur Park until she ran out of money.

In Koreatown, her high school Spanish was of no use. Nor was her English. These shopkeepers in their tidy shops looked away from her. "My son is lost," she said. "This is my son. Have you seen him?" The men were silent and wary. But a few of the women let her place David's picture in their windows. And as the doors closed behind her, Drew wondered if they would move quickly to the window and take the flyers down. This Los Angeles was foreign to her. The Southern California in which she grew up was full of English words, and the faces were either black or white. Miles away—in the valley and along the coast—her friends were walking that California. Laura had driven to the South Bay where all the faces were still white and every coffee shop made espresso. Karen and Karen's sister had gone north over the hill to Encino and Sherman Oaks. The neighbors two doors down had offered to cover Santa Monica, and the man across the street who worked in Orange County had taken a hundred flyers to put up in the shopping malls there.

Chuck had recruited half a dozen teachers. Two of the men were African Americans, and they had volunteered to tack up posters in the churches and liquor stores of South Central LA. His gay friend, a tenth grade English teacher, would blanket West Hollywood.

"You'll need at least a thousand more flyers," Ruth had told Drew. "I'll have them ready by two P.M. Chuck can pick them up during his free period and take them back to school."

"How do you remember he has fifth period free?" Drew had asked.

Ruth shrugged. For twenty years she had run the office at a large plant that cleaned costumes for the movie studios. She had been responsible for sending out as many as two dozen trucks a day, half of them for the emergency pickup or return of confederate uniforms whose wearers had stumbled into a sound stage swamp or, once, one of Lana Turner's negligees that had been stained by the nervous dog with whom she was sharing a scene. Ruth closed her own dogs in David's bedroom and reached for Kiley's hand. Watching her mother and her son leave for Copymat, Drew had wanted to call them back. She had wanted to insist that Kiley stay locked safely inside the house behind the barrier of marigolds and bouganvillea. But safety was last week's illusion. To get David back, she had to teach herself to live dangerously. She left a message for Chuck at the school office, picked up her purse, and headed east.

Moving west now, heading toward the outrageously expensive restaurants and colorful condom stores on Melrose Avenue where teenagers roamed in packs on Saturday night, Drew found herself in front of Paramount Studios. She had once worked for a producer who had his offices at Paramount, and every Monday she had driven to the studio to bring him the scripts she had read the previous week. Almost none of the scripts she read—not even the few good ones that she enthusiastically recommended—had been made into movies. If this were a movie, she could drop 100,000 leaflets from an airplane, letting them rain down on Los Angeles. If this were a movie, David would come safely home. "Oh, Christ," she remembered her producer saying of a script in which a serial killer threw a second grader from the Golden Gate Bridge, "the public won't stand for this. Doesn't this dork of a writer have any brains?" If this were a movie, it would end like *Without a Trace,* that Fox movie starring Kate Nelligan, where a dozen police cars turn on their sirens and blow their horns in triumph as they bring the kidnapped boy back to his mother.

But it wasn't a movie. Drew taped a poster to the high white walls of Paramount just outside the DeMille gate. It was up to her to find her son.

CHAPTER 19

David Hulse, Dave Stewart, Dave Hollins who played third base for the Phillies and was second in the league to Barry Bonds in runs in 1992, David Justice, David Nied, David McCarty, and Dave Winfield who'd been an outfielder forever and had played on maybe six teams. David had bought grab bags of old cards—some as old as 1990—and he tried to think of other faces he had seen. There was Dave Fleming, too. And David Cone. At home, in the shoe boxes on his bookcase, David Greene had cards for all of them. He must have half a dozen Dave Winfield cards. You couldn't help getting Dave Winfield even if you didn't want him.

They had gone back to the motel after lunch, and Denver had shoved David inside. David thought that Denver was going to hit him again and he put his hands in front of his face, but the man had only pushed him on to the bed and told him to stay there. For ten minutes David lay on the bed without moving. Usually Denver hit him and then was kind. But sometimes—if David didn't move and made no sound—the anger went out of Denver's eyes before he hit or kicked or jabbed David in the ribs.

Even lying with his back to Denver, David could tell when the anger went away. Denver was breathing more slowly and less noisily now. David's father had never hit his mother, but the anger between Chuck and Drew—the ice-cold words with which they struck each other—had made David vigilant.

David sat up and reached for the stack of baseball cards on the bed table. Denver paid no attention to him. There were, perhaps, sixty cards. He had simply grabbed a handful of unsorted cards and put them in his backpack. He turned them over one by one and slipped out the cards he wanted to hide, his fingers sliding down the slick plastic coating. There were only four, including the David Hulse he had won from Denver. He would have to get Denver to trade. Denver had hundreds of cards in his gym bag.

"Daddy!" He wrote the word and then tugged at Denver's arm. When Denver looked at him, he added, "Trade?" He smiled the smile he used when his father was late picking him up and he could feel the rage starting in his mother. He pushed thirty cards at Denver and wrote, "Please."

"Sure, Andy," Denver said and took a stack of cards from his gym bag.

There were two Dave Winfields in the pile Denver gave him, one of them from 1991 when Winfield was with the California Angels. There was a Dave Stewart, too, pitching for Oakland. "Trade ten?" David wrote and slid one Dave Winfield to the bottom of the ten cards he wanted Denver to trade him and one into the middle with Dave Stewart second from the top. He barely looked at the ten cards Denver chose before writing, "Yes."

"Fooled you," Denver said triumphantly. Too late, David realized that Denver had taken a 1992 Ultra Award Winner Cal Ripken. It was the most valuable card he had with him, worth maybe four dollars.

Denver looked at David, his gray eyes puzzled. "You ain't usually so stupid," he said.

"Butthead," David shouted at himself. "You stupid, stupid butthead." Then he picked up an index card and wrote, "No trade." His hand was trembling, and the marker slipped and stained his fingers with yellow ink.

Denver had been holding the Cal Ripken in front of David's face. When the boy reached for it, Denver pulled the card away. "Ain't that too bad," he said. "It's mine now." With a child's malicious glee, Denver dangled the card out of David's reach.

It wasn't only the flesh eaters who could be cunning. Gazelles could turn and twist and deceive and make the huge jaws close on air. David stood on Denver's bed and grabbed at the card. The bigger fuss he made, the less suspicious Denver would be.

"Crybaby," Denver taunted and karate chopped at David's thigh with open hand.

Off balance, David fell into the well between the beds, scraping his knuckles on the thin carpet. He lay on his stomach until Denver pulled him up. David closed his eyes and braced himself for another blow. But Denver was Daddy now. "I'll give you a chance to win it back, Andy," he said, his hands gently brushing David's hair.

"Thank you," David wrote. He could not have said the words without Denver knowing they were false. But lies could not leach through cardboard. On paper the words were what they seemed. Slyly, David added, "More cards. Buy me more, Daddy."

Denver had stopped at a gas station and torn the advertisements for baseball card stores from the phone book chained to the telephone booth. "Damned if we ain't got lots to choose from," he said greedily, as if he came from a place where there was no choice of toys.

Second Base Memorabilia was the closest, and there was a parking space in front of the store. But the shop was crowded, and Denver stopped outside the door. David tugged at him. For a moment it seemed that Denver would pull the boy away. Then he changed his mind. He leaned forward and whispered into David's ear, "You point to the cards you want, and don't you go wandering away." He kept his hands on David's shoulders as they moved to the counter and waited next to another father and son.

David pointed to the thickest packets—a 1996 Topps Major League and a bag of leftover worthless players the store had wrapped in plastic and was selling cheap. Most likely there'd be a David in the bag, and at least he'd have a lot more cards to trade for Denver's cards. When Denver pushed five dollars across the counter and waited for change, David reached in his pocket and pulled out his David Hulse. He had no plan except to drop the David cards everywhere, like Hansel's pebbles in the forest. He put his hand, with the card in his palm, on the edge of the glass. When Denver tossed him the new packs, David left David Hulse behind.

"Hey, kid." The twenty-two-year-old manager of Second Base Memorabilia had barely outgrown his own trading days. "You left one of your cards."

Panicked, David ran awkwardly back and pushed the smiling Texas Rangers outfielder into the Ziploc bag full of tarnished Saturday heroes. Dave Hulse had played in thirty-two games in 1992 and batted .304. Before he turned toward Denver again, David had buried Hulse in the middle of the bag.

"Clumsy," Denver said. "Lose your head if it wasn't buckled on." His voice was fussy around the edges. Once more he sounded as if someone else's words were in his mouth.

Unable to say aloud that he was sorry, David walked with a puppy gait, tilting his head until he had nuzzled his way into the space between Denver's arm and ribs. With every lie, he grew better at deception.

"I'm hungry," Denver said. "Let's eat."

Denver was always hungry now, and he ate with a greediness that was nearly gluttony, wolfing down hamburgers, french fries, chili dogs—whatever the world of fast food had to offer. He seemed, when he was eating, to be close to ecstasy. "Damn, that was good," he would say as the last bite slid down his throat, and his voice would have an edge of sadness. No matter how much he ate, he was hungry a few hours later.

"KFC," David wrote.

"McDonald's," Denver said. "I want a couple of their cherry pies."

For a few days David had enjoyed the unprecedented freedom of cheeseburgers for breakfast, Coke and pizza at midnight, Reese's peanut butter cups whenever he asked for them. Once, Denver had bought a pound bag of M&Ms, and they had finished it in an hour. Now his stomach lurched at the thought of more fried food. He wanted—surprisingly, he craved—an apple and the carrot sticks his mother always kept in the refrigerator.

This McDonald's was upscale. They sat at a table topped with wood grained Formica. Denver's food—quarter pounder, chocolate shake, two cherry pies—sprawled into David's space. David drank milk and pretended to eat Chicken McNuggets. He had asked for them because they came with tubs of mustard sauce. He made a show of opening a tub of sweet-and-sour sauce and dipping a McNugget. With his other hand, he slipped the mustard into his pocket. His bruised knuckles stung when he brushed them against the coarse denim of his jeans. Someone was eating Chicken McNuggets at the next table, too, and on the far side of the room two bored little girls in pink shorts were making a stack of plastic tubs.

"Let's go, Mommy." The five year old rocked in her wood-grained plastic chair. "Go," echoed the three year old. "Soon," said the mother, half finished with a strawberry shake. "Now," said the five year old imperiously. Commanded by David, Drew might have hurried—as this nameless mother did—to finish her drink and wipe her mouth and pick up her purse.

Covetously, David watched them leave their debris on the table. The stack was six tubs high, so two had to be mustard. Maybe more. Drinking his milk, with his face blank and his eyes closed, David planned the way he would steal the tubs. He was good at stealing. That was a secret not even Danny knew. After he reached into the candy bin at the drugstore, he would pay for the bar in his hand but not for the one he had pushed up the sleeve of his sweater. He would always take the stolen candy to the thin branches at the top of his tree and eat it there, high above everybody.

As Denver was tearing the wrapper from his first pie, David mimed an invisible napkin and pointed at the napkin dispenser across the room.

"Better get me some, too," Denver said, his mouth red with clotted cherry.

Denver's eyes followed David to the counter. Carefully, David counted out half a dozen napkins and started back. Denver was still watching when David's arm knocked the stack of tubs to the floor. Three were mustard. Quickly, David picked up the tubs and put the other three back on the table. He had pushed the mustard packets into the sleeve of his pullover.

Denver wiped his mouth with two of the napkins and slit the box that held his second pie. Sitting a narrow table's length away, David shook the mustard into his lap. The sharp edges of the foil scratched his fingers as he pushed the mustard deep into his pocket.

While Denver ate, David stroked the two inch cubes. Below them, in the bottom of his pocket, waiting at the plate for his turn to swing, was Dave Winfield. Winfield was the Toronto Blue Jays' designated hitter in 1992.

"Let's see what you got," Denver said.

David, cornered, had no place to run.

"Come on. Let's see what you got," Denver said again. But he was not asking for the secret in David's pocket. Instead, Denver reached across the table for the plastic bag of baseball cards. He pulled the bag open and spilled out the two dozen throwaways. Then he tore open the copper-and-black tinfoil of Topps Series One where Jim Edmonds was swinging for the Angels, Tom Candiotti was pitching for the Dodgers, and Don Mattingly was running out a hit for the Yankees as he had been doing for more than a dozen years.

"Trade you," Denver said, holding up Topps No. 219, a Future Star card for New York Yankees shortstop Derek Jeter, who was *Baseball Weekly*'s minor league player of the year in 1994. Denver could simply have taken the card, but whatever rules he lived by prohibited him from seizing it or even demanding that it be traded.

This time David was cautious. "Later," he wrote. "Maybe." Denver tilted his head back and let the last rivulet of chocolate shake flow to his mouth. Waiting, David fished for his rubber bands and began to sort the players into teams. There were, by chance, three Kansas City Royals with their royal blue batting helmets and royal blue sleeves. "Do the outside edges first," his mother would always say when they put together jigsaw puzzles. "That will help you see where the inside pieces go." David had started by moving Colonel Mustard around the Clue board in his head. Then the David cards followed Colonel Mustard down the secret passage between the study and the kitchen. Each step led, unbidden, to the next. Royal, Royal, ROYAL. He held the three cards in his hand. Royal Motel. He could fill in the middle with more cards, different cards. He could tell a story. He could tell his mother where he was.

Suddenly, with awful urgency, David had to go to the bathroom. Afraid that he was going to pee on the floor, he tugged at Denver's T-shirt. "Can't you wait?" Denver asked. Dancing up and down, David shook his head. "Well, go on, then," Denver said, pushing him toward the bathroom door. "But hurry up."

Urine sprayed so quickly that David's hand was wet, and the drops made a sticky circle on the floor. When the stream dribbled to an end, David washed his hands. Then he took a rubber band and tied a tub of mustard to a David card and to the second baseman for the Kansas City Royals. The cards curled around the tub, and the package listed to the side like a sinking toy boat. David put the packet behind the hot water faucet and turned to unlock the door. But what if Denver opened the door? What if Denver wanted to pee? Caught in the silent space between predator and prey, David put the packet in his pocket, took it out again, put it back. In the end, he left it behind and ran to Denver holding up the lure of Derek Jeter in his pinstriped uniform.

"You want to trade?" Denver asked.

David smiled and nodded. He took Denver's hand and pulled him toward the car.

About fifteen minutes after Denver and David left the restaurant, a teenager at the end of his shift was sent to clean the bathroom. He mopped the imitation brick linoleum, put more soap in the dispenser, and threw the wet packet of mustard and baseball cards into the trash.

CHAPTER 20

By late afternoon on Friday, West had removed the piano teacher from his list. The man had spent the Memorial Day weekend south of the border, "down Mexico way," as the old song went. The trip had been an accident. He had been pulled into the car by three friends who were heading for Ensenada and wouldn't take no for an answer. "Blind luck," he said to West. "Dumb blind luck. I'll be damned." More accurately, in this case he wouldn't be damned.

James Arthur Rogers Jr. was another story. Now twenty-one, the boy who had sent his eight-year-old brother to the hospital two years earlier spoke the language he had learned in thirty-two court-ordered visits to a psychologist. He was very sorry for what he had done to Joey, Rogers said. He had lacked impulse control. Now he had learned to sublimate his anger. At the suggestion of his psychologist, he had taken up football and was a reserve line-backer on his junior college team. While he was talking, Rogers chewed the inside of his lip; a small drop of blood landed on his chin. West had the sense of a volcano that might be dormant but was by no means extinct. No matter how many hours of therapy had been poured into the crater, the stresses that had caused the last eruption had not been drowned. West noticed that Joey Rogers—his ribs healed but his eyes still wary—never walked within reach of his brother's fists.

Jim Rogers had been at the Galleria on the Saturday afternoon David Greene went missing. He had, he said, gone by himself to look for a present for his mother's birthday but hadn't found anything he wanted to buy. He had walked over to the Galleria around four o'clock and returned home around six or six-thirty. He wasn't really sure of the time. After looking at a photograph of David Greene, Rogers said he didn't think he had seen the boy. There were a lot of kids running around the mall, but he hadn't paid much attention to them, he said.

West watched Joey Rogers lace up his Rollerblades for a game of street hockey. The boy had chosen a chair across the room from his brother.

"Need a goalie?" Jim tossed a puck from hand to hand.

Joey shook his head. "It's not a real game. Just three or four of the guys."

West did not believe that everyone who was prodded or provoked viciously enough was capable of murder. There would always be some people who would stop short of killing. But James Arthur Rogers Jr. was not one of them. West watched Rogers throw the puck—a little harder than necessary—to his brother. Rogers could have seen David Greene at the Galleria, could have hated him for some unknown reason, could have pulled him out of the mall and beaten him to death. Rogers lived six houses from the hedge where the boy's bloody shorts were found. If David Greene were dead, he might have been killed by Rogers's fists. But if David Greene were still alive, this young man struggling so hard to appear calm was innocent of everything except envy and anger. And Angus West could not allow himself to believe that David Greene was dead.

"Who wants to take the comic book shops?"

There were two thousand flyers, a six-pack of Diet Coke, and two bottles of white wine on the coffee table. For the last half hour Drew had lost herself in the details of organizing the ten people who sat in the living room of her house. Or, rather, what she had lost was the weight of melancholy that she had carried like a backpack filled with stones for almost a week.

Bob Sellars raised his hand. "I know most of the stores around here. I can make sure Hi de Ho and Golden Apple keep a lookout for David."

Drew filled two more squares on the rough chart she had drawn earlier in the evening. On Saturday, Bob would hit all the comic book stores from Sunset Boulevard south. Allan Adams, who taught with Chuck, would canvass the Valley. Drew's depression was not gone. She could feel it lapping at the edges of her heart. But she was grateful for the task that had made it recede, if only for half an hour.

Chuck had not volunteered to swoop down on pizza parlors in Torrance and Rosemead. He had no compass in his head. Coming out of a familiar restaurant, he would turn the wrong way. Driving home from dinner at a friend's house he would find himself heading east when he had intended to drive west or north when his route was south. "You're going the wrong way," Drew used to say with an exasperation that was lacerating. "I don't understand. We've been here a dozen times." It was Drew's competence that Chuck had hated most.

One of the bottles was empty. Awkwardly, Chuck pushed a corkscrew into the other one. If the geneticists were right, David's ineptness at throwing a baseball had been passed down from father to son. But had Drew's talent for organizing been a present of Ruth's genes or a lesson taught at her mother's knee? Early in Drew's marriage, Ruth had defined—and dismissed—Chuck as an absentminded professor. He never forgot a historical date, the meaning of a battle, or the importance of a Supreme

Court decision, and he could teach such things brilliantly. But he wandered through daily life guided by an inadequate map.

Drew refilled Bob Sellars's glass. She had no way of knowing how many of the people who sat on the couch and hardwood floor of her living room believed that what they were doing would make a difference. She didn't even know how many of the friends who would be spending their weekend searching for David thought that David was still alive. But why couldn't David be with someone who would see what a special boy he was and be kind to him and buy him baseball cards?

"I'll take the baseball stores on this side of the hill and west of Hollywood," Drew said. "I know where most of them are. David hasn't spent his allowance on anything but baseball cards for a year."

"Ditto," said Laura Matranga. "Danny and I can take the card shops in the Valley."

Drew filled in the last three squares. Art would canvass the baseball stores in Hollywood and downtown Los Angeles. Ruth would stay home with Kiley and answer the telephone. With hundreds of flyers already taped to trees and store windows, someone should be calling. Chuck would be Ruth's backup. He had borrowed Allan Adams's cellular phone. Drew passed the number out to everyone in the room. Anyone who discovered anything was to call Chuck.

Chuck's suitcase was in the hall outside Kiley's bedroom. Tiffani had packed clean underwear and shirts and brought the suitcase to school. Drew had put clean sheets on Kiley's bottom bunk.

"What can I do?" Kiley asked, and Drew gave him a dozen pencils to sharpen. He handed the sharpened pencils to Laura. "Daddy's sleeping in my room," he told her. The Matrangas had been divorced since Danny was three.

When the others left, Laura stayed behind. Drew poured the last drops of Trader Joe's house special into Laura's glass. At a Stanford film series during her sophomore year, Drew had seen an old James Mason movie the central metaphor of which she had adopted. Like Salome dancing before King Herod, people wrapped themselves in seven veils. Intimacy demanded that one or more veils be shed but never the seventh veil. No one except saints and doomed lovers ever dropped the protective seventh veil. For a few years, Drew had shed five veils with Chuck. But by the time their marriage was over, she was wearing all her veils and an overcoat besides. With Laura, more than once Drew had briefly lifted the sixth veil.

"What would you do if Danny died?"

"I'd go on," Laura said. "I'd probably get myself pregnant by the first man I could find with good genes and a decent sense of humor."

"If it weren't for Kiley, I think I might commit suicide," Drew said. "At least I'd think about killing myself." She licked the rim of her empty glass. "I think about it now sometimes, about taking sleeping pills and getting into a warm bath and slipping under the water the way Thomas Heggen did. That seems such an easy way to die. I suppose I wouldn't do it, though. Kiley would stop me; I couldn't abandon him that way."

Laura touched Drew's shoulder. "Do you think that David's dead?"

Drew told Laura the truth. "If he's dead, I can never make things right. So I have to believe that he's still alive."

West had spent the evening in Hollywood waiting for John Scherdsky to come home. Home—at least according to the Department of Motor Vehicles—was Apartment D in a bungalow court built during the thirties. The court had, at one time, been painted bright pink and planted with date palms and banana trees. The palms, at least, had thrived. They towered over the squat brown buildings and dropped their unripe dates by the hundreds on the cracked concrete stoops and path. Whatever California had promised the Midwesterners who had lived in such courts when they were new and whatever dreams the emigrants had brought to Los Angeles with them, had long since been swept away by the Santa Ana winds. However bright its paint sixty years ago, the

Cozy Court was now just another dead end with rusted screens. Nearly every street in Hollywood had its share of Cozy Courts.

No charges had been filed against Scherdsky in Sherwood, since the boy at whom Scherdsky waved a box cutter had just walked out of the toy store with a video game hidden under his sweater. But Scherdsky did have a record. The LAPD had cited him for two or three barroom brawls and a drunk and disorderly. He was drunk when he stumbled back to the Cozy Court at midnight.

West caught up with him on the bottom step of Bungalow D. "John Scherdsky?"

West was a head taller than Scherdsky, so the little man's punch caught West in the middle of his chest. It was followed by a left jab that raked West's ribs and a haymaker aimed at his chin. But West turned, the punch grazed his cheek, and, sodden from too much whiskey, Scherdsky lost his balance and fell. Before he could get up, West was sitting on his back.

"So take the damned car," Scherdsky shouted as loudly as he could with his mouth pressed against the cracked cement. "It's a piece of shit anyway."

West handcuffed the little man's hands behind his back and pulled him up. "I'm a policeman, not a repo man."

"I'm a welterweight," Scherdsky said. "Or was."

According to his driver's license, Scherdsky was fifty-two years old. Liquor and life had upped the ante. With his watery blue eyes and leathery skin, he could have passed for sixty-five. He was, West thought, the least likely toy salesman he had ever met. But then, Scherdsky had only been temporary Christmas help at Toys Unlimited. And he hadn't lasted until Christmas.

"Thirty-two fights," Scherdsky said. "I could have been someone."

We all could have been someone, thought West.

"My manager sold me out." With the slurred insistence on telling the truth that is sometimes found at the bottom of a shot glass, Scherdsky added. "My legs sold me out. But I could take a punch." His fists had just sold him out in another way, but he seemed to have no interest in the fact that he was handcuffed and in danger of being dragged off to jail for slugging a policeman. He leaned against West and began to snore. West unlocked the hand-cuffs and felt in Scherdsky's pockets for a door key.

Everyone gets through the night as best he can. The living room and hall of Scherdsky's small bungalow were piled with paper bags, neatly folded and reaching to the ceiling, and with balls of string and rubber bands and stacks of plastic foam and plastic bags. Some of the paper bags were taped to the windows, protection against the light. Dust as thick as talcum powder rained on West as he guided Scherdsky to the tiny bedroom at the end of the hall. Whatever company the paper bags provided was missing from the bedroom. The bed was cheap and made of metal. Scherdsky curled up and was asleep. West took off Scherdsky's shoes and put them next to the mattress. Halfway to the door and without planning it, West turned back and tucked a five dollar bill into the nearest shoe.

West had not expected that one of Sherwood's files would lead to David Greene. But sitting in his car outside the Cozy Court, he realized that he had hoped. Hoped without reward. Whoever had taken the boy was still formless, lost in the blackness of the night city that surrounded him.

It was after 1:00 A.M. when West drove to Drew's house. Although he waited with the engine running, he could see no light and hear no noise. Inside, each person was isolated in sleep and did not hear him drive away.

Drew had the oddest dream. She was perhaps nine years old and living in a town she had never seen except in the television shows of her childhood—*My Three Sons* and *Lassie* and *Mayberry R.F.D.* In the dream she wore a pinafore and left all the doors of her house unlocked and was completely, absolutely safe.

Lying on the thin mattress that covered the wooden slats of Kiley's bunk, Chuck groped through tangled landscapes with broken glasses dangling from his ears and woke to the sound of Drew's breathing a room away.

Ruth dreamed a dream she had not had since childhood, a nightmare that she had left behind more than fifty years earlier. In it she was pursued by a huge ant, gigantic and malevolent. Just as when she was five and the insect had followed her night after night, she reached a fence she could not climb and, when the creature's black forelegs touched her shoulder, woke up.

At Ruth's feet and curled against her back, the dogs twitched and moaned and moved their feet in frantic pantomine. Whatever the dogs were dreaming, they did not say.

CHAPTER 21

David counted his treasures. Lying motionless in the dark, he added and subtracted, multiplied and divided them. David was afraid of the dark only when he was alone in it. Denver was more than strong enough to keep the creatures of the dark from devouring him. Even stupid Kiley was strong enough to keep the monsters away. Maybe because Kiley didn't believe in monsters.

David had grown bolder. No more than an arm's length away, Denver was still awake. Yet David let himself imagine going home. More dangerously, he lay in the dark and planned his way home. He was afraid of Denver's rage and Denver's knife. He was afraid that he would somehow let Denver know that Andy Ellis didn't exist, afraid that something in his eyes or his walk would make Denver realize that Andy had disappeared. But he was no longer afraid that Denver could read his mind. Imprisoned in this motel room behind mud-splashed windows and a triple-locked door, he couldn't talk but he was free to think.

After dinner, they had gone to two more baseball card stores. Hardly caring what he bought, David had been crafty in leaving

163

his lopsided packages behind. In the first store, he had hidden the packet of mustard and cards behind display boxes on the counter. In the second shop, he had dropped the packet into an almost empty box that held packs of Donruss. Anyone refilling the box would find it.

Hidden in the stacks of cards on the table beside David's bed were eight David cards and half a dozen Kansas City Royals. He had one old Royals team card and, wonderful luck, a card for Shawn Green. The Shawn Green had come in a Fleer Metal Universe pack he had chosen at the second store. If it had been in one of the packs that Denver bought, David would never have dared to trade for it.

In the intelligence test David had taken in first grade, he had been shown a series of pictures and asked what was wrong with each one. With every right answer—a missing ear or a tree with roots at the top—he had been shown a picture with a subtler flaw, a barnyard scene in which the sheep had one horse's hoof, a bird whose wings didn't quite match. His first wrong answer had come on a picture that was used to test seventh graders. Now he lay in the dark and formed pictures in his mind. He would use the Shawn Green card at the next store. No. He would save it. He had to be sure whoever found the card would know what it meant. What else could he leave? He saw himself leaving a trail of agates. But the polished rocks wouldn't mean anything, not even to his mother. He couldn't leave his baseball mitt. It was too big, and Denver would know it was missing. Maybe he could write a message on his magnetic scrabble. "Help. David Greene." Were there enough E's? But it was dangerous to write a message. What if Denver opened the board?

Denver was asleep now, his mouth pressed against his pillow, his restless hands scraping at his sheet. David turned until he could see the bulk of Denver's body. The black shape in the other bed twisted, but it did not wake. For the first time David was awake while Denver slept. Greene the great. Greene the greatest.

"I'm hungry," David wrote. "Food." He made a fist and shoveled imaginary food into his mouth. He wanted pancakes, lots of pancakes with strawberry syrup. He had awakened this morning, Saturday, with a birthday-morning excitement. Today they would go to three, four, five more baseball shops. He stuck his hand in the pocket of his jeans to make sure the packages were still there. Greene the great.

During the week in which they had lived together in this motel, they had silently divided the room between them. Denver's gym bag was under his bed; his cowboy boots and tennis shoes were lined up near the window. He had thrown his clothes into the top two drawers of the room's broken dresser, leaving the bottom drawer for David. The room's one chair, overstuffed with sagging cushions that had once been yellow, was as much Denver's property as the boots. David had never tried to sit in it.

On the second day, Denver had taken David's comic books; he let David read them, but he kept them on the floor by his bed. "Mine," Denver had said, and David had not tried to argue. Denver's knife was always in his pocket. Except at night. Denver put it under the pillow when he slept.

David owned perhaps a quarter of the room's space, the part of the room that was farthest from the door. He didn't use the dresser. There was a drawer in the nightstand in which he kept his baseball and mitt. The top of the nightstand was a shrine to the rest of his treasures. He had piled the polished rocks so they formed a cone like the rock heaps hikers build to signal a direction. He had placed a stack of baseball cards on each side of the rocks. Nothing that Denver had bought him was on the nightstand. He put the glasses in his shoes each night and kept his clothes in the black gym bag.

For a week it had been Denver who always woke hungry. "I'm starving," he would say and search among the bags on the floor for leftover onion rings or a half-eaten candy bar. This morning was different.

"Food," David pantomined again.

"I ain't hungry," Denver said. He sat sluggishly in the yellow chair, his fingers tracing the bronco on his belt buckle.

An hour later, David tried again. "Breakfast," he wrote. "I'm hungry."

Denver said nothing, so David added, "Please, Daddy."

Until now, Denver's energy had been the central fact of each day. Denver had hit, stroked, devoured, stuffed his mouth with food and his gym bag with baseball cards. Now he was torpid, a rattlesnake in the sun. It was as though the antic excitement he had worn for days was a skin that he had shed on the floor of the dirty room. It was as though whatever game he had been playing with David wasn't fun anymore.

David crossed out "Breakfast" and wrote "New cards."

But trading cards no longer seemed to interest Denver. Angry at his own passive father, a reckless David had allowed himself to go with swaggering Denver. Now he was stranded. David felt the packages in his pockets, the ships that would sail him home, and began to cry.

"Andy." The name was almost a question.

David filled a card. "Yes, Daddy."

Then the old Denver was back. "Sure, Andy. Let's get more cards."

A mile beyond the motel, there was an International House of Pancakes, and David pointed toward it and pulled at Denver's arm. But the man drove on. He stopped at a hamburger stand at the back of a closed car wash. David sat on one of the tall stools while Denver bought each of them a hot dog. David reached for the thin plastic rectangles of mustard and saw that there were plastic tubes of ketchup mixed in. Miss Scarlet. Colonel Mustard and Miss Scarlet. His mother had to know what the ketchup meant. He closed his fingers over half a dozen of the ketchup packages and dropped them into the pocket of his jacket. He was reaching for the mustards when Denver grabbed them first and tore them open. After Denver squirted mustard on both hot dogs, there was only one tube left. David carried it back to the car hidden beneath the steamy wax paper that covered his breakfast.

The two card shops were only a few blocks apart. Three Strikes sat at the end of a minimall next to a one-hour photo store. Grogan's sold *Partridge Family* lunchboxes and green Kryptonite rocks—the saleable debris of old movies and television shows—as well as sports cards.

"Hey, Andy, look at this," Denver said, reaching for an Indiana Jones hat from *Raiders of the Lost Ark*. In the car, David had had no opportunity to slide the ketchup into the package he would leave behind. He waited for Denver to turn away, so he could slip the ketchup beneath the rubber band. But Denver, expansive, cracked an Indiana Jones bullwhip. He was wearing his cowboy boots today and his cowboy personality. When David didn't applaud, he cracked the toy bullwhip against the boy's back. David was not hurt by the spongy rubber, but he understood the warning. Since the divorce, David had learned to be watchful. When he and Kiley spent weekends with Chuck, he had taken over Drew's job of reminding his father that Kiley would be waiting at the side gate after soccer practice or must be driven to school by 8:00 A.M. Monday morning for an assembly. He leaned over and picked up some enameled starfleet pins from *Star Trek* and handed them to Denver.

At the beginning, Denver had played David like a fish. He had enticed the boy to nibble at the bait and, when David was well hooked, had alternated between reeling him in, allowing the line to go slack, and then suddenly reeling in again until the boy was dazed and almost broken. David didn't have the strength to reel Denver in, but he had learned how to pacify and distract him. While Denver was choosing between half a dozen *Star Trek* artifacts, David slipped ketchup into both packages.

"What'll it be, fellow?" Grogan asked David. Grogan was at the top end of middle age and the top end of middle weight, and most of the extra pounds circled his stomach. At the stores they had visited, the clerks had asked their questions of the man with the money. Denver had chosen and paid. David had not been invisible; he had simply been of no interest to them. But this small shop was Grogan's toy. He had opened it after he retired from the county fire department with a decent pension a year earlier.

"My boy'll take a couple of packs of Upper Deck," Denver said. "Me, I'll take the pin." He pointed to the triangular enamel badge he had pinned to his T-shirt.

Although it was Saturday morning, the shop was empty. Grogan's was just beginning to make inroads on the bigger, gaudier Three Strikes four blocks away.

Grogan brought his leathery face—baked in the smoke of a thousand fires—closer. His eyes, smoke-damaged too many times, had been the cause of his retirement. "Who's your favorite ballplayer, son?" he asked as he handed David two packs of cards.

David tried to answer. Warmed by the sympathy in Grogan's voice, he tried to say, "Help me." But he could only make hoarse croaking sounds.

"Cat sure has got your tongue," Grogan teased.

David took a step toward Grogan, but Denver put his arm around the boy and pulled him closer. "Most often, he can talk your arm off," Denver said, with the smoothness of butter, "but he's got laryngitis, and the doc says not to talk 'til he sees him on Tuesday."

"No," David tried to say with his eyes. "Don't believe him."

But the door to the shop opened, and three brothers with Saturday allowances burning the palms of their hands pushed and shoved in their need to be the first to choose. "Got second series yet?" shouted the oldest.

"Just hold your swing, Riccardo, until I get through with these customers," Grogan said. He reached for Denver's twenty-dollar bill. He was a shopkeeper now with his next sale on the front burner and no time to play. With the counter blocked by the three boys, David looked for a place to leave his packet. He finally hid it behind a display of Thermos bottles decorated with Scooby Doo and Huckleberry Hound.

There were ten cards in every Upper Deck pack, each card a gaudily colored scene framed by a copper-colored border along the bottom. David found one Royals player in his second pack—Johnny Damon. But it was another card that he held tightly in his hand, running his thumb across the slick plastic. An unimportant outfielder had just hit the ball and was running toward first base. He was pounding the ground with his head down and his arms spread like birds' wings, and it seemed as if he would fly beyond first base and no one could catch up with him, not ever.

When they reached the minimall, there was only one empty parking space. The space was across the lot from Three Strikes, so that David had to walk behind Denver's car to reach the store. For the first time, he was close enough to see the license plate. At the motel, the zoo, and the other shops, Denver had made sure that David was pushed into or pulled out of the car from the front, and dirt had been rubbed into the dun-colored front plate.

"Hurry up," Denver said, pulling David past the car. There was mud on the rear license plate, too, but David could read one letter, K.

Three Strikes was full of posters. From one wall, quarterbacks released footballs that seemed intended for the wide receivers on the opposite wall. Pitchers aimed blurred balls at batters across the room. Beneath the posters were locked cabinets, their glass shelves holding hundreds of plastic-encased special cards—Michael Jordan, Johnny Unitas, Nolan Ryan, Kareem Abdul Jabbar. Flourescent lights bathed decades of heroes in milky radiance. Awed, David forgot his goal and moved softly from counter to counter.

"Christ," Denver said, moving with him. "Don't I wish I had these."

Yes, David nodded, and for one moment he was himself again, whole. Hand in hand with Denver, he walked the central aisle of this cathedral—acquisitive, reverent, and yearning to have the strength that filled the shelves.

They were in the shop too short a time to be noticed. "Let's go," Denver said. Whether he was suddenly wary of the waiting people—at least a dozen men and boys—or angry that so much was unattainable, or merely annoyed by the line at the cash register, he turned away and pulled David toward the door. Once more divided, hunted and hunter, David had only time to reach into his pocket and drop his packet on the glass of the last counter, in plain sight.

Denver didn't look back.

David had wanted to stay in the card shop, touching what he couldn't have. As Denver pushed him to the car, he turned back and stumbled. As clever as David was, and as careful, it was impossible for him to know what minor thing would trigger Denver's memories and his rage.

"Why should I buy you anything?" Denver said as he started the car. "Andy is a bad boy. Why should I care about him?"

They had barely left the parking lot when one of the clerks found the packet. "Look at this, Steve," he said, handing it to the assistant manager.

Steve poked at the mustard. The cards were throwaways, not worth a second glance. He made a jump shot, and the packet tumbled into the wastepaper basket.

CHAPTER 22

It was Chuck who opened the door to Angus West at 7:00 A.M. on Saturday morning. Chuck hadn't shaved yet, and he was wearing a button-up white shirt and green pajama bottoms. Drew felt a need to explain.

"Kiley wanted his daddy."

The doorbell had startled the dogs. Barking, they raced one another to the door and joustled against West until they were reassured by a half-familiar smell. Drew found that she was trembling, as though the doorbell were a cosmic starter's gun.

"I'd better get dressed." Embarrassed, Chuck stated the obvious.

The dogs trailed into the kitchen behind Drew and Angus. There was too much to say, so Drew said nothing as she filled a mug with coffee and handed it to West. In the six years since his wife left, West had never sat, drinking coffee, in someone's kitchen two days in a row. And only a few one-night stands with long hair and bright red lipstick had been in his kitchen at all. For half a decade, Ellen's coffeepot had been as solitary as its owner.

Drew's kitchen made a strange war room. A copy of the day's

assignments had been pinned to the front of the refrigerator with a Mickey Mouse magnet, displacing one of Kiley's drawings. Drew and Laura had glued a large Southern California map to cardboard, and Laura had brought a box of colored push pins left over from Danny's science project. If any of the searchers found something, a blue pin would mark the spot. When people who had seen the flyers called, yellow pins would be pushed into the map. For now, the map leaned against the spice cabinet next to the yellow legal pads on which Ruth and Chuck would log the calls.

Ruth put a Thomas Bros. street guide on the table. It would be Ruth's job to make a list of all the stores that had been visited and to dispatch the troops to nearby shops. During the last few days Ruth had lost some of her armor, the hard crustacean shell that protected the soft white flesh within. Brisket was already eight years old, and she had awakened at six this morning grieving for the loss that—no matter how long Brisket lived—would come too soon. She cursed herself for having given her heart away one more time.

After she had walked the dogs, Ruth found a biscuit mix in the cupboard and began to prepare biscuits. Long before Chuck and Kiley were awake, Drew joined her and, wordlessly, rolled the dough. While the biscuits were baking, they sat at the kitchen table and drank the first coffee of the day together. Now, just as Chuck and Kiley sat down and Drew put pots of jam and a plate of biscuits on the table, the telephone rang.

"I've seen your boy."

The woman was old, with a voice of cracked leather.

"Where?" Drew asked. "When?"

"Out my window. I always look out my window. I see so much out my window."

Then there was a new voice, rich and black. "I'm sorry," the new voice said. "We saw your boy's picture at the market, and Mrs. Matthews insisted I write down the number."

"You haven't seen David?"

"Mrs. Matthews is sorry about your boy. She wants to help."

Drew could hear soft crying that might have been the rustling of leaves.

"Tell her 'thank you,'" Drew said and held the phone for a long minute before hanging up.

West watched Drew's open palm defiantly brush tears from the corner of her eye. "I should have told her," West thought, and he wondered why he had not prepared Drew for the narcissists and sadists who would find their own pleasures in David Greene's disappearance.

Too late, he gave the required lesson. "There are always a lot of calls," he said. "Most of the people who say they've seen David won't have seen him. Some people will be calling for the reward. Others won't be lying to you, but they'll have bad eyesight or want to help too much. And some will call to hurt you. Don't believe them when they tell you David's dead."

Chuck put his arms around Drew, and Drew did not pull away. David and misery united them.

"So tell me who to believe," Ruth said. "I'll be taking the calls today." She sat across the table from West, her voice as controlled and unemotional as his. "How do I judge? What are the clues?"

"Keep them talking," West said. "Most people will give themselves away if they talk long enough." He was about to add, "Go with your hunches," but didn't. He didn't know this brusque, square woman, and he had no idea what her instincts would tell her. "Ask how they learned about David. If they saw the flyer, where was it posted?"

One of the dogs pushed against West's knee, and he leaned down to pat it. There was another thing he would have to say. Why the hell had he gotten involved in this? But he knew why. He scratched the dog's ear, delaying what he must say next.

"You haven't told us something," Drew said suddenly. Without knowing how, she had read the stiffness in West's back and the way he gripped his coffee with tense fingers.

"Whoever took David may call," West said. "You have to be ready for that." He looked at Ruth. "He probably won't tell you he has the boy, but he may hint at it. You have to listen for someone who seems on the edge of bragging or someone who wants too much information from you. You have to . . ."

The telephone rang again. Ruth offered the phone to West, but he shook his head. She reached for a yellow pad and one of the pencils Kiley had carefully sharpened the night before.

"Hello."

To the other people in the kitchen, the conversation was an alternating current of questions and silences. "Where did you see him?" "When?" "What was he wearing?" "What makes you sure the boy was David?" "Can you describe the man who was with him?" "Isn't Serrano a block past Western?" "Can you give me that phone number again?"

Twenty years of running an office, twenty years of arguing over invoices and tracking lost shipments, paid off now. Drew's questions would have been too sharp. Chuck would have been blown off course with every answer. Ruth was, as usual, in control.

"I'll have someone come talk to you," Ruth said. "Will you be home for the next hour?"

Chuck pushed the first yellow pin into the map at Serrano Avenue near Third Street. There was a new tenant in the garden court across the street from the woman who had called, Ruth said. He had been there less than a week, and he had moved in with a boy the woman was certain was David. The man was always shouting at the boy.

West reached for the pad and copied down the woman's name and address. And so it was decided what role he would play in today's search.

Drew was parked in front of B&B Sportscards in Beverly Hills half an hour before the store opened at 9 A.M. On the dashboard was a list of fourteen card stores. She closed her eyes and planned the day—Santa Monica Boulevard west, with a jog to All Sport on Pico and back up and then west again to Ivan's Sports and Comics on Fifteenth Street. She should hit the shops in Santa Monica before she headed south. Going south to the beach cities, she could avoid the worst of the freeway traffic by taking the back road past the sewage plant. Drew was something that had been rare in her mother's generation and was a dime a dozen in hers— a native of La Ciudad de Nuestra Señora, La Reina de Los Angeles. She had the city in her head.

Drew heard a key in the lock of B&B and opened her eyes. She reached the store's owner almost before he was inside the shop. "My son is missing," she said. Color photographs of David were in her hand. "Have you seen him?"

By 1 P.M. Drew had covered card shops in Beverly Hills, Santa Monica, Culver City, and Westchester. Then she had driven farther south to the beach cities. She had taken the road along the cliffs at the edge of the ocean, and against her will her spirits had risen with the seagulls that circled the sunlit sea. It was like the times she was angry with Chuck and still could not keep her body from responding to his touch. She had no right to feel the beauty of the day, but she could not help herself.

El Segundo, distinguished by its sewage plant, was easy, but it was almost impossible to find a parking space in front of the trendy boutiques and cappuccino bars of Manhattan and Hermosa Beaches. In those beach cities, it seemed that everyone wore shorts or spandex and rode the waves.

It took almost two more hours before Drew was finished with the beach cities and headed inland to the flatness of Gardena, Torrance, and Lawndale. The color pictures of David were facedown on the bucket seat next to her. She could not bear to turn her head and catch an unexpected glimpse of her son in his Astros uniform, posing on one knee, bat in hand, for this year's Sherwood League picture. In one store in Santa Monica and another in Redondo Beach, clerks thought they might have seen David, although they couldn't be sure. Nor could they remember when the boy who might be David had come or if he had come alone. Drew took their names and phone numbers for West. West could sort out the possibility of truth while she could only say, "Look out for him. Please."

She handed a flyer to every clerk and half a dozen more to each manager. "David loves baseball cards," she told them. "And he's smart about them. Please tell people about him. Show them the posters. If he has a choice, this is where he'll come."

In pizza parlors and malls and comic book shops from the valley to Long Beach, the same questions were asked. "Have you seen this boy? "Has this boy ever been here?" And the same answers were given. "No." "Never."

"Want to stop for lunch?" Laura Matranga asked her son. Danny shook his head. "Not yet." "Aren't you hungry?" "I don't want to stop looking," he said. Laura kissed the top of his head and reached for the next address.

"This is stupid," Ari Goldman had said to his wife that morning. "David's dead." But, at 9 A.M., the Goldmans, who lived in the pink stucco house down the block, had gotten into separate cars and driven in opposite directions. Joan Goldman wanted to show David's picture in the galleries and pavilions and shopping plazas of the expensive suburbs that surrounded Sherwood. She had a hunch, she had told Drew the night before. Ari had taken the assignment he was given—two dozen pizza parlors along with a suggestion that he try to put up flyers in any McDonald's, Burger King, or Jack in the Box that was nearby.

West rang the doorbell of the small house on Serrano. The woman who answered the door seemed sound of mind and body and not overly greedy for attention. When West was a young detective, spending his days interviewing the public-spirited citizens who had provided the LAPD with tips on various gruesome crimes, his sergeant had defined the tipsters broadly as "cuckoos," "weirdos," and "Look into this one, West." West's own classification system had been more subtle. He gave motive equal weight with sanity. The forgetful old man who had dutifully voted in every election since 1936 and was once more doing his civic duty might be more believable than the young woman with twenty-twenty vision who delighted in telling and retelling what she had seen.

"Mrs. Wilson? I've come about the boy you think might be David Greene."

Mrs. Wilson told the same story she had told Ruth on the phone—a stranger across the street, a silent little boy. Although she had only seen the boy two or three times, she had wondered about him even before she saw the poster in the window of a Korean electronics store. Yes, she did pay a lot of attention to what was going on. The neighborhood had changed so much in the last ten years. She was sixty-four, recently retired from a job in the coat department at Bullock's. Actually, it was the store that had retired, gone out of business, and she had been too old to think of getting another job.

As far as Mrs. Wilson knew, the boy was still in the apartment across the street. They almost never went out, she said.

West walked the street in front of the court and then the alley behind it. He doubted that the first phone call would deliver David Greene wrapped in blue ribbon and ready for the journey home. It was never that simple. But Theda Wilson had new glasses and a firm chin. West was sure she had seen a boy who looked like David Greene.

The mail slot was in the apartment door, and all the circulars that had been dropped on the porch were addressed to Occupant. Behind the closed blinds, a television set roared. West stood to one side and pounded on the door. He had decided to be a plumber. There probably wasn't an apartment in Hollywood without a leaky faucet or a clogged pipe.

No lie was necessary. The boy who opened the door was David's height and weight, but he had brown eyes and a narrow mouth.

"You want something?" the boy asked.

"I want to talk to your father."

"He's sleeping."

"It's late to be sleeping."

"He's drunk."

West slipped past the brown boxes that lined the walls of the living room, silent evidence of transition. The boy sat down in front of cartoon animals skewering each other with cartoon swords. There was a box of Cocoa Puffs on the couch, and the boy ate the cereal by the handful, spilling a little more on the floor each time.

"You want some milk?" West asked.

"Isn't any," the boy said.

"Would you want some milk if there were milk?"

Startled that what he wanted would be of interest to anyone, the boy looked at West and answered, "Yes."

West bought half a gallon of milk at the convenience store around the corner. When he had filled a bowl with cereal and milk and handed it to the boy, he went into the bedroom and woke the man who was lying facedown on one of the twin beds.

"Who are you?" the man asked. Like the boy, he had a narrow mouth, but his breath was rancid. "Who the hell are you?"

West showed his identification and watched the man's belligerence melt into alarm. "Is it Joe?" He lurched past West into the living room.

The cartoon animals were now swallowing dynamite sticks in the form of lollipops. "Hey, Daddy," the boy said. "Look at this."

With reassurance came sobriety and anger. "What the hell are you doing in my apartment? Get the fuck out of here."

From the time he was ten, West had been aware of the advantage of his size. But he was fifteen and on his high school wrestling team before he learned how to use his size as a defensive weapon. There was no need to break people into pieces if they chose to break themselves. He made his bulk into a wall against which the man's anger was blunted. "I'm looking for a missing boy," he said, his voice as tranquil as a sea of glass. "Prove to me this is your son."

"Fuck you," the man said, but this time the words signaled defeat. Even as he said them, he reached for one of the cartons stacked against the wall. He found a photo album and handed it to West.

A plump baby drooled at the camera from the safety of his mother's arms. A toddler in green corduroy reached for a plastic truck. A three year old rode piggyback on the man's shoulders.

"Where's your wife?" West asked.

"Ex-wife. In Las Vegas. She dumped me and the kid for a better life dealing blackjack." His words were acid and ate holes in the air.

"Fuck Mommy," the boy said.

"Fuck Ellen," West thought. She had left for a better life that was, undeniably, better. But Ellen had left no boxes behind. She had packed the best of his life—his seven-year-old son—and taken it with her. He could, he supposed, call the county and get a social worker out to investigate whether the man standing in front of him was a fit father. But he knew he wouldn't. He knew he believed that even a drunken parent was better than no parent at all.

Left alone, Ruth and Chuck drifted into the polite truce that had been their way of coping with each other during Drew's marriage. Chuck rarely argued with anyone, and Ruth had reluctantly accepted Chuck as the father of her grandchildren. They had seemed to get along well enough, but they had both complained to Drew.

By one in the afternoon, most of the searchers had reported in at least once from pay phones in various fast food emporiums. Depending on personal taste, the pizza parlor contingent had settled on Chicago style, thin crust, or deep dish for lunch. Drew had eaten nothing, but she had called Chuck twice to ask about the phone calls.

"Is there anything?"

"No."

"No trace of David? No one recognized the picture?"

"The policeman is checking the calls out." Chuck knew she wanted more, and he did not know how to provide it. She had always wanted more than he was able to give. So he said, "It's Mommy," and handed the phone to Kiley.

"Did you find David?" Kiley asked.

"Not yet," Drew said.

"Will you find him today?"

"Maybe one of us will find him," Drew said and felt her tongue walk the narrow truth between elation and despair.

West had also called twice, and Ruth had read him names and addresses from her half-filled yellow pad. There had been nine more phone calls. Two were from men who had begun with, "How much is the reward?" One of the men had insisted on being paid the reward first, before he would tell Ruth where he had seen David. "Don't you believe me, lady?" he had asked. The other had told her he had seen David in a vision and had previously found several lost objects, including a missing dog, by conjuring them up in dreams. The second man had cheerfully left his name and phone number.

The ten yellow pins on the map formed no pattern. They were separated by inches that meant miles, and four of them were stuck beyond the empty hills that divided the city from the valley.

The telephone rang again. It was a woman's voice this time. "I live in Tarzana," she said. "I'm sure I saw that missing boy yesterday."

Kiley pushed the new pin into the map. "Here," he said. "David's here."

CHAPTER 23

D rew entered Grogan's two or three hours after David and Denver left. It had, in the end, been a good day for the shop, the best Saturday business in the four months the store had been open. It was not that Grogan wanted to make a fortune. He wanted to make a thousand dollars a month net profit, which would be enough to keep his wife from nagging him about wasting his time and his pension. He was talking to her on the phone when Drew arrived.

"But, Gail . . ." Grogan's face was as red as the dyed cherry on top of a hot fudge sundae. "Because I need to be here. It's Saturday. I'll do it after church tomorrow." For most of their marriage, Grogan had slept at the firehouse three nights a week and had taken his meals and his companionship there even more often. Whatever wonders Gail Grogan had expected from her husband's retirement had not occurred.

Freud said that one should be skeptical of accidents. But an innocent person can be mowed down by someone else's nonaccident, as Drew was now. Three of Grogan's fire station buddies were leaning against the counter—big men with rough tongues who had gotten in the habit of ending their shifts by dropping into the shop for one of the beers Grogan kept in the refrigerator in the storeroom.

"I see Gail's not letting up on you any," one said.

"If you're freezing in bed at home," said the second, "we'll kick Schultz out of your old bunk."

They had known and ribbed one another for twenty years, but the barbs could still hit vulnerable spots. Grogan barely looked at Drew's poster. "Sorry, lady," he said.

Drew tried again. "If he should come in . . ." She had never been good at artifice, had never painted her face with anything more than lipstick. But she tried to snare Grogan with a begging gesture and a smile.

"Yes," Grogan said, turning his back on Drew. "Sure. If he comes in, I'll call you."

Each time she closed the door of a store behind her, Drew felt the ache of another lost possibility. When she left Grogan's she felt the stab in her stomach as well as her heart and realized that she had had nothing to eat all day except one cup of coffee and half a biscuit. Early in a childhood lived without religion, Drew had replaced God with mythology. She should, she knew, stay without food now, offering her emptiness as penance to whatever unseen forces ruled her world. But, like Persephone nibbling on pomegranate seeds in hell, she stopped in the 7-Eleven at the other end of the minimall from Three Strikes for a pack of Life Savers. When she put the candy in her mouth, she felt ashamed, as though she had failed another test.

Three Strikes was still crowded, and Drew had to wait while the men and boys took their turns at the front counter. She was the only woman in the shop, and some of the men looked at her curiously.

After five minutes, only two teenage boys remained, and they were debating their choices with the necessary solemnity before deciding what to buy. "What can I help you with?" The co-owner of Three Strikes was Drew's age. He had been a fullback in high school. His partner, who never worked on Saturday, had gone a step further—second string center at Cal State Fullerton.

"My son is missing," Drew said. She handed him a flyer and the color pictures of David.

"Gee, I'm sorry."

"Have you seen him?"

He held each snapshot to the light, then shook his head. "Maybe one of the other guys did, though." He shouted for the young clerk. "Hey, Paul, you seen this boy?"

"No," the boy said and passed the snapshots on to the assistant manager. "You seen him, Steve?"

Steve gave the photographs back to Drew. "I'm here most of the time. I didn't see him come in."

The three men circled Drew, a circle of masculine protection too porous to serve as a shield. "If there's anything we can do . . ." the owner said. Drew acknowledged their attempt at chivalry. "Thank you. Look out for him. Please. David loves baseball cards. He's been collecting since he was six. He's got hundreds—more than two thousand—of them. We don't know what's happened. But if David could decide where to go, he'd go where he could buy baseball cards."

The teenage boys were standing at the cash register now, and Paul turned away to help them.

"It's stupid," Steve said. He was twenty-two years old and in his next to last semester at Cal State Long Beach. "But . . ." He had a surfer's streaked blond hair and bleached blue eyes.

Drew pounced on his embarrassed hesitation. "You might have seen David?"

"No," Steve said. "Just something weird that happened this morning."

"Weird?"

"Something was left here." He pointed to the counter near the front door. "A package of junk."

Drew the organizer, Drew who kept the irrational world at bay with graphs and lists and cryptograms, Drew who created maps in her head and navigated home on strange surface streets when the freeways were becalmed, reached for this straw. "Do you have it? Can I see it?"

"I threw it away," Steve said, feeling uncomfortable that the important oddness of a missing child had caused him to think of the other odd nonsense. "It was nothing."

Before she spoke again, Drew watched Steve open two boxes filled with packs of basketball cards and arrange them on the shelves behind the counter. "It was nothing," he said to reassure her.

"I'd still like to see it," Drew said. "Please."

The package had slipped to the bottom of the wastebasket, and it took Steve a moment to find it beneath some empty cans of orange soda. He wet a rag and wiped the orange soda from the cards and condiments, but a few more orange drops rolled from the plastic ketchup onto his palm as he handed the package to Drew. She stared into the determined face of Dave Winfield, aging designated hitter. The ketchup made no sense to her nor did Brent Mayne, catcher for the Kansas City Royals with his mask off, staring up at a ball only he could see. And the orange and white tub of McDonald's hot mustard sauce was too far removed from the wooden yellow game piece representing Colonel Mustard for her brain to make the connection. But she couldn't throw the package back in the trash can. Why was there a ballplayer named David?

"Weird," Steve said again. He turned the Winfield card over and read the legend on the back. "That's a cheap card."

"No one's left stuff like this before?"

Steve shook his head. "Un-uh."

Drew put the ketchup, mustard, and Kansas City catcher back inside the rubber band and placed the package on the dashboard, but she held the Dave Winfield in her hand as she drove the four blocks back to Grogan's. Drew believed in the malevolence of the God whose existence she doubted. She believed in an untrustworthy universe and the spitefulness of fate. A friend's forty-year-old obstetrician had died playing Ping-Pong on his patio. He had slipped and hit his forehead on the table. The eighteen-year-old cousin of a different friend had been struck by lightning while sitting in a rowboat on a sunny day at a family picnic. But she could not allow herself to believe that David was dead, and she could not allow herself to believe that the baseball card she held in her hand had been a random choice. How many baseball players were named David?

The firemen had finished their beers and left, but Grogan was waiting on two middle-aged men in running shorts who were buying out the store's stock of movie cowboy memorabilia—from Tom Mix and Hopalong Cassidy to Gene Autry and Roy Rogers. One of the men laid a hundred dollar bill on the counter and then added a twenty. Grogan gave him forty-seven cents change.

This time Drew didn't smile. She held out the packet from Three Strikes. "Have you found anything like this?" she asked.

"You're the lady whose boy is missing." With his friends gone and money in the till, Grogan seemed embarrassed by his earlier surliness.

"Someone left this package at Three Strikes today," Drew said. "It was left on one of the counters."

Grogan shook his head even before he took the package apart. "The cards aren't worth anything," he said.

"You might not have found it yet."

"You think it has something to do with your son?" Grogan asked.

Drew wanted the answer to be "Yes." But it wasn't. Not yet. "I don't know," she said. "Can I look?"

Grogan squeezed past the cash register. "I'll help you."

Unlike Three Strikes with its inventory of heroes safely locked beneath glass, the open shelves at Grogan's were crammed with lunchboxes, toy sharks, spaceships, plastic *E.T.* Christmas ornaments, and boxes of cheap sports cards. Since the store was small, the first impression was that someone had too carelessly prepared a rummage sale. Grogan wiped off a dusty Millenium Falcon. "Great movie," he said.

It was Grogan who found David's packet wedged between a pyramid of lunchboxes and half a dozen plastic Thermos bottles with Saturday-morning cartoon characters stenciled across their pastel surfaces. This time the baseball players were G. Jeffires, third baseman for the Kansas City Royals, and David Justice of the Atlanta Braves. If there were Justice, Drew thought, David would be home.

She held a tub of mustard sauce from KFC and a duplicate of the other sliver of ketchup encased in white plastic, and she felt— as usual the thought came to her in a literary metaphor—as though an iron band around her heart had snapped. In one variation of the story of The Frog Prince, the prince rides home with his princess while four iron bands around the heart of his faithful coachman break apart, one by one. It can't be coincidence, Drew thought. David must have left these. And the first band was shattered. But that was as far as she could go. From David but not David. Three thick iron bands remained.

Drew pushed the photographs of David into Grogan's hands. "Are you sure you didn't see him?"

Grogan rubbed his eyes and looked at blurred color snapshots of a boy with long honey-colored hair. "My eyes aren't very good anymore," he said, "but I don't think so."

The pay phone down the block from Grogan's was broken. The streets of Southern California are a landscape of palm trees and broken phones. Drew moved from one gas station to the next listening to dead air. "Damn," she said over and over again, so burning with impatience that she felt feverish.

"I'll be home by six," she told Chuck from the phone at a doughnut shop in Gardena. "When the sergeant calls, tell him to come back to the house."

"What have you found?" Chuck asked.

Drew realized the absurdity of trying to explain over the telephone what she had found—a package of things that made no sense, a connection as fragile as a cobweb. "I'm not sure," she said. "I'll show you when I get home."

She went first to the last card shop on her list, a small store on Hawthorne Boulevard. "Not much room to hide anything here," the man in the Dodgers warm-up jacket said. "Anyone left something here, I'd find it in a minute." No, he added, he had never seen the boy in the photographs.

Then she drove west, back to the beach cities, squinting at the sun as it began its late afternoon descent into the Pacific Ocean. She drove as much by instinct as by sight. If you grew up in Southern California, you learned how to deal with the sun just as teenagers in frozen states learned what touch on the steering wheel would keep a car from sliding on the ice. Whatever later use movie stars and gangsters would make of Ray-Bans, sunglasses had not begun as an affectation. Drew leaned over and opened the glove compartment. If her sunglasses were there, they were buried beneath too many tapes and road maps to reach for in the sticky traffic. So Drew pulled the visor down and looked through half-closed eyes while, minute by minute, the sun dropped lower and its rays spread like syrup to ensnare more four-wheeled ants.

In Redondo Beach, Hermosa, and El Segundo, the clerks looked at the packets Drew handed them and shook their heads. Stopping at each of the stores she had visited earlier in the day, she worked her way up the coast and into Beverly Hills. No one had found a similar package. There was no other trace of something that might have been left by David.

The five of them ended the day where the day had begun—at the kitchen table. Drew had not reached home until seven, and Kiley had thrown himself on her as soon as she opened the door.

"You've been gone too long," he said, his hands pulling her down.

Before West arrived, Chuck and Ruth puzzled over the cards, while Kiley took the packages apart and put them together again and then took them apart. Too late Drew thought of fingerprints. But the packet from Three Strikes had been wiped clean before it was handed to her, and she had had to show both packages to the clerks at the other stores. Only Kiley was eating, and he had left a peanut butter fingerprint on J. Eisenreich before Drew managed to take the card away.

Drew flushed. "I'm sorry I didn't think of fingerprints sooner."

West held the cards by the corners and spread them out. With all the people who had handled the packages, there would be little chance of getting usable prints. "I'll send a friend of mine out tomorrow anyway to see what prints he can lift from David's room," West said.

The kitchen smelled of coffee and summer fruit. Kiley had finished his sandwich. "Wipe your hands," Drew said, "and don't touch those" as he reached for the tubs of mustard. Beneath the old-fashioned ceiling fixture—oval glass with frosted glass swans—the cards lay mute and gave away no secrets. From Chuck at one end of the table to Drew at the other, the four adults formed a bell curve—A to F, disbelief to certainty. "It's not much," Chuck said. "Some kid playing a joke."

Drew attacked. "Why do both packets have a baseball player named David?"

"Coincidence?" Chuck wanted his son back as much as Drew did, but he had long since replaced magic with history. Chuck lived in a world of facts.

"Two packages with baseball players named David has to be more than coincidence."

"If these came from David, the other things would mean something to us," Chuck said, looking at the ketchup. "And they don't."

For half an hour, they had been trying to find some meaning in the other things. They had examined the mustard to see if the packages had further identification. Each of them had read the statistics and history on the back of the four cards. "Brent

Mayne—Born: 4/19/68, Ht: 6'1", Wt: 190, Bats: Left, Throws: Right, Birthplace: Loma Linda, California." They had tried to find an anagram or pattern in the names of the players and the manufacturers of the cards. They had even added and subtracted the numbers of the cards and the players.

"It's accidental, Drew," Chuck said in the tone he used when half the class had misunderstood an exam question and he had to lead them toward reasoning out the right answer. "You want to believe David's alive so much that you . . ."

"No," she yelled. "It's not a coincidence! Not two packages. Two packages have to mean something."

While Drew felt the same fury she always felt when Chuck lectured her and Chuck felt the same hurt he always felt when Drew was angry with him, Kiley retreated from his parents' quarrel by grabbing the KFC mustard sauce and using it to push the taller tub from McDonald's around the table. With the half of her brain that knew when the glass of milk was about to be spilled or the tub of mustard to fall from the table, Drew reached out and caught the McDonald's before it hit the floor.

It was not that Drew leapt to conclusions like a trout to a well-tied fly. She was, in ordinary situations, more cynical than her ex-husband. In their wariness toward the world, Chuck and Drew had been a perfect match. But new ways of knowing had come to Drew eight years earlier with the amniotic fluid. While Chuck slept through the baby's impatient screams, Drew had awakened, more often than not, a heartbeat before her son's first cry.

Kiley lifted the bright yellow tub of KFC mustard sauce and walked it along the table, while Drew stared vacantly at the face of Colonel Sanders in his black bow tie. The understanding came with a rush that was visceral, as though the sac that held the baby had broken once more, with the fluid again flowing down her legs and onto the kitchen floor.

"Colonel Mustard," she said. "That's David's message. He took the Clue cards with him. He's leaving a clue."

West turned skeptical eyes towards Drew. "And the ketchup?"

Drew shook her head. "I don't know."

West was a policeman now. "Instead of leaving the packet, why didn't he ask for help?"

"I don't know." Drew shook her head again. "For some reason he has to talk to us in riddles."

"Why? If he can walk into two card shops and walk out again, why does he have to talk in riddles?"

Drew had no answer.

"You can't change the facts," Chuck said. "Not by believing in magic."

West pushed his cup toward Ruth, and she refilled it. He did not look at Drew. He knew he should side with Charles Greene—two rational men dismissing the fantasies of a mother who needed her son too much. Logic said that the packets were part of some kid's game and the David cards one of the million random things that just happen. Every policeman knew of two suspects born on the same day or of a mugger and his victim meeting up with each other a week later at a ballpark hot dog stand. Coincidence. Things that happened. In West's case, the year he joined the LAPD and was directing traffic, Allen Stewart Rodman and Alan Stuart Rodman had sideswiped each other at the intersection of Figueroa and Ninth Street. He saw himself putting the two packets on Chief Zarelli's desk and listened, in his head, to the chief's laughter.

It was past Kiley's bedtime, but no one had told him to go to bed. Half asleep already, he climbed into Drew's lap. Drew's long brown hair shadowed Kiley's face as she rocked him.

West picked up the two Kansas City Royals cards and handed them to Drew. "Suppose you're right. Suppose David left the packets. What is he trying to tell us with these?"

That David was with G. Jeffries or B. Mayne made no sense. The sharp edges of the cards pricked Drew's fingers. She stared at the blur of the crowd as Jeffries, batting glove in his hip pocket, headed for the plate in 1993.

Ruth, who was sitting next to Drew, was used to unhappy endings. At sixty, she had outlived two marriages, both her parents, and her youthful idealism. She and Drew had not paid emotional attention to each other for years. But, if they were choosing teams, she would stand by her daughter's side. She would choose to be on Drew's team even if that team had already lost. "If David were going to Kansas City, could he know that?" Ruth asked. "Is he trying to tell us where he's going?"

"He might," said West, "be trying to tell us where he's been."

The local phone book—covering the area from West Hollywood to Malibu—was full of Royal Motels, Cafe Royales, Royal stationers, car washes, and dry cleaners. There was even a Royal movie theater. And that area was the tiniest sliver cut from the pie of Southern California. Logic said that the phone book contained chimeras and that chasing them down the pages was as useless as trying to hold soap bubbles. Common sense said that the packets were meaningless. But West had known from the beginning that he would not refuse to help a second time.

Ruth pulled the phone book toward her and dialed the Royal Rest Inn. "We're looking for an eight-year-old boy who has been missing for a week. The story was in the *LA Times* on Wednesday. Has anyone checked in recently with a young boy? He's a little over four feet tall, and he weighs about sixty-five pounds. . . ."

Chuck, who had never been sensitive to undercurrents— Drew had often spent the drive home from a dinner party filling Chuck in on what had happened while he sat in the same room, oblivious—did not realize at first that logic had lost the game. "Be logical," he had often said to Drew when she skated toward the thin ice of assumption. It took five minutes before he understood that he was isolated. He got up and poured himself another cup of coffee. He wasn't thirsty. But he needed to get away from the three heads bent over the telephone book.

"There must be hundreds of Royal restaurants and shops and motels between here and San Diego," Drew said. "We'll need to get phone books and try to figure out where each of them is located. It might take days." She looked at West. "Yesterday, you said we had another week. At most."

West could offer no reassurance.

Chuck stood in the center of the kitchen and looked at the ceiling above Drew's head. "Tiffani . . ." he began, and then stopped. Still staring at the glass swans, he started over, rejoining the others without believing in what they were trying to do. "There's an easy way of getting information like that," he said. "With a computer. Tiffani knows how. The papers I wrote for the junior college journal, Tiffani surfed the Internet for material. She could bring her laptop over and make up lists of addresses." He still had not looked at Drew.

The divorce had been the same mixture of agony and relief to Drew as it had been to Chuck. The difference was that Chuck had not been willing to end the marriage until he had found someone else to look for his mislaid glasses and make the beds. Drew saw herself opening the door to Tiffani and inviting Chuck's new woman to join the life Chuck had left behind. The mind picture made her shudder, and her hands trembled. The coffee in the cup she was holding splashed down Ruth's shirt.

Even before Chuck stopped talking and hid his face behind his cup, Drew knew what her answer would be. But she still found it difficult to say Tiffani's name. "Yes," she said. "Ask . . . her . . . to come. As soon as possible."

CHAPTER 24

"Why should I buy you anything?" Denver had said the words half a dozen times on Saturday afternoon. Once, he had added, "No one bought me baseball cards."

When they left Three Strikes, Denver turned the nose of the car north. Sometimes he rode the freeways. More often, he drove through places David had never been before, the neat suburban streets of Duarte, Montebello, Monrovia, and Arcadia. David tried to memorize the street names, but there were too many streets and the names were too strange to him. They drove for hours with the wind at their back and no destination.

Once David wrote, "More cards?" That was when Denver hit him and said, "No one bought me baseball cards." After that—for as long as he could—David sat without moving as though he wasn't in the car at all. It was the way he had lain on the bed in the motel waiting for Denver's anger to go away. But, no matter how long they drove, Denver's anger didn't go away.

A week earlier, Denver had gone hunting. What he had brought back to the Royal Motel was raw material rather than raw flesh. Raw material for the movie version of his life in which he could switch the scenes around and change the past. But making the past stay changed is always a problem. Denver was the name the man had chosen for this home movie. With the new name had come the opportunity for a new beginning and a new ending, for a fiction in which mothers didn't run away and a good daddy loved his son. Denver did not yet know that this attempt to change the outcome of his life was failing, as all the other attempts had failed.

Eventually David got so hungry that he tugged at Denver's arm and shoveled a forkful of imaginary food to his mouth. That time, Denver hit him harder.

They drove in silence. Denver had punched the power button on the radio, and the music had trickled away, so there was no background of gals and guys throbbing with immense, unsatisfied longings. They drove east, away from the sun. They drove until Denver had exhausted himself.

They returned to the motel about the time Drew spread David's packages across her kitchen table. Now it was David who searched through the litter on the floor. That Denver was not hungry could have warned David. But it didn't. Chocolate shakes and barbecued rib sandwiches, warm pie and french fries had given Denver the energy to create his dream life. Cheeseburgers and hot dogs had been the fuel that helped to sustain the fantasy. But now he had no interest in food.

David found some cold french fries and half a dozen M&Ms. There was a stale chocolate doughnut, and he lay on his bed and licked off the chocolate before he stuffed the dry cake into his mouth. Then he pulled the blanket over his head so he could not see the stranger that Denver had become. But he could still hear Denver walking up and down the room, his boots crushing the plastic and cardboard containers. He could hear Denver whispering to himself, "Andy is a bad boy. Daddy punishes a bad boy."

David was not sure when he fell asleep. But he awoke, still fully dressed, in the middle of the night to find Denver scrubbing the bathroom washbasin. It was the sound of running water that had awakened him. Denver wiped off the handles of the water faucets and then squirted ammonia on the bathroom door, using one of the motel towels to wipe the door from top to bottom and along the edge. He was wearing rubber gloves—as he had that first night.

Everything was gone from the floor. The straws and soft drink cups and Styrofoam clamshells had been crammed into a plastic bag. Denver's cowboy boots and his gym bag and the stack of comic books that used to belong to David were gone, too. Denver was wearing tennis shoes and his hunting shirt, *Lethal Weapon 3*. While David watched, Denver polished the top and sides of the dresser and then, with even greater care, the handles on each of the empty drawers. When the grime of the window and windowsill turned the towel black, he placed it in the bag by the front door and picked up another already soaped towel. He wiped down the metal frame of his bed and then started on the bedside table with its mosaic of cigarette burns.

It wasn't until Denver had scrubbed everything else—the moldings, towel bar, light switch, and shower handles as well as the chains and locks on the door—that he told David to get up.

"Go piss," he said. He followed David into the bathroom and waited. When the boy was through, Denver wiped off the metal handle, the porcelain bowl, and both parts of the seat. The bottle of ammonia was almost empty. The sharp smell hung in the air and made David cough. Denver reached for the toilet paper holder—a wooden bar on a wire frame. He threw toilet paper and bar into his sack.

"Sit here and don't touch anything," he said as he pushed David on to the bed. He unzipped David's gym bag and held it against the end table. Then he swept everything on the table into the open bag. He threw the ball and baseball mitt and the green toothbrush on top and zipped up the bag again. After he had wiped the drawer and top of the table and run his towel down each curved leg, Denver pulled David up, jerking the boy's arm for extra emphasis as he said, "Don't move." Then Denver pushed the mattress onto the floor and wiped the frame and the springs to which David had been handcuffed. There was still a drop of dried blood where the spring had cut David's arm when he writhed in panic in the dark. While David stood and watched, Denver stripped the beds and found a sock tangled in David's sheets. Then he tugged the mattresses back on to the beds, took the pillowcases and the rest of the towels, turned off the light with his gloved hands, and opened the door.

"Game time," he said. It was 3 A.M.

There was no moon, and the stars were distant and dim. David stopped at the threshold and began to cry. He was afraid that if he stepped into the dark, it would rise like black water over his head and he would drown.

"Hurry up," Denver said impatiently. "What are you, a fraidycat?"

Denver stepped closer, and his breath was moist on David's neck. "Andy is a fraidycat, a pussy," and his hands left the acrid smell of ammonia on David's hair.

In that moment David knew he must not let the man discover that he was afraid of the dark.

David was already too full of secrets, so full that he could hardly move from the weight of them. But he stopped crying and clamped his lips together, even though he ached to give the secrets back, to tell them to Denver so he could be rid of them: "I'm David Greene. I'm leaving a trail so my mother can find me. Don't make me go outside in the dark because I'm afraid that the dark will swallow me." But he mustn't tell Denver anything. If Denver knew this secret, he would have the power to hold David down in the dark until he choked on it. David shook his head in a fierce "No, I'm not afraid" and stepped into the night.

There was no wind, and the only sound came from the chunks of broken beer bottles splintering beneath his feet. The pockets of David's jeans were still full of packets. Just before he opened the car door, he dropped one on the ground. Denver pulled forward and to the right and then backed up, the car wheels crushing the packet and leaving the tires smeared with mustard and ketchup. The David card stuck to the rear tire for a few blocks and then fell into the street.

Five miles away from the motel, Denver emptied the plastic bag into a supermarket Dumpster. Then he picked up a box of rotten fruits and vegetables that had been left next to the Dumpster and poured out strawberries, cucumbers, and oranges so green with mold that there was no orange to be seen. They splattered as they covered the towels marked ROYAL MOTEL.

CHAPTER 25

Drew watched Tiffani's hands type meaningless combinations of letters and numbers filled with periods and backward slashes. They were small hands with frosted pink polish on the acrylic fingernails. Tiffani carried her youth as heedlessly as Pasha carried his tennis ball. Her right ear had been pierced four times, and she wore a semicircle of zircon studs of different sizes in the lobe. Her hair was cut short, like Winona Ryder's in the 1994 movie *Reality Bites*. In her left ear, she wore a dangling silver ankh. That Egyptian symbol of life, so trendy during the 1960s, had recently become a Generation X artifact because it was favored by Death, the heroine in the Sandman comic books. Tiffani also wore baggy jeans and a brown suede vest from Aardvarks, one of the expensive vintage shops on Melrose Avenue, and her overlarge breasts pushed against the soft suede. The result of hair, clothes, and jewelry intimidated Drew even though she realized that it wasn't quite successful. Like the haircut, the clothes were slightly out of date.

Watching Tiffani's fingers dart from keyboard to mouse and back again, Drew felt the weight of the eleven years that separated her from the girl with whom her ex-husband was living. But the barrier was not the elasticity of Tiffani's fresh, young skin. For Drew, the mastery of youth was contained in the fact that Tiffani's hands were fluent in a foreign language that Drew had hardly begun to learn.

It was Drew and the three golden retrievers who had opened the door to Tiffani half an hour earlier. Chuck had stood up at the sound of the doorbell. He had sat down again when Drew, unwilling to allow Chuck to play host in the house he had abandoned, said, "I'll get it."

"I'm awfully sorry about David," Tiffani had said on the doorstep. "He's a neat kid."

"Come in," Drew had answered. For the Greenes, "Come in" was formal language. People were usually waved into the house with a "Hi."

Drew led Tiffani into the kitchen and metaphorically handed her over to Chuck. Standing across the room from Tiffani, Chuck made the introductions by long distance. Tiffani cradled her laptop against her chest to deflect Drew's excruciating politeness. The computer's pale blue canvas cover matched the blue of her eyes.

Kiley woke up long enough to say, "Hi, Tiffani," before sleep pulled him down again. He was sleeping on Ruth's lap now, and, after a brief head shake of acknowledgment, Ruth focused her attention on the dogs and the child. West was, as usual, impassive as Tiffani bent down and pushed the plug of the laptop into the socket next to him.

"Would you like some coffee?" Drew asked, reaching for the pot.

"I don't drink coffee," Tiffani answered. "Got some tea? Just hot water and a teabag would be fine." As Drew turned on the teakettle, Tiffani added, "Herbal tea, if you've got any."

CompuServe promised that postal addresses were only keystrokes—plus nineteen dollars and eighty cents an hour—away. Tiffani took a quick but indirect route. Whenever she wanted to surf the Internet, she piggybacked onto her brother's computer at

USC. At a salary of nearly fifty thousand a year, Jake—four years older than Tiffani—installed computer networks for the academic departments at the university. When Tiffani was eleven, fifteen-year-old Jake had given her his outdated Radio Shack computer and his passion for computing. A couple of times Tiffani had tried to explain that passion to Chuck. Unsuccessfully. What her fingers knew, her tongue could only call "an exciting world."

It was a world without awkwardness or embarrassment about sitting in the kitchen of a house belonging to the ex-wife of your lover, a woman who had a Phi Beta Kappa key from Stanford while you had to drop out and find a job after two years at Santa Monica City College and a semester at UCLA. Within minutes, Tiffani was driving full speed down the information superhighway. That's what it felt like—driving as fast as you could with the gas pedal pushed to the floorboard. In less than an hour of exploring CompuServe's Phonefile and Bizfile databases, Tiffani had lists of all the businesses in Southern California whose names started with Royal, Royale, or Royalty—from Royal Motors in Beverly Hills to Royal markets in eleven cities and the Royal Pet Mortuary. Showing off, she configured the lists in several ways—by geographical area, by city, by kinds of businesses, and alphabetically—before handing the disk to Drew to print.

It was midnight now. The coffee was cold. The tea was colder. Kiley was in bed. Since Chuck would be going home with Tiffani, Flame was sleeping in Kiley's bottom bunk. West had left noiselessly an hour earlier. Silent as an Indian, he had disappeared without a word.

Who est had driven to Todd Carter's apartment in the Marina. Sherwood preferred its officers to live within the city limits, but no one made a fuss when they didn't. Carter lived in one of those swinging singles buildings deified on *Melrose Place*. Although it was past 11 P.M., a small group of twenty-somethings was hanging out by the swimming pool. The pool was heated; the beer was cold. Todd was wearing a Sherwood PD sweatshirt over his black trunks.

It was impossible not to notice West. Even if the others had been standing, he would have been taller. Play-wrestling on a chaise longe with a girl in a bikini, Todd sat up abruptly and sucked in his stomach. He started to say, "Hey, West," but it came out "Sergeant?"

"Got a minute?"

"Sure."

"Maybe we could go to your apartment?"

"Sure." Todd grabbed two cans of beer from the cooler and loped ahead of West up two flights of stairs. The building had been contorted so that every apartment had a view of the boat harbor. Todd handed West a beer and asked, "What's up, Sarge?"

"Did you finish making those lists of dead and missing kids?"

Todd was a good enough detective to realize where the conversation was going to go—down a steep slide that could land him in the toilet. "Yeah," he said.

"You don't happen to have them here?"

Todd shook his head. "They're in my desk."

"I need a copy."

West had left Todd no room to maneuver. He could say, "Sure. Glad to oblige. Happy to steal police documents for you." Or he could say, "Fuck off. Never mind that you're the best detective we have. You smell like shit to Zarelli, and anyone who comes near you is going to smell like shit, too."

"You're suspended," Todd said.

West agreed. "Yes."

"I'm not supposed to give you anything."

West agreed again. "Yes."

"If I give you the lists and Zarelli finds out, I'm in deep shit."

"Yes."

Todd sat on one of the bar stools that separated the postage stamp kitchen from the postage stamp living/dining room with its picture window and picture view. "So why should I stick my neck out?"

West could have said, "Because a child's life might depend on it," or "Because I don't think Trout killed the boy," or "Because you've got balls enough to do it." Instead, he asked a question.

"Why did you finish the lists?"

The young detective was startled. "What?"

It had been a mistake for Todd to sit down. Only a few inches shorter than West and with the home court advantage, he had more or less held his own when he was standing. West looked down at him. "It was a bitch of a job. And, with me gone, no one was going to be on your tail. No one was going to give a damn about those lists."

"Oh, Jesus," Todd said.

West smiled for the first time. "Since you made them for me, I think you'd better give them to me."

"When do you need them?" Todd asked.

"Tomorrow morning. As early as possible."

"I could go in at nine."

West smiled again. "I'll buy you breakfast at Ship's at nine-thirty."

"The Greene boy is still alive then?" Todd asked.

"Yes," West said.

W est had always been a creature of the night. As a young police-man, he had loved being on duty through the dark hours. Ellen had never understood his willingness to take the night shift. Larks and owls. In this case a lark and a bat. At twelve, West had imag-ined himself as the Caped Crusader, perched on the rooftops of Gotham City and ready to apprehend evildoers in the dark streets below. He spent much of August that year climbing up and down the roof of his house on a rope he had knotted and attached to the eaves. By the next summer he had discovered girls and surfing. But he had never lost his sense of being at home in the dark.

For the second night in a row, he arrived at the Greenes' house after midnight. This time, they were all awake. Drew had taken

Tiffani's lists and cut them into geographical chunks. The same friends who had walked the streets on Saturday would let their fingers do the walking on Sunday. Earlier, West had drawn a ten-mile circle around the two blue pins on the homemade map. Every Royal car wash, laundry, office supply store, sandwich shop, and motel within ten miles of Three Strikes and Grogan's would be visited by West, Drew, Laura, or Karen and Bob Sellars. They would start as near as possible to the baseball card stores and move out in concentric circles like ripples on a pond. Once again Chuck and Ruth would wait by the telephone. And Tiffani? Her computer zipped into its canvas bag, she sipped cold tea and stared past Drew—Drew had similarly spent the evening staring past Tiffani—and could hardly wait to be home and sleeping next to Chuck.

"I'll be going," she said. "You don't need me anymore."

"We'll need you tomorrow," West said.

"Huh?" Surprised, Tiffani pulled at the ankh.

"I'll have lists of . . ." He started to say "boys who have been killed" but changed the words to "several types of police cases. I need those lists run in as many ways as you can come up with—by name, by address, by the age of missing boys, and by when and where the boys were reported missing." He would give her more details in the morning. Away from this house, he could be blunt about the other things he wanted—cause of death, unusual circumstances, if the dying had been deliberately prolonged, if any features of the crimes had puzzled the police or sickened them and, of course, suspects in both the solved and unsolved deaths and disappearances.

"You've got the lists on a disk?"

West shook his head.

"They're paper lists?" In Tiffani's mouth, the word *paper* sounded like the name of an unpleasant bug.

"Yes."

"You've got to be joking." What she really wanted to say was, "No way." Each name on the list, she explained, would have to be scanned into a database before it could be manipulated. So would all the other information. It would take forever to create a useful format.

West dismissed Tiffani's "forever." "I need it by tomorrow evening," he said. It was the first time West had used his flat, demanding policeman's voice on Tiffani. "Just tell me how we can do it."

It was not possible to refuse. "I can't do it by myself," Tiffani said slowly. "But Jake can probably get some kids from the Database Group to type in the information. If you'll pay them."

It was Drew who asked, "How much?"

Uncertain, Tiffani made a guess. "I suppose a hundred dollars each would do it. Then Jake or I could manipulate the data for you."

It was almost the first time Drew had looked straight at Tiffani. "I'll pay them," she said.

Earlier, when West went to check out the man who had asked for a reward, Drew had insisted on giving him bribe money—two hundred dollars. She had pushed the money into his hand and closed his fist around it. Since the night she had taken his face between her hands and forced him to look at her while she told him David wasn't dead, it was the first time she had touched him.

Tiffani unzipped her laptop and plugged it in again. This time, she logged in with Jake's P.P.P. ID—CozyJ—and password and stuffed a message into his E-mail box. Under "message," she typed: "Bro. Bear—Need help. Cub." Their nicknames for each other had come years ago from a favorite picture book.

"I can give him the lists about 10:00 *a.m.*," West said.

Tiffani stared at the screen. If Jake was still at his computer—and he probably would be since it wasn't even 1 A.M.—Xbiff would beep at him to check his E-mail, and he'd send her a message back. If not, she'd do it the old-fashioned way and page him.

The Royal Savings and Thrift in West Los Angeles was not open on Sundays. The Royal Theater had a recorded message. Nobody at the Royal Market in Boyle Heights spoke English. And could the voices at the Royal Pet Wash in Reseda and the Royal Thai restaurant in North Hollywood be trusted? "No, lady, no boy here," the manager of the Royal Thai told Joan Goldman to whom Drew had given two pages of addresses in the east valley.

Around 2:00 P.M. on Sunday afternoon, Chuck drove to the Royal Theater which played foreign language films—mostly Chinese and Latin American movies since Italian films had been out of favor for several years. Chuck had none of Drew's aggression or tenacity. And he was too well aware of the absurdity of David sitting through *Horseman on the Roof* to be unembarrassed by his errand. He showed the posters of David and accepted with relief the statements of the manager and the girl in the ticket booth that they had never seen the boy. On the way back to Drew's house, he stopped to buy cream cheese and half a dozen bagels to take to Kiley. Before the divorce Chuck and David had walked to Sherwood's bagel shop most Sunday mornings for the week's supply.

The morning turned into afternoon, and the afternoon into evening. Six or seven of the searchers brought their chunks of Los Angeles back for someone else to finish tomorrow, Monday, when they had to be at work. Several others phoned Ruth with the names of the delicatessens and car dealers they had already eliminated. Ruth had taped one of Tiffani's alphabetized lists to a kitchen cabinet, and she crossed off the stores that had been screened. Seven or eight times someone told Ruth about a "gut feeling" or a "hunch" that someone was lying or might know more. Ruth made a separate list of those places.

They were, all of them, amateurs at the game of detecting. The professionals would have done it more deftly, with less chance of error. But the professionals were busy. In Los Angeles, they were busy with street gangs, carjackings, rape, and murder. Reports were dutifully taken on lesser crimes, and occasionally a burglar was inept enough to be caught in the act. If it were left to the professionals, one deputy might have spent one day on a missing child.

Chuck, who lacked stamina, left around seven, even though he knew Tiffani would not be at the apartment. Tiffani and her laptop were with Jake, running electronic impulses through their fingers. It was still light, a warm June night that softened the hard edges of the search, and Ruth and Kiley played with the dogs on the grassy strip next to the driveway. Ruth left the kitchen window open, so she could hear the phone. Like human siblings, the dogs had different skills. Brisket, a sloppy performer in the obedience ring, had a nose that might have belonged to a bloodhound. He had earned his T.D.X.—Tracking Dog Excellent title—with amazing ease. Good-natured Pasha was always willing to try, although he wasn't particularly good at anything for which people gave trophies to dogs. Flame had the potential of being a star in competitive obedience. He had earned his C.D. (companion dog) in three consecutive trials with scores in the high 190s. While Kiley bounced balls against the garage door for Brisket and Pasha, Ruth, whose energy had always annoyed Chuck, heeled Flame up and down the grass. Eventually the five of them went inside, and Ruth read the other four a fairy tale.

At 8 A.M. on Sunday morning, West had given Lesson A in How to Investigate to Karen and Bob Sellars, Laura, and Drew. He was using them to play the odds. In police work as in horse racing, longshots often won but favorites were still a better bet. The odds said that whoever had left those packets at Three Strikes and Grogan's had not dropped in from Mars. The odds said that he lived somewhere within the ten-mile circle West had drawn on the map.

West followed up with Lesson B. "Show David's pictures to the people who run the shops on either side of your target store and across the street from it. If anyone tells you he's seen David, get as much information as you can and leave. Call in and give the information to Ruth. I'll be calling her every half hour, and I'll follow up. If you think one of the places on your list is suspicious, just back away and call the house. If something doesn't feel right, let me handle it."

The four of them would be spokes on the wheel, moving outward in different directions from the two baseball card stores. The list West was carrying was different. Solutions required separating the possible from the impossible, refining the possible into the probable and improbable, dividing the probable into the most and least likely. Mistakes could be—and often were—made at every fork in the mental road. It was possible that David Greene was being held in the back room of some Royal Cleaners or in a building next to a Royal Deli. It seemed a lot more likely that he was sleeping in a Royal motel or eating in a Royal restaurant or playing video games at the Royal Arcade. It seemed likely that, if the boy was clever enough to leave clues, he was clever enough to leave clues that someone had a hope of following. It seemed likely that, during the week he had been missing, David Greene had spent a lot of time under a Royal Something sign. But those things were only likely if . . . if the packets had been left by David Greene, if the message had been interpreted correctly by the boy's mother, if David Greene was still alive.

The list West had given himself contained the names of every Royal eating joint and sleeping place within the ten-mile circle. But he was intending to go first to the Royal Arcade, which was less than a mile away from Three Strikes. During the previous days, West had doggedly checked out the telephone tips and the suspects from the Sherwood Police Department files. Now he felt the excitement of hitting a target on the firing range dead center. He knew about small boys and video games. An arcade would be as much of a lure to an eight year old as a sports card shop. If he had guessed right, and he was sure he had guessed right, David Greene had been to the Royal Arcade.

The others had started their searches early, but West did not reach the arcade until eleven o'clock. After buying Todd Carter bacon, eggs, hashed brown potatoes, and deep-dish apple pie, he had driven to USC to meet Tiffani and give her the lists. Tiffani's brother had rounded up half a dozen students to scan in the information for ninety dollars apiece. Jake had said to tell West that they might have a usable database for him by 9:00 P.M. Tiffani would call when it was ready.

Despite its name, the Royal Arcade was small and shabby, filled with games that had been popular several years earlier, including AfterBurner and Mortal Kombat. The floor was covered with gray indoor-outdoor carpeting with the torn seams patched by gray duct tape. But David Greene wouldn't have noticed the shabbiness, West thought. His son had never seen anything but the games. Like Jack, David Greene would have seen only the enticing screens with their epic wars.

As soon as West opened the door, he was battered by the sounds of battle between kickboxers and thugs, knights and dragons, submarines and sea monsters, helicopters and terrorists, humans and nuclear mutants, androids and aliens, Arnold Schwarzenegger and Predator. A row of pinball machines stood against one wall, with a row of race cars on the wall opposite. West threaded his way through the noise—the crescendo of explosions, the crunch of broken bodies—and found the manager in an alcove at the back.

"No seen boy," the manager said, without looking at the photograph. To West, he was indeterminably Asian—Cambodian perhaps—and too old for this job. "No seen any boy ever."

Since it was Sunday, the arcade was full of boys practicing ritual mass murder for a quarter a game.

"You go," the man said. "You clear out." He made a shooing motion with his hands as though chasing away chickens, and the words blew like wind through gaps in his yellow teeth.

West flicked open the leather case that held his badge and arced the silver metal with a quick thrust into the man's face and out again before his eyes had time to focus on the Sherwood Police Department logo. "If I don't get information, I call Immigration," West said. The man in front of him might be legal, but, even if he were, the chances were ten to one that he had a brother, a nephew, or a couple of cousins who had steamed illegally under the Golden Gate Bridge.

"What you want?" There was less terror than resignation in the man's voice. The devils he could not frighten away had to be appeased.

"Look at these photographs," West said. "Take a good look."

This time, the manager took a good look, squinting at the color pictures and then holding them at arm's length up to the bare lightbulb in the alcove. "No seen boy," he said again. He seemed to say the words regretfully, as though afraid that not having seen the boy would be worse trouble than having seen him.

"You're sure?" West asked in his heaviest voice, although he had seen no involuntary jerk of the man's hands and no flicker of recognition in his eyes.

"Sure," the man said defiantly.

West was sure, too, sure that the Royal Arcade would have drawn David Greene like arcades had always drawn Jack. . . . He forced himself to stop thinking of Jack. Then he turned on the manager and clawed him with his voice. "You're lying. The boy was here." The man was a foot shorter than West, and he shrank and closed like a flower fighting a wind strong enough to shear off petals. "No," he kept saying. "Me sure. That boy not here."

Finally West believed him and jerked away and moved down the rows of fantasy machines, waiting until each player had been incinerated or fallen from the highest turret of the castle or drowned in a pit of toxic waste. Then he blocked the coin slot with his body and forced each boy to look at David's picture. The boys shook their heads and shrugged their shoulders and, after West had moved away, put another quarter in the box.

Roughly, West pulled Thunder Blade away from the wall and felt in the cockpits of the race cars and on the undersides of the pinball machines and along the cord of Virtua Fighter. He found no packets. Eventually, he had to give up.

"Shit. Piss." Street Fighter II was no longer kicking the street free of criminal scum. "Shit, piss," the manager said as he dug into the innards of the jammed machine. "Shit, piss," as he kicked the door shut.

It would be a long day, West knew, as he walked toward the door. He had taken a shortcut and started at what he thought was the center of the web, and the shortcut had led nowhere. Now it was his turn to work his way outward along the sticky strands. As he left the Royal Arcade, synthesized machine voices sent him on his way: "Once the Casket of Doom has opened . . ." "He lives only to avenge himself against the aliens . . ." "It's time to hunt."

CHAPTER 26

It is always cold in Southern California before dawn. Even in June, there is a raw dampness to the night that surprises strangers. The desert is the coldest, and that surprises them the most. David had zipped up his jacket, and he sat with his head down and his shoulders hunched, but the jacket was too thin to block out the cold. Forty years ago on a morning like this one, Denver and David would have been driving through groves of orange trees, and the sky would have been orange, too, glowing with the flames from the smudgepots that kept the fruit from freezing. But Orange County had no oranges now, and the 10 Freeway was a ribbon of concrete surrounded by concrete.

Interstate 10 started in Santa Monica, California, and ended in Jacksonville, Florida; started in the fog of the Pacific Ocean and ended in the moist twenty-four-hour-a-day southern heat. David rolled himself into a ball with his hands clenched between his jacket and his shirt and sat shivering while Denver drove through the dawn. Denver never talked to David now. They drove in silence past Azusa—A to Z in the USA—Pomona, San Bernardino, and then into the desert. The sand was gray and full of tumble-weeds, and the roadside stands, not yet open on a Sunday morning, had signs advertising date milkshakes. They drove east, and some-where past Coachella but not yet near Blythe the sun came up and blinded them.

"Damn, I'm tired," Denver said then. He said the words abruptly, as though he had suddenly realized that it was more than twenty-four hours since he had been asleep.

A few miles farther on, Denver left the interstate and drove slowly down an access road so filled with the night's debris from the desert that sand crunched like glass beneath the tires. Warmed by the sun, David sat up and hoped that the silent man sitting next to him was hungry. Denver had to be hungry; he had to be hun-gry because David, himself, was starving.

In another life, David had whined, "I'm starving" to his mother the three or four times a messenger brought an urgent script and a Hollywood bidding war meant that he had to wait an extra hour for dinner. He had commanded, "Hurry up. I'm starving."

Yesterday David had eaten a hot dog for breakfast and stale french fries and a doughnut for dinner. Now he ate the hot dog again in his mind, but the remembered taste didn't make his stomach ache less. Denver hadn't had anything for dinner; Den-ver had to be hungry.

But Denver wasn't hungry. He drove past a Dairy Freeze and a shack advertising beer and ribs. David watched Denver's face and knew it wouldn't do any good to pull at his arm. Whatever Den-ver was feeling, it wasn't hunger. Whatever Denver was looking at, it was nothing David could see.

David put his hands in his jacket pockets and felt the smooth plastic edges of his packets. There were three of them, and he had two more in his jeans. But the Royals cards didn't mean anything now. And maybe he was too far from home for his mother to fol-low. For his mother to find him, he would have to . . . The thought frightened him so much that he broke it in two. He stared through the car window at the sand, but the thought came back as though blown into his face by the wind. He would have to write his name and phone number on the cards. Fear of Denver welled up like vomit in David's throat. If Denver saw the cards, he would know there was no Andy. David shivered again as he remembered Denver walking past his bed and whispering over and over, "Andy is a bad boy." If Denver saw the cards, he would do something terrible. But, beneath the fear, was something equally strong. Beneath the fear was a sudden anger that filled David so completely there was no room left for hunger.

About ten miles from the interstate, Denver stopped at a motel on the outskirts of some nameless desert town that had two trailer parks and no main street. "Stay down," he told David and pushed him to the floor. "Don't move." David crouched with his face against the gas pedal, and Denver swung out of the car with that crazy animal grace and charmed the old lady who had walked slowly from her living room behind the motel office when he rang the bell.

"Ma'am, I'm bushed," he said. "Been driving almost twenty hours. Down from Oregon. I think I could sleep for a million years."

"Most of the rooms are open this early in the day," she said. "You want to take a look?"

In a brackish town like this one, most rooms were always open, which was why Denver had chosen this place over the motels whose neon signs waved along the highway. "You pick for me, ma'am. A room in the back where there won't be much noise."

She patted gray hair into place. "Room six's got a nice new television. And it's around the back."

"Sounds good," Denver said. "You got a real nice place here, ma'am." He paid and wrote the first name that occurred to him— John Jenkins—and had turned to go when she pushed the pad back to him.

"I need your license plate number," she said.

Denver wrote down letters and numbers that were close to the truth, but he scrambled the numbers as much as he dared. The woman might take a closer look at his car. Already, she had moved around him to look through the office window. "That's not an Oregon license," she said.

Denver shook his head and started to say, "California," when she squinted at the mud-smeared plate and said, "New Mexico? Not many states have yellowish plates." Denver had thought to find carelessness in this backwater and had stumbled on a connoisseur of license plates, a seventy-two-year-old Christian widow who would soon be on her way to church and who liked her records to be as tidy as her soul.

"My brother's car," he said, smiling while she patted her hair again. "I'm giving it back to him down in El Paso. I'll be starting out with the birds tomorrow."

The woman would not bother to wash off the mud so she could check the license, but, even if she did, anyone might mix up the numbers on a car he didn't own.

The room was unexpectedly clean and light, and the toilet wore a Sani-Clean paper band. The standard two double beds were covered with tan chenille bedspreads, and the soft blankets were newly washed. There was sand on the windowsills, unavoidable with the desert starting a yard beyond the back wall of the motel, but the paper cups were wrapped in plastic. Room 6 was next to an alcove with an ice bin and a vending machine full of Pepsi and Mountain Dew and another stocked with candy bars and corn chips. The vending machines did a better business than one might have supposed. During the week, the motel got more than its share of men in pickup trucks and hard hats who were building something or tearing something down.

Pushed toward the motel room, David veered and ran to the machines. The sight of candy bars lined up behind glass had brought the ache in his stomach back. He held on to the candy machine with both hands. He was too hungry to care if Denver hit him.

When Denver tried to pull David away, David's foot banged against the metal with a sharp clang. The strident harshness of the sound rose and hung—it seemed endlessly—in the air.

"All right," Denver said quickly. He reached into his pocket and poured coins into David's palm.

David stuffed three quarters into the coin slot and started to pull the lever beneath the packages of chocolate cookies. Before the lever was fully out, he let it drop back into place. He had two dimes left; Denver had given him ninety-five cents. The cookies cost sixty-five cents, and nothing in the neat rows behind the glass cost less than forty cents. If he bought the cookies, he could buy nothing else; and Denver might never let him come back to the machine. "Hurry up," Denver whispered into David's ear as the boy spent fifty-five cents for a Hershey bar and the remaining money on cheese crackers.

Inside the room, in payment for the candy, Denver slapped David's face. David held tight to crackers and chocolate as Denver slapped him a second time. Then Denver turned away from the boy and closed the heavy drapes and blocked out the sun. When he had locked the door and bolted it and tied his belt to the door-knob and to the chair he propped beneath the doorknob, he tossed David's bag on to the far bed. He had said nothing to the boy since he had whispered, "Hurry up."

David tore the wrapping from the cheese and crackers and, not bothering to use the red plastic dipper, stuck his fingers in the cheese and smeared it on the crackers. When he had eaten all the crackers, he tore the cheese well into two pieces and licked the specks of cheese that remained. He had pulled off the wrapper of the candy bar and had the chocolate halfway to his mouth before he jerked his hand back and dropped the candy on the table next to his bed. This bedside table was a bright, unscarred wood that smelled of lemon polish. As part of his private magic, David always delayed opening the packs of baseball cards he bought, sometimes for an hour. Now, with the same self-will, he allowed himself to eat only the first row—three squares—of chocolate. He let each square melt in his mouth to make it last longer. To keep himself from eating the rest, he opened the gym bag and began to stack his cards and rocks on the bed table.

"Won't be here long enough to bother doing that," Denver said. He slipped one handcuff on David's wrist and pulled up the mattress to lock the other cuff to the bed frame. The cold metal dug into the scabs that were left from the last time Denver had handcuffed the boy. David shook his head frantically and pointed to his toys and to the bathroom which was a few steps beyond the bed. "Please," he mouthed. "Please, Daddy."

Not yet completely disinterested in David's comfort, Denver found an old curtain cord in the closet and tied, with intricate knots, one end to the bed frame and the other to the handcuff on David's wrist. "You make any noise and . . ." Denver rattled the loose handcuff.

David reached for his markers and wrote, "I'll be good," in atomic gold.

Denver took the gold marker out of David's hand and picked up the rest of the colored pens. "You won't need these anymore," he said. Denver had placed his bag on the floor between the beds. David watched while the man unzipped the bag and threw the markers in. They disappeared beneath the surface of Denver's clothes, and David, stripped of his second voice, hugged his polished stones to keep Denver from taking away another piece of his life. But Denver had no more interest in David and his things. Without looking at the boy again, he took off his boots and jeans and slid beneath the soft blanket.

Already the desert heat was rolling in. Sunlight, directed downward by the thick drapes, spilled on to the floor. David lay, rigid as death, on tufts of chenille. If he moved or breathed, Denver might reach over and take something else away.

If David had been lonely before, when Denver talked too fast and bought him things and gleefully pushed food into his willing mouth, he was desolate now with Denver receding from him, and home so far away that he could never find his way back without drawing a path with his markers. The homesickness trickled down his body with the sweat, the liquid ache pooling behind his knees. But he did not move.

Denver slept restlessly for twenty minutes. Then he stood up and lurched to the air conditioner high up in the wall and twisted the dial. Cool air rumbled out, and he let it lap at his face for a moment before he turned and fell back into bed.

An hour went by and then another, and still Denver didn't

move. David kicked off his shoes and jeans and crawled between the sheets. And Denver, who had always been angry in sleep—his elbows digging into the pillow, his feet gouging the sheet, his hands tearing at the blankets—lay as though transformed into stone.

David lay soaked in loneliness. If he had been a boy with more friends and fewer secrets, this isolation might have forced him to give up. If he had been a poster boy—chosen first at games and as cafeteria monitor—he might have been paralyzed by adversity. But hidden thoughts and solitary ways are a kind of vaccination against the terrors of solitude. And David was stoked by anger, by the fury that his mother called his Dragon Rage. He had learned in his mother's womb or at her knee that he was entitled to strike out at the world, and he hated Denver with a fierceness that made him brave. He closed his eyes and still could not erase the picture of his markers tossed into Denver's bag and zipped so easily away. He opened his eyes and tried to lean far enough so that he could touch the bag with his free hand. Toes digging into the mattress on the opposite side, he teetered six inches short. He scrambled back into the middle of the bed and, lying motionless, counted to five hundred. Across a chasm of five feet, Denver had not moved.

The next time, David slid beneath his bed and swam along the carpet, pulling the cord as far as he could and then stretching his free hand until he could reach into Denver's not quite zipped bag. Lying on his stomach on the floor, he made his blind hand climb the side of the cool, slick, nylon bag. He was afraid of what the bag might contain—a siren to warn Denver or something alive that had metal teeth to bite down and hold him until Denver woke—but he forced himself to open his fingers and search through the clothes for a marker. He needed one marker, just one.

The colored pens had sifted to the bottom, and David pawed the edges of the bag. When he brought up a pen, there was something attached—a rolled-up, ragged piece of heavy cloth.

In the splinter of sunlight on the floor, the cloth had words and pictures: *Play Town*. It was one of those sturdy primer books that baby hands and teeth cannot destroy. David had had three or four of those books. One of them had a picture for each letter of the alphabet. Like his outgrown clothes, David's books had been passed on to Kiley.

This book with *Play Town* on the cover was much older than David's books; the cloth was crushed, and some of the bright colors were almost rubbed off, as though the book had been held and read a hundred times. The first page had pictures of a mailman and a milkman, with *Postman* and *Milkman* underneath. The second page was a market with a man weighing fruit and a little girl eating an apple. The third page—David stopped breathing—the third page was a white farmhouse with fields of corn on both sides. *The Farm.* And on the page across from the house was a tall tree with a tire tied on it and a black-haired boy swinging in the tire and a big brown dog lying next to the boy, and the caption, *Having Fun.* On the back of the tree page there were farm animals—a cow, a pig, chickens, and a horse neatly labeled—and a farmwife holding a freshly baked pie. And that was all. The rest of the book was missing.

There was writing on the cover, so faint that David could barely make out the words, even in the spill of sun: "Happy 2nd Birthday, Andy, from Mommy."

A secretkeeper knows when secrets are dangerous. David rolled the book up again and stuck it as far down into Denver's bag as he could reach and buried it beneath the weight of Denver's clothes. As though he sensed the fingers disturbing his underworld, Denver moaned. David sprawled beneath the bed, a turtle with no shell. If Denver woke. . . . But Denver only moaned once more and then was quiet.

The bed was a mountain, and David barely had enough strength to crawl to the top and lie, facedown, panting into the pillow as his body was overcome by its own daring. He lay there for fifteen or twenty minutes. Then, in the dark beneath the covers, he took each of his five packets apart. He brought the cards to the surface. In the artifical dusk of early afternoon, he put the Kansas City Royals into the stack of baseball cards on the bedtable. On the back of every David card, in Martian purple, he carefully printed *David Greene* and his phone number, including the area code. But on three of the cards, plastic coated, the writing vanished even as he wrote. On the other two cards, cheap card-board images of Dave Winfield, the purple ink spread and blurred but did not disappear. When he had rubber banded the packets again, David stuffed all five into his jacket pockets and hugged the jacket next to him in bed and lay his cheek on it as he used to do—and sometimes still secretly did—with his yellow rabbit.

Even as he lay curled with his head on the jacket, David knew he had to return the purple pen. Denver might have counted. Or Denver might have some magic way to know if a marker was missing. During the week in which he had been Denver's pris-oner and Denver's son, David had learned how to deal with the man. But the Denver who had pulled him out of bed in the middle of Saturday night and who had sat silently next to him during the long hours of desert was someone new—someone impervi-ous to David's smiles and puppy meekness. It was as though the sand had shifted under David's feet and half buried him. "Get up," he kept telling himself. "Put the marker back." But it was another thirty minutes before he could make himself sit up.

David was halfway out of bed when the whiteness of the sheets gave him a dangerous idea. White as paper. He slid under the cov-ers head first, and, unable to see what he was doing, printed *Help. David Greene,* and his phone number on the bottom sheet just above the place where it twisted over the edge of the mattress. Fear of Denver made his fingers tremble, and the letters had wavy edges like words written in the sky. If Denver tore this bed apart and found the words, he would know David wasn't Andy. But maybe Denver already knew that David wasn't Andy. Or maybe the way Denver was acting he didn't want Andy anymore.

When the purple pen was back in Denver's bag, David began to shiver. Burying himself beneath the blanket and bedspread, he hugged the jacket again and folded his arms across his chest and made small animal noises. It was a long time before the shivering stopped. To comfort himself, he reached for the candy bar and ate another row of chocolate squares. After that, he couldn't stop himself from eating it all.

Sometime in midafternoon, he fell asleep.

CHAPTER 27

The ransom note arrived on Monday morning in the mail. The words had been cut from Friday's *Los Angeles Times*. "I have your son. I want $100,000. Wait for word." Whenever possible, the author had used headlines, but apparently "I" had not been displayed in prominent black type in Friday's paper.

Drew was alone when the mail came. She had been trying to write a report on a script that was an imitation of an imitation of the *Die Hard* movie that had wowed audiences in 1988. In *Die Hard,* dozens of hostages had been held prisoner in a high-rise building with only Bruce Willis to save them. In the scripts and movies that followed *Die Hard,* dozens of hostages had been held prisoner in airports, submarines, trains, buses, and space stations by increasingly psychotic terrorists and mad bombers. The faceless herd of hostages in the current script was imprisoned in a subterranean cavern in North Dakota, at least until one more movie superhero easily penetrated impenetrable defenses and rescued them. "Trite," Drew wrote. "Cookie-cutter heroics."

It was the last week of school. Kiley was in the Sherwood Ele-

mentary School auditorium learning the song the two kindergarten classes would sing on Thursday for the graduating sixth
graders. Since final exams were over, Chuck was trying to keep
under some sort of control eleventh graders who had nothing at
stake. Through trial and error during his nine years as a teacher,
Chuck had learned that movies worked best on these last few days
before summer vacation. To add a slight trace of American history, Chuck was spending the week showing his eleventh graders
two of Hollywood's epic pronouncements on World War II—*The
Longest Day* on Monday and Tuesday, *Tora, Tora, Tora* on Wednesday and Thursday. Ruth had taken the dogs to the valley for an
agility class. On the way back, she would stop at the market for
half a gallon of milk. Life goes on and spreads to fill the void. The
dogs had missed most of their classes this past week. Unlike the
students and teachers at Sherwood High who were sick of school
after nine months of it, the dogs were eager to go back to weave
poles and bar jumps.

When the mail came, Drew opened the gas bill first and then
the ransom note.

Drew had learned a lot in eight days. She put the note and the
torn envelope in separate plastic bags, being careful to hold each by
one corner. She looked at the envelope through the plastic. Her
address had been typed, and the letter had been mailed in Santa Barbara—a hundred miles up the coast from Los Angeles—on Friday.
A hundred miles was nothing. One hundred thousand dollars
was nothing. She had four thousand dollars in the bank, and she
could mortgage her future for the other ninety-six thousand.
Drew dialed Angus West's phone number so quickly that she mis-
dialed and had to punch the buttons a second time. But West
wasn't home. The voice on the answering machine gave nothing
away. It repeated the phone number and added, "Leave a message."

West had struck out on Sunday. So had the other searchers. No
shopkeepers or garage mechanics within West's ten-mile circle

had seen David Greene. This morning, Karen Sellars would visit the eight or nine stores that had not been open on Sunday, but West doubted that she would discover any sign of David. With an appointment to meet Jake and Tiffani at USC at 10:00 P.M., West had not finished his list either. The dozen Royal Motels he had visited had been bright places with helpful managers who were eager to be of service to the police and who seemed to have nothing to hide. But there were still two motels left to check at the farthest edge of the circle.

Despite Tiffani's disdain for paper, Jake had provided West with a three-inch-thick stack of hard copy. By midnight, West's rarely used dining room table was covered with the results of Jake's manipulations. West had stayed up until 2:00 A.M. trying to find common denominators in the inventories of dead boys, missing boys, boys presumed dead, boys dispatched with meat cleavers, shotguns, wire nooses, boys who had vanished so completely that the earth might well have swallowed them.

Just before dawn, West dreamed again of LaChandra Johnston. This time, the dream was muted. The girl, wearing clothes of leaves and twigs as though she had been unearthed, circled him, then touched him lightly on the shoulder and ran away. Back from the grave for a game of hide and seek, LaChandra ran deep and then deeper into woods, and West pursued until he woke.

There had been enough reconciliation in the dream for West to wake untormented. By 8:00 A.M., he was driving south on the 405. It was neatness that made West simmer in the freeway traffic soup. He had drawn a ten-mile circle. He would have preferred to spend the morning trying again to force a pattern into the four years of police reports. But, whether through instinct or adherence to some law of probability, he had drawn a ten-mile circle, and tidiness demanded that the Royal Court in Hawaiian Gardens and the Royal Motel in Gardena be checked out.

The Royal Court was closed, a victim of the recession that put its chill hands around the throat of Southern California in the early nineties. There were plywood boards across the office windows, and what had once been a border of geraniums was too dry to give life to weeds. The sign that had in the best of times proclaimed ROYAL COURT read AL COU. But there was also trash in the parking lot and doors that had been kicked in and then shoddily repaired. More than rats slept behind the broken doors. Without water, gas, or electricity, it was still a safer harbor than the world beyond the doors.

The last Royal Motel seemed hardly less barren than the Royal Court. Someone had recently hosed down the building in a futile attempt to turn the gray stucco white again. Long streaks of dirt dribbled from roof to foundation amid curls of peeling paint, and brown water had formed half a dozen shallow pools in the parking lot. There was a vacant lot behind and to one side of the motel and, on the other side beyond the parking lot, the foundation of some house lost to rot or fire. The pitted street at the front led eventually to a freeway exit. The freeway could not have been too far away since the air was full of roaring. It was not a place where anyone was likely to ask questions. A person who had kidnapped a child could easily lose himself here.

Before he opened the rusted screen door of the office, West walked to the end of the parking lot—Room 12—and through the vacant lot, crushing stalks of wild wheat that came nearly to his thighs. From the time he was a young patrolman, West had found himself needing some understanding of a place before he could understand the people who had chosen to live or hide there. In the early years he had been mocked for walking perimeters and bending to feel the heat of the asphalt in a junior high school yard where rising tempers and temperatures had sent one Hispanic and two black ninth graders to the hospital. Eventually, a sergeant gave this boundary walking a name—"West's prowling again"— and it had been accepted.

The slender, coltish man with watchful eyes who faced West across the front desk was not frightened of badges. "So?" he said when West laid his identifcation on the counter between them. "This isn't Sherwood."

West showed him David Greene's picture. "I'm looking for this boy."

"I can't help you."

"Can't or won't?" West said mildly. Muscle would get him nowhere with this man—at least, not yet. Twenty-three years old, Mario Hernandez was part Italian, part Mexican, part redneck; and all three parts knew how to skim a little cream from the prostitutes who rented rooms by the week and how to coax out a little bribe from the businessmen who rented rooms by the hour. He earned a steady fifty dollars a week by accommodating the drug dealer in Room 5. He had seventeen hundred dollars buried in the vacant lot and dreamed of Cuernavaca.

"I run a clean place," Hernandez said. They both knew Hernandez was lying. More, they both knew that Hernandez was amusing himself by letting West know he was lying.

"Then you don't mind if I look at your guest book," West said.

With a flourish, Hernandez blew dust off a black ledger and pushed it toward West. Of the last dozen guests, seven were named Smith. The two Ms. Smiths paid weekly. Three of the five Mr. Smiths had paid eighteen dollars an hour. All the entries were in the same handwriting.

"A lot of Smiths," West said.

Hernandez smiled with white shark's teeth. He was nimble and lithe, and boyishly confident that neither his mind nor his body would ever let him down. Beside him, West seemed oversized and dull. "It's the most common American name," Hernandez said, completely unruffled by West's bulk and occupation. In seventeenth-century Spain, he would have been a dangerous swordsman. He thrust again: "Followed by Garcia."

"Do any of the Smiths have this boy with them?" Plodding on, West put the color photographs of David Greene in front of Hernandez again. "He might have been here since last Saturday."

Hernandez shrugged. His eyes were dark, and the bones of his wrist were delicate. When he had three thousand dollars in the coffee can buried beside stalks of wheat and anise, he would drive across the border and live for a long time with a girl he knew in Cuernavaca. He would leave the Royal Motel and a year of unpaid room taxes to its trusting absentee owner, Khairul

Chowdhury, who lived in Arizona. Since Hernandez was industrious and frugal—he didn't sample the wares offered by the man in Room 5 and there was always a girl or two who would cook him a free dinner—he thought he would have enough money by December. He looked up at West and rubbed his thumb against his middle finger gently, fingering something invisible.

"Maybe," he said.

Beneath the glass that covered the counter were an ancient sheet of unenforced motel rules and postcards featuring the wonders of Disneyland. West put a ten dollar bill on Mickey Mouse's head. Beneath long lashes, Hernandez looked bored. West rolled a twenty dollar bill and held it between his fingers like a cigarette.

Hernandez wondered what he could invent to sell the policeman. Not for a minute did it occur to him to tell West the truth of what he might have seen or thought he heard. Noticing things was dangerous. Telling what you noticed was more dangerous. "That boy was here for one night," he tried and then waited for West to give him a clue to what he should say next. West said nothing, so Hernandez, greedy, improvised. "Three days ago. Maybe four. He cried for his mother."

West's face remained impassive, but, on the word *mother,* the money between his fingers moved, and Hernandez was agile enough to ride the air current. He put a long, thin finger on David's face. "He wanted his mother. I'm sure it's the same boy. What's his name?"

"Bobby," West said, baiting a trap.

"That's what the man called him. Bobby." Hernandez reached for the easily earned thirty dollars. Before Hernandez could relieve Mickey Mouse of his ten dollar burden, West had his fingers around the young man's wrist. It was the speed with which the big man moved even more than West's unshakeable grip that made Hernandez realize he had misjudged the policeman.

"Let's start over," West said. "Have you seen the boy?"

Bravery turned to bravado, but Hernandez's features had not yet hardened into adult cement and he managed to look guileless. "Yes. Of course."

Lies never made West angry. People who shaded the truth were an occupational hazard. Nor was he discouraged by lies. There was almost always some truth to be found underneath if you squeezed the lies hard enough. The fingers around Hernandez's wrist tightened, and now the shark's teeth belonged to West. "Have you seen the boy?" he asked, leaving an inch of space between each word.

Hernandez seemed half a dozen years younger now. "No."

West dropped Hernandez's arm and, regaining some pride, the young man did not allow himself to rub his wrist. To Hernandez's surprise, West put the ten dollar bill back on Mickey's head. "Could someone have a boy in one of the rooms without you seeing him?"

Hernandez answered carefully. "Most people who come here don't want to be noticed. And I'm not here at night." He was supposed to be there, of course, but most nights he had a better place to sleep.

"What about the maids?"

"Maid," Hernandez said. "The rooms are cleaned on Tuesday." The invoice Hernandez sent Chowdhury every month charged for maid service three days a week. The name on the invoice was Maria Sanchez. The place Hernandez slept most nights was Maria Sanchez's apartment.

West waited. His stillness flustered Hernandez as much as what had happened a moment earlier. Used to thrust and parry and with an acrobatic tongue, the young man was thrown off balance by patience.

"None of the regulars could have a kid," he said. "We got a guy comes Tuesday and Friday afternoons with different sluts, and another guy bangs his secretary every Wednesday. The ho who works out of six's got a couple of kids, but they're with her mother somewhere out of state."

"Strangers?" West asked.

With the elasticity of youth, Hernandez already had most of his confidence back. "Hey, would you stay in a junkyard like this?"

West accepted the question as rhetorical and waited some

229

more. There was no need to tell Hernandez the odd things people were capable of.

"We're cheap so we're on the greaser circuit. We get Mexicans with a bunch of kids most nights," Hernandez said. "Going down to T.J. We're next to the freeway, so we get some people too tired to care where they sleep. None of them stay more than one night."

West still had a hunch that Hernandez had something to tell. He spread out the twenty dollar bill and placed it next to the ten, covering Space Mountain. Hunches—the pricking of one's thumbs, the chill that climbed the spine—were the currency of a good detective. You couldn't admit that in court, of course. You had to say that you had noticed a gate ajar or a ground-story window open, and so you had investigated. On his first day in court two months earlier, Todd Carter had said he had a hunch where the burglary suspect—a boy of nineteen who looked quite presentable in a coat and tie borrowed from the public defender— might have gone to hide. When the public defender was through ridiculing the police's hunches, the jury acquitted the boy in less than two hours. West had bought Carter a beer and told him it was the good detectives who had hunches.

There was a long silence while flies went randomly in and out through quarter-size holes in the screen. West showed no discomfort. He left it to others to hack at silence with their icepicks.

At last, Hernandez reached for the money, and this time West did not stop him. "Maria heard something," Hernandez said. "When she came to clean the rooms last Tuesday, she thought she heard a kid crying in Room Twelve. The sign to keep out was on the door. And I didn't hear anything." Nor had Hernandez wanted to hear anything. And he had told Maria that what the customers did was none of her business.

Hernandez had last seen a car in front of Room 12 on Saturday night. He didn't think it had been there Sunday. But, then, on weekends as well as weekdays, Hernandez spent as little time as possible at the Royal Motel. So long as the room was paid for— and the stocky white man in Room 12 had paid until Wednesday—it wasn't his concern whether there was a car there or not.

When, nine-millimeter semiautomatic Beretta in hand and with the safety off, West slipped Hernandez's pass key into the lock of Room 12 and kicked the door open, the smell of ammonia was still strong enough to sting his throat. He was assaulted by the emptiness of the room and by the care that had been taken to make it empty. The man who had rented the room—Hernandez had guessed he was at least thirty but probably no older than thirty-five and an inch or two under six feet tall—might not have stolen David Greene, but he had known that ammonia would destroy fingerprints and he had had some reason to wipe the room clean.

"Hey," Hernandez said, "most times they trash the rooms." He had trailed behind West, boyish curiosity taking precedence over learned indifference. Methodically, West looked under the beds, behind the shower curtain and, wrapping his hand in the bottom edge of his shirt, opened every drawer. After the error of the Royal Arcade, West knew he should feel some satisfaction. But there was no proof that David Greene had ever been in this motel room. And Hernandez's description of the car—a gray Honda five or six years old—and of the man who drove it fitted at least two million automobiles and men.

Hernandez touched West's shoulder. "I know something," he said in a light, tentative voice. "It's worth money."

West handed him another twenty. Hernandez held the money loosely in his hand, as though certain that, this time, it would not be pulled away.

"The car had New Mexico plates. The guy had covered the plates with mud real well, but one of the letters was K. Saturday morning, I asked him where he was heading next, and he said he was going home."

Before he left, West walked the edge of the parking lot. When he had explored the first six feet of the vacant land behind Room 12 and found nothing, he moved across the parking lot from east to west and back again, weaving around the puddles. He checked the Dumpster; it was empty. On his second circuit of the parking lot—from north to south—West saw the baseball card at the bottom of one of the deeper puddles of muddy water. It was a cheap Topps cardboard, and the face of the player and the legend at the bottom had already peeled away. But the royal blue sleeves were visible and so was *Royals,* written in cursive across the headless player's chest.

West had looked at the ransom note half a dozen times. Now it sat on the table in front of Drew—a sheet of white paper torn in half and filled with crooked words pasted on with rubber cement. "I have your son," tilted upward. "I want $100,000" slid down, so that "son" and "I" formed a peak. Beneath them, "Wait for word" sat prim and straight at the bottom of the mountain. Of course they wouldn't wait for word. It was not yet noon, and Todd Carter was on his way over to pick up the note and take it to the crime lab.

West could have brought the letter to the SPD. He could have handed the plastic wrapped sheet of drugstore white paper to Lieutenant Zane and been vindicated for his refusal to believe that Trout had killed David Greene. The trouble was that West couldn't force himself to believe in the guilt of the anonymous fingers that had pasted the words on the paper.

As soon as Drew had handed him the letter, West had phoned Zane with the news. "Come back," Zane had said.

With the unforced silence that always made Zane nervous, West had simply waited for the lieutenant to continue. "I can get Zarelli to cancel your suspension," Zane had said. "Come back early."

When West said nothing, Zane lowered his voice and whispered what he was not supposed to say. "Zarelli told me to ask you to come back. If the boy's alive, the chief's going to look bad. If you come back, the City Council won't ask as many questions."

"You'd better put a tap on the Greene phone," West said.

"What about . . ."

"I'll think about it."

Drew had placed the sodden baseball card on a paper towel decorated with blue geese. "Goosey goosey gander, whither do you wander?" Whither did David wander? She shook her head to clear it of the nursery rhyme. "They can't both . . ." She motioned toward the baseball card and the envelope.

"No," West said. "We can't believe both."

"If the person who wrote the note has David in Santa Barbara, the other messages mean nothing?" Drew was not really asking a question.

West had walked the parking lot half a dozen times and found no trace of other things that might have been left by David Greene—no mustard, no ketchup, no card glorifying a ballplayer named David. This card might have been dropped by one of the Mexican children leaving the motel. It might have blown out the window of a passing car. If entered as evidence, it would be considered immaterial, irrelevant. Weighed next to the proof of the ransom note, this card and the two packets would be insubstantial—the remnants of some unknown child's unknown game.

"I don't believe they mean nothing," Drew said.

This time, West's silence was turbulent.

"You said the man in that motel room had erased all the fingerprints. Someone heard a child cry. And there was a baseball card." Listmaker Drew Greene was reorganizing chaos. "I don't believe they mean nothing," she said again.

West was sure the ransom note was a hoax. But he had been wrong a hundred times before. He had been wrong yesterday when he was sure that David Greene had gone to the Royal Arcade. And even if the ransom note were a bad joke or some amateur's way of reaching for the brass ring, what did they do next? How did they follow the gray car that had disappeared from the motel parking lot Saturday night or Sunday morning?

None of West's thoughts penetrated the granite of his face, but Drew read them anyway. More and more, since Friday morning when West had come to the house to tell her that he thought David was alive, Drew had been able to read the hieroglyphics of his smooth surface. "I think . . ." Drew hesitated for a second and then plunged into the deepest water. ". . . I know that David left those packets." What Drew also knew in the moment of saying the words was that she was wagering the whole of her future on them. She stood up, still and straight, and with her height and leanness she seemed for an instant like a carved figure on the bow of a ship headed into perilous seas. Then she was Drew again, maddeningly insistent. "How do we follow the car?"

"We don't have enough of the license plate to trace the car," West said. "I had Todd call New Mexico anyway."

"But you think he's going home?"

West had thought from almost the beginning that the man who took David Greene was shrewd and, quite possibly, crazy. But there are lots of ways to be crazy. This man was no Trout flashing his craziness in public. The clever young manager of the Royal Motel had found the man in Room 12 no odder than anyone else who paid his money for a room there. He had been cunning enough to successfully hide the boy and successfuly create a facade of sanity.

"What about those lists you had Jake and Tiffani"—the name came easier to Drew now—"collate? There wasn't anything there?"

The lists were on the dashboard of West's car. Even though he recognized the absurdity of withholding the neatly calculated deaths, he had found himself leaving the lists behind when he entered the house. "I haven't found anything," he said. "We can try again."

The night before, West had not known what he was looking for. He had stumbled through the thicket of bloody facts and searched for the odd sentence at the bottom of a page that would make the hair rise on his neck. He had gone to bed at 2:00 A.M. without finding it among the ninety-three pages of printouts. Now he began where he had ended, his hands lingering on each page as though he were reading Braille.

West was no listmaker. He had taught himself the mechanics of police work—when to tighten the screws, where to place the bolts; and he was patient enough to build a decent machine. Yet, half the time, he didn't build a machine at all but simply used the screws and bolts as handholds on which to vault to some conclusion.

Drew was the practical one. For centuries women had gotten up from childbirth to wash the bloody sheets. And if there were now Laundromats and Maytags instead of the pump in the barnyard, the sheets still had to be washed. Drew knew what she was looking for—some connection to New Mexico—and she found it forty minutes later. West had been afraid that Drew would be crushed by the weight of pain contained in Jake's terse lists. But she checked her imagination at the door and read the alphabetized columns of the dead as though the names were clues to an ordinary crossword puzzle. Drew could not allow the names to be anything more than game pieces. And she followed each dead boy across twenty-five different ways of organizing the facts of death and built a picture from a line here and a fact there and another midway down the next list: "Gaines, John Robert, 9 years old, body found in the Kern River on August 12, 1992, sixteen days after he was reported missing. Cause of death, strangulation. Stepfather suspected. Nothing proved."

Guns and fists were the preferred weapons; and of the deaths whose time was known, few children had been killed in the optimistic light of morning.

"West."

He responded to her tone. "You've found something?"

Drew pushed five pieces of paper toward him. Alan Beckstein had disappeared from a mall in Orange County in October of 1993. It was that fact which had made Drew look for other mentions of his name. A year later Alan Beckstein's skeleton had been found in the mountains near the ghost city of Mogollon in southwestern New Mexico. From marks on his breastbone and clavicle that seemed sharper than the teeth marks on other of his bones, it appeared that he had been stabbed. His body had been identified by dental records through one of the missing children registries. When he disappeared, Alan Beckstein—the only child of Anne and Edward Beckstein of Costa Mesa—was seven years old.

He would be ten now—he should be ten—Drew thought, as

she dialed the telephone number that went with Alan Beckstein's name and address.

"Hello." It was a woman's voice.

"Anne Beckstein?" Drew couldn't afford to hesitate. "I'm calling about your son."

"How did you get this number?" The voice had become raspy, as though the word *son* had stripped it raw. "It's unlisted."

"This is Drew Greene. I'm calling about my son. David. He's been missing for nine days, and I think he was taken by someone who lives in New Mexico, by someone who's taking him to New Mexico, by the same man who killed your son." Within a single sentence, Drew had moved from knowable fact to uncertain evidence to terra incognita. "I live in Sherwood. Will you help me?"

They met in a coffee shop, just off the San Diego Freeway, midway between Sherwood and Costa Mesa. They recognized each other, were marked for each other, by a sad desperation as visible as clown paint on each face. Anne Beckstein was four months pregnant. "It's a girl," she said. There was no need to state the obvious— that a girl would not be as painful an everyday reminder of her loss.

Alan had gone to the mall with some neighborhood teenagers, she said, and the boys had met some girls and forgotten about him. When the police had failed to find him, she and Edward had hired a private detective. The detective had not found him either. Anne told the story without emotion, deflecting pain by walking as lightly as possible across the memory.

"I'm sorry," Drew said, whispering the words as though to say them loudly would add to the weight of Anne's loss.

"This is Alan." Not, "This was Alan." The boy in the school photograph Anne took from her purse was forever fixed in second grade, unchanging and unchangeable.

"Oh, God," Drew said and handed Anne a photograph of David. The two little boys—stocky and square with the same blue-gray eyes—could have been brothers.

They ordered coffee, but neither of them drank it. After Alan was found—was identified—Anne said, she and Edward had hired the detective again to look for his killer. They had wanted to avenge Alan. They had failed. But the detective had brought them some reports and a geological survey map of the area where Alan had been found. She had brought them for Drew.

When Drew left fifteen minutes later, Anne said, "Good luck with finding your son."

"Good luck," Drew answered. "With the baby."

Anne sat with her hands cupped around the cold coffee. "I hope," she said.

If Drew had forced herself to forget David to keep from dulling the sharp edge of her search, Ruth had forgotten David in the physical exertion of running beside Brisket and directing him into the tunnels and down the crossover dog walk of an advanced agility course. Over the double bar and a sharp left through the tire and right over another bar and right again was enough complexity for her mind to hold, and she was grateful for the exhaustion she felt when she sat panting on the grass after she had also brought Pasha and then Flame past the eighteen obstacles to the finish line. After resting less than five minutes, she took Pasha out of his crate and practiced weave poles with him in a far cor-ner of the field. Before class, Ruth had driven up to Oxnard to check her house and pick up her mail. On all the drives up and down the freeway, Brisket lay with his head on Ruth's lap. She drove the fast lane with one hand and used the other to stroke his ears.

By the time Ruth's van pulled into Drew's driveway and the dogs crowded into the kitchen, impatient for the biscuits that were their rewards after class, Drew had reserved two seats on the 5:45 P.M. plane to Albuquerque, one of the few flights where you didn't have to change planes or stop in Denver. They would get to New Mexico at 8:15. In Albuquerque, she and West would rent a car and drive southwest to the Gila National Forest, where Alan's skeleton had been found.

"You don't mean it," Todd Carter had said. "It's . . ." He was too green at his job not to hesitate before challenging West. "It's . . . crazy." That was not the word he had intended to use. "Not crazy, but it's like looking for a needle in . . ." He started over. "You don't know that this guy's going to New Mexico. You don't know that this guy had anything to do with the Beckstein boy. And, even if he did, he's probably smart enough never to go near those mountains again."

West had said the same things to himself. And to Drew. She had refused to hear them.

"You said he told the motel manager that he was going home."

"He might have been lying," West said.

"You didn't see Alan Beckstein's picture."

Drew sat next to West on the couch and asked, "What choice do we have?" The logical answer was the choice to stay in Los Angeles and let the New Mexico police do whatever they might do with the wisps of information West could provide. The trouble was that it was also logical for New Mexico to ignore the information until proof in the form of another dead boy was presented to them. And West had waited thirteen years for this chance to keep another child from dying.

Carter gave up. "Oh, hell, what do you want me to do?"

Ruth sat on David's bed stroking Brisket's head. They had been companions for so many years that each could fit effortlessly into the physical and emotional space offered by the other. When Ruth thought of Pasha and Flame, it was with affection, an emotion diluted from what she felt for Brisket who had entered her life within months of the time her second husband had left it. Through the open bedroom door Ruth could hear Kiley sobbing—his hiccoughs of grief and anger punctuated by "I don't want you to go."

Stroking Kiley, petting him, Drew rocked her son until his tears were only damp spots on her cheek and collar and he could put his arms around her neck and whisper into her ear—saying the words aloud was impossible—"You might never come back."

He wanted certainties that life didn't offer. Not even fiction was a gilt-edged security. In *James and the Giant Peach*, Kiley's favorite book, James's parents were eaten in broad daylight by a rhinoceros.

"I'll come back," Drew said.

Troubled by Kiley's sobs, Flame nuzzled the boy and then lay on the floor next to him. Eventually, Kiley slid from his mother's arms and, turning his back on her, gave his passion to the dog. His face was so flushed that he would have seemed feverish if his forehead had not been cool to Drew's touch.

"Want some coffee?" Ruth asked.

Drew shifted from being a mother to being a child and let Ruth lead her to the kitchen table and put a mug of coffee in her hands. After phone calls to Sergeant Fish—an unimaginative, florid-faced, but decent detective who would head the Sherwood Police Department's hunt for the writer of the ransom note—West and Carter had disappeared. A message had been left for Chuck at Sherwood High telling him to come to Drew's house as soon as possible.

Above Drew's head the glass swans chased each other. "You don't mind if Chuck stays here, too?" Drew asked her mother. "It'll make Kiley feel better."

Ruth shook her head. They sat silently for more than a minute before Ruth was able to say what she had brought Drew to the kitchen to say. "Take Brisket with you."

Drew didn't need to ask why. Four or five times Drew had gone with David to watch Brisket and Ruth track. Her mother had driven down from Oxnard and Drew had driven up from Sherwood and they had met in a county park on the Los Angeles/Ventura border. Once, David had laid the track, walking through the scrub brush and up the hills with a small stuffed bear inside his shirt to make his scent on it as strong as possible and then dropping the bear at the end of the track for Brisket and Ruth to find. Brisket had followed the scent left by David's footprints for nearly half a mile. Even when David had turned and jumped over a fallen tree, Brisket had only lost the scent for a moment.

"But I can't," Drew said. "You won't fly him."

Ruth had never put her dogs on airplanes. There were too many horror stories about crushed crates and dogs suffocated or baked to death in airless cargo holds. So she limited herself to competing in California, with an occasional overnight drive to Las Vegas or Eugene, Oregon.

"Brisket could track David in the mountains," Ruth said. Her voice had its usual unemotional steadiness. Where Drew was tender enough to show how deeply she felt each of the cuts and scrapes inflicted by outrageous fortune, Ruth dwelt inside a forest of scar tissue. "And we've been doing something new. Variable Surface Tracking. Footprints that are three or four hours old. On pavement. Where there's no crushed vegetation to help the dog. Brisket's already good at following the scent of footprints on sidewalks and inside stores."

Drawn by his name, Brisket padded into the kitchen and stood at Ruth's side. In counterpoint to the silver patches scattered through Ruth's dark hair, Brisket's muzzle was flecked with gray. In human terms, they were roughly the same age.

Both women bent down to pet the dog. Ruth pulled her hand back and let Drew bury her fingers in Brisket's thick chestnut ruff. Brisket moved toward Drew and licked the salt trails of Kiley's tears from her face.

CHAPTER 28

Denver shook David awake. It was after dawn on Monday morning. David had awakened during the night to find Denver sitting motionless in one of the room's two armchairs. The boy had fled back to the safety of sleep.

This time, Denver made no effort to wipe his presence from the room. Perhaps this motel was simply a stepping stone too lightly touched to be imprinted, a waystation between the solid past and the already determined future. There were many ways of getting to where Denver had to go. Denver had never come this way before and would not use this road again.

There was neither tenderness nor roughness in Denver's touch. His "Get up" was a cowboy's "Get along" to the steers he had rounded up and was driving to the stockyards. David reached toward the nightstand for his markers before he remembered and let his hands drop. He turned to Denver and mouthed, "Daddy."

"Daddies punish bad boys," Denver said. His tone was neither angry nor regretful. The fantasy of a good daddy had been shed. What was true was true and couldn't be changed.

David pulled on his jeans over dirty underpants. He still had one pair of clean socks. As soon as Denver turned away and bent down to put on his boots, David felt in the bedclothes for his jacket and slid his arms into the wrinkled sleeves. Immediately, he stuck his hands in the pockets and was comforted when his fingers touched the curved edges of the five packets.

Methodically, Denver erased David from the motel room. After stuffing the candy and cheese wrappers in the pocket of his jeans, he plumped up David's pillows, straightened the sheets, and pulled the chenille bedspread taut. He left his own bed unmade. Before noon, the housekeeper would put fresh sheets on Denver's bed, fresh soap in the bathroom, and a new strip of Sani-Clean around the toilet. David's message, written in purple on the bottom sheet, would not be discovered for five days.

In the cool desert morning with pink ribbons fading from the edges of the sky, Denver took the gym bags to the car. Then he walked along the path of dime-size white pebbles to the front of the motel to make sure there were no half-open doors or morning sounds. But the only sound was made by Denver's boots on the rocks. He had motioned for David to sit on the unmade bed and wait, and he had not bothered to lock the door. Even if someone had warned him, Denver might not have believed that the docile boy, sitting listlessly on the bed, had his pockets full of messages. After the first few days, no boy had ever tried to run away. Even when they struggled at first, the boys were soon paralyzed by fear and confusion. Denver, alert to external danger, his eyes and ears focused outward, accepted what had always been as what was.

If Denver misunderstood David, the boy had no tools with which to understand Denver. Chuck had never held a knife to his throat. Drew had not run away when he was six and left him behind, had not saved herself and sacrificed her son. David had met with human sacrifice once in a comic book, but the cloaked lord of darkness was eight feet tall with red eyes and a headsman's ax. If he had his markers and index cards, David would have written, "Why aren't you my nice daddy anymore?" It would have been a plea, but—since David was his mother's son no matter what the situation—it would also have been a request for information.

"Duck down," Denver said after he had pushed David into the car. David crouched beneath the glove compartment until they were two miles from the motel. When Denver let the boy sit up, the coolness of the early morning was gone, and heat was already sifting into the car. David unzipped his jacket and sat with his hands in his pockets. One . . . two . . . three . . . He counted the five packets over and over again. He had thought of leaving a packet behind in the motel room, but he had already left one message there, and five was not enough for all the miles between here and home. With the morning sun in his eyes, he knew they were driving east. He had learned things like that in Indian Guides. Even after the divorce, his father had taken him and Kiley to Indian Guide Powwows. So he knew that, every minute, here was farther from home.

They stopped eventually in some small Arizona town. Like a snake that gorges and then fasts, Denver had eaten nothing since Saturday morning. Smiling without smiling, he followed the waitress to a table in the back. The diner was small and almost empty, and there was a miniature jukebox on each red Formica table; Denver put a quarter in for Johnny Cash.

"Coffee?" The waitress was middle-aged with swollen feet. Her blonde hair had dark roots, and she wore it in a style that had been fashionable a decade earlier.

"Two Cokes," Denver said. He ordered—pancakes and eggs over easy with biscuits, sausage, and home fries—without looking at David. He might as well have been sitting at the table by himself. "And two of those doughnuts," he called after her. "The ones with the sparkles."

When the food came, Denver ate stolidly but without enthusiasm, as though he had run out of fuel and needed restoking. David was the greedy one. He reached hesitantly for the pancakes and when Denver did not pin his wrist or push his hand away, he stuck his fork through four of the thick circles and pulled them onto his plate and poured half the pitcher of syrup on top. Then he shoveled the food into his mouth, his head bent low, barely six inches from the Formica tabletop. Like a dog who fears an intruder at its bowl, David swallowed without chewing, and syrup coated his cheeks and dripped from his fork to his fingers.

The pancakes, saucer size, came nowhere near filling David's emptiness. When he looked up to see what other food Denver didn't want, he saw instead that the waitress was watching him. He had listened to enough lectures about his table manners to feel embarrassed, and he dropped his hands into his lap and sat up straight. The waitress was standing behind Denver and about thirty feet away. With the peep show over, she pulled a pad from her pocket and began totaling the bill of the old couple having breakfast at the corner table. Too late, David knew what he should have done, what he would do now if she would only look at him again.

A moment later, she did. David grabbed a doughnut with both hands and stuffed it into his mouth. The pastel sprinkles cascaded down his chin. Wordless, he could only talk with his body. Deprived of pens, pencils, chalk, and crayons, he had to write his desperation in air. He chewed with his mouth open. He spread too much jam on the half biscuit Denver had left and crammed it into his mouth on top of the doughnut and licked his fingers. Notice me, he wrote with his hands and mouth. Remember me.

Then the fry cook spun a plate toward the waitress and she turned away. Denver had put his fork down and was leaning back in his chair and sucking the last drops of Coke from the ice in his glass. David touched the edge of Denver's plate and looked up at the man.

Denver pushed the plate toward the boy as he might have pushed it toward a dog waiting hopefully beside the table. David emptied everything Denver had left uneaten—half a sausage, the spidery edges of egg white, and a few spoonfuls of ketchup and fries—into the circle of syrup on his own plate and ate it wolfishly. When it was gone, he was still hungry. As they were leaving, he touched Denver's arm and pointed toward the doughtnuts stacked in a pyramid beneath their plastic dome on the counter. He didn't think Denver would hit him for asking. But if Denver did hit him, the waitress would notice.

"Half a dozen of those frosted doughtnuts to go," Denver said. "The chocolate ones and a couple with nuts. My boy's still hungry." He was playing daddy again but without conviction.

On the table they had just left, stuck in syrup in the middle of David's plate, was a packet of mustard, ketchup, and Dave Magadan at bat for the Houston Astros. Now David had four packets left.

CHAPTER 29

As soon as Chuck arrived—having gotten another teacher to cover his sixth period class—Kiley shifted his allegiance to the parent who would not be leaving town. In an illusion of control, Kiley was riding Chuck piggyback when the doorbell rang an hour later.

Chuck opened the door and blinked at Tiffani. It was Chuck's quaintly owlish look behind horn-rimmed glasses that had first attracted Drew. Chuck was wearing wire rims by the time Tiffani came to work at Sherwood High, but she, too, had responded to Chuck's intelligence combined with his need for a guide through the thickets of daily life.

Caught playing family, Chuck did not know how to respond. On the telephone, the long cord carried into Kiley's bedroom so that Drew would not hear, Chuck had told Tiffani of the hypothesis that had been constructed from her data and of Drew's refusal to listen to reason. "I'm not crazy," Drew had said. "I can't just sit here and wait. I have to follow David. Even if I'm following him to the wrong place, it's better than not following him at

247

all." Unconscious of the fact that he was echoing Todd Carter, Chuck had spoken of needles in haystacks. He might have used the words "wild-goose chase." "You didn't see Alan Beckstein's picture," Drew had said.

Kiley, not willing to share his father, held on more tightly. Unsure how Drew would react, Chuck said, "I didn't expect you over, Tiff."

While Chuck was struggling with why Tiffani was standing amid the marigolds an hour after they had said good-bye at the copy machine, Drew opened the door wider. "Has Jake found out something else?" she asked.

"Me," Tiffani said and tugged at the ankh. She was carrying her laptop in its robin's egg blue case. Ill at ease, she ran the fingers of her other hand through her hair until the short yellow strands seemed like petals ruffled by the wind. "I had an idea."

It was an electronically driven idea, and, as Tiffani explained it, the balance in the room shifted. The barely computer literate pupils moved closer together while the twenty-two year old in her cowboy boots under a long sheer crinkle skirt stood a teacher's length away from them. "With a search engine like Alta Vista or Yahoo I can do a search using keywords like those mountains in New Mexico where they found that boy. There are lots of reports on crimes. There are—you know—hundreds of papers on any subject. I found Chuck a Ph.D. thesis at Michigan that had stuff about the buffalo slaughter and the railroads. If I try enough sites, I might find another missing boy. Or something. And then—you know—you could prove you were going the right way."

To Tiffani's surprise, she was looking at Drew and not at Chuck. Like Ruth and Angus West, Tiffani had been dragged along by Drew's refusal to accept the possibility of losing her son.

"Please," Drew said. "Please try it. Try anything."

Kiley rode his father into the kitchen. Digging his heels into Chuck's side, Kiley forgot for a moment that his mother was abandoning him. He remembered as soon as Chuck dropped him in a chair and started looking for teabags.

"They're in the cupboard to the right," Tiffani said. There was on Tiffani's face a fondness that Drew remembered from the early, playing-house years of her marriage. Before David and Kiley, she had found Chuck's sweet ineptness adorable. They had stayed up until 2:00 A.M. drinking red wine and debating the relative merits of Ingmar Bergman and Oliver Stone. They had overdosed on egg rolls, historical relevance, and Kung Pao chicken and made love in the morning.

Tiffani plugged in her laptop, and Drew turned the kettle on. Unaware of the thoughts of either woman, Chuck found the teabags and handed them to Drew.

"Thanks," Drew said with a warmth that came from the remembering and that made Chuck look at her as though there was some trick in the word.

Tiffani watched Drew pour hot water into a Heal the Bay mug with steady hands. She had never particularly wanted children. Or maybe she wanted a child at some hazy future time but not until she was thirty at least.

"I had another idea," Tiffani said as Drew handed her the tea. This time, even Chuck could sense Tiffani's embarrassment. It seemed to Tiffani that what she was going to say was lame, some weird thing out of *The X-Files*. But the other night and again now, Drew seemed to be commanding her to help. "When I surf the Net, I talk with a lot of people, you know, chat groups, and news groups, and maybe I could ask some of them to look out for David. There are websites for all sorts of things and places. I looked some up before I left school today, and there's a good link for New Mexico. Maybe people who live in New Mexico . . ."

Drew had the atlas open almost before Tiffani had finished. Arizona in green and New Mexico in yellow shared a single page. Drew's hand could travel across the representational space in the time it took her heart to beat twice. "Had we but world enough and time." They had too much world, hundreds of miles of world, and too little time to explore it. "Here," Drew said, tracing the cities along Highway 10, "or here, from Yuma, Arizona, down Highway Eight." With one finger she could cover the hundred miles north from Lordsberg, New Mexico, to what used to be

Apache lands. "And anyone who lives in the towns here. There's a hundred miles of national forests. And God knows how much private land. If someone saw David or the car, we'd know where to go." Her hands moved with a precision she didn't feel. I want a sign, she thought, a vision, an angel tapping me on the shoulder. I want to believe in something more than myself.

The telephone rang then and Kiley said, as he had said with each telephone call for nine days, "Someone's found David."

Drew didn't recognize the voice. It was a man's voice and slightly hoarse. For an instant she thought it must be the writer of the ransom note and was afraid that she and West had created an illusionary world and that everything they had insisted on believing was false.

"Mrs. Greene?"

"Yes."

"This is John Grogan."

It took Drew a moment to remember who Grogan was.

"I didn't recognize the boy in the snapshots you showed me Saturday. The color pictures. But when I looked at the poster you left, the black-and-white picture . . . My eyes aren't very good, and I'm not sure, but a boy who came in Saturday morning could have been the boy in the poster. I didn't think so at first because he had black hair, very short, and he was wearing glasses. But now I think it might be the same boy."

"Was the boy with anyone, Mr. Grogan?"

"He was with his daddy," Grogan said. "They looked a lot alike. The thing that makes me remember is that the boy couldn't talk. His daddy said he had laryngitis."

"Grogan saw him," Drew shouted as she hung up the phone. "David is alive." She looked up to see that Chuck, overcome with love for his son, was crying.

Through the rush hour traffic, Drew sat in the front seat of the van next to her mother. West sat in the back with Brisket and a hastily purchased airline crate. Ruth had covered the top of the crate with large red LIVE ANIMAL THIS SIDE UP stickers. In her lap Drew held David's yellow rabbit Ziplocked into its own plastic bag and, in a smaller Ziploc bag, a pair of David's dirty socks. The rabbit's ears were broken, one eye was missing, and patches of hair had been rubbed from its back and paws—the signs of love. It was the unharmed animals with luxurious fur and both shoe-button eyes intact that had been abandoned. Love the destroyer began early. In his love, David had devoured the yellow rabbit. What had she done in her love? She had mixed it with too much anger and too many conditions. Cringing, she remembered her coldness after David's last baseball game, when he had dropped two fly balls in a row. Flawed, she had wanted a flawless son.

"You remember how to harness Brisket?"

"You showed me four times."

"You'll remember to buckle . . . ?"

"You showed me four times."

"You remember that when he finds the scent he'll seem very intense with his head low and his shoulders forward?"

"Mother!" Drew said.

"I just want to be sure," Ruth answered.

Both Ruth and Drew were glad for this wan echo of their serious quarrels. The comfort of arguing kept the unthinkable at bay.

At the airport, West checked Brisket's heavy nylon bag and carried his own light one to the departure gate. Ruth stood at the plate glass window looking not at the huge white body of the plane but at the hole in its underside. She would stand there, staring down at the baggage carts, until Brisket was loaded. The baggage handler was to look up and wave as soon as he had put the crate aboard.

Ruth felt rather than saw Drew move to her side. The two women waited together and watched the crate disappear. The people, too, were being boarded.

"Thank you," Drew said.

"I love you, you know. I just don't show it very well." Even now, Ruth's voice was steady.

For years, it had been Ruth who had reached for Drew and Drew who had squirmed away until Ruth stopped reaching. Now it was Drew who put her arms across her mother's back and kissed the cheek that smelled of the orange peel shampoo Ruth had used to lather Brisket. Drew had not touched her mother more than perfunctorily in a dozen years, and her hand brushed the loose skin of Ruth's upper arm which sagged beneath her short-sleeved blouse. Everyone was a hostage to time one way or another. At sixty, Ruth had kept her energy and the muscles in her legs, but time had dissolved the firmness of her arms. Wasted time. Lost time. "I love you, too," Drew said.

West had been one of the first to board, and he sat, his legs twisted uncomfortably, next to the window. He could have had an aisle seat, but that was no better unless he kept his feet in the middle of the aisle to trip the flight attendants. He was too tall to be comfortable anywhere but first class, and no one traveled first class on a policeman's salary. The discomfort didn't make him angry. West was used to paying for the advantages of his size.

They would be flying east into the night, overtaking the night instead of fleeing from it. This time as always, the moment when the airplane left the ground was alchemy to Drew, the miraculous change of a thing into something better. The awkward, oversize machine lumbering down the runway became lighter than air. If the transformation was not quite straw into gold, Drew disbelieved it in the same way. It was a marvel to her still.

"Would you like to buy beer, wine, a cocktail?" The stewardess held the little bottles aloft.

West shook his head. Except for beer, he had not had a drink since he had walked out of the Sherwood Police Department to search for David Greene.

The plane was less than half full, and so the middle seat between Drew and West remained empty. They put their bags of peanuts and their plastic glasses of tomato juice and Diet Sprite on the tray table of the empty seat. If the plane had been full, Drew would have taken the middle seat, but she was grateful for the space between them. She thought of it as breathing space. During those first few days, West had been opaque to her. Now Drew felt she could close her eyes and put her fingers to his face and read what he hid there. She still remembered how soft his hair had felt when she had taken his face and pulled it down; and she was disturbed by the tingling in her fingers as she remembered.

"When we get to Albuquerque . . ." She was talking just to break the silence.

West had seen the countless ways in which human beings respond to death and devastation—from disbelief to glee, from the woman who insisted, "He can't be dead; he's bowling," to the man who politely excused himself and went into the next room and blew his brains out. He had watched a father who, told at supper that his son was dead, had leaned across the table and speared another piece of meat and eaten it with relish. He had, however, rarely seen anyone fight as hard as Drew.

Sealed together in air or by air, they had the enforced intimacy of people who had met a moment ago and would part a moment from now so that whatever was said or done in the present would be without permanent effect. The land below them was invisible. It was the land that Drew's fingers had traced on the map, but erased by clouds, it might as well not have existed.

"David called them cumulative clouds," Drew said. "When I gave him the right word, he said he knew they were cumulus clouds but he preferred his word because they were like lots of spoonfuls of whipped cream piled on top of each other." She made a small gesture with her hand. "I don't even know if I talk about David more because he's gone. I think about him more— almost all the time—but when you have children you use them as touchstones. I remember the month something happened because David was in nursery school then or Kiley had just gotten over chicken pox. They date the world for me. And validate it." The elegant twist of language was deliberate. Drew was no more capable of shoddy language than West was capable of shoddy detective work. They each took pride in what they did best.

"I have a son," West said. He did not look at Drew. It had been so long since he had shared anything of himself that he was awkward at it, like a tennis player attempting to serve years after he last picked up a racket.

Drew, who needed to know everything about everything, had sense enough to keep quiet.

West continued to stare straight ahead. "He lives in Connecticut with his mother and stepfather. He's thirteen."

When Ellen had taken Jack away, West had assured his son that nothing would change between them. He would always be Jack's father; Jack would always be his son. But, two years later, Ellen had married another man, and the boy, then nine, acquired Daddy Ron. Ellen had done nothing to sever West's connection to his son. Time and space had done that nicely on their own. And Ron was a decent man. He would have had to be, for Ellen to marry him.

Most adults learn ways to avoid the painful emotions they felt so strongly as children, and Drew's anger had always been her barrier against terror. She had been safe behind the wall of her rage. But there had been a price for safety, a deadening. If . . . when David's safe again, Drew thought, I don't think I'll be the person I was a week ago.

Tiffani sat at Drew's kitchen table with Drew's son on one side of her and Drew's ex-husband on the other. Ruth had not returned from the airport yet, so Tiffani was the shadow mistress of this house as she poured more boiling water from Drew's blue enamel teapot into Drew's environmental mug. It was a creepy but not entirely unpleasant feeling, and she remembered the tea parties she had forced on Jake and her mother when she was six.

"Fuckit," Tiffani said as she started a search. It was neither a curse nor an obscenity, merely an acknowledgment that something of import was beginning. Drew might have said, "Here goes nothing," and Ruth would surely have spoken of "taking the plunge."

Tiffani had logged on Jake's USC computer, and she typed in

his user ID and then his password. She could sit in Drew's kitchen and search the Web in Germany or Australia. All the universities in the world were a big reference book if you knew what you were looking for. Even the government archives were available. Tiffani typed in keywords. She was looking for a paper or Ph.D. thesis that would link crimes against children and New Mexico.

Ten minutes later, she had three windows open, cluttering the screen of the laptop. Luckily she had sixty-four megs of RAM—an expensive birthday gift from her brother—to keep the disk swapping down to a minimum. She was running two different searches in two different windows and, at the same time, using the third instance of Netscape to go to the most promising links. The Internet was unbelievably large, and the two searches were yielding hundreds of hits all over the globe. Unless she was lucky, it wouldn't be short, and it wouldn't be easy. Even if she only went to the most promising links, there could be twelve to fifteen hours of searching. She looked at her wrist. She was wearing a Swatch watch Jake had given her for her fifteenth birthday. It had a black plastic band and a green and blue face that she had once thought was the height of coolness. She decided to search the Web for an hour. Then she would log on to her main news group, Dawn Patrol, and see if Zorro or Weber Fan or Lissome Pink or any of the others lived along the highways where David might be going or knew anyone who lived there. She'd try the other chat groups and see what the New Mexico website had to offer. In the E-mail of people she only knew by pseudonym, she'd leave messages about an eight-year-old boy who might have short, black hair and not be able to talk and a stocky man in his thirties who drove a gray Honda Civic with a K in its New Mexico license plate. If she had no luck, she'd go back to Netscape.

Chuck leaned over to see what Tiffani was typing, and Kiley, frightened and jealous, put his hands over his father's eyes.

"I want a peanut butter sandwich," Kiley said.

It took Chuck three tries to find the bread, knife, and peanut butter. But, without being asked, he made the sandwich exactly the way Kiley liked it, trimming off the crusts and then cutting the sandwich into four quarters.

"Peanut butter?" he asked Tiffani.

She nodded without taking her fingers off the keyboard, and Chuck made her a sandwich, too.

CHAPTER 30

David finished two of the doughnuts before the car was back on Interstate 10. Even though he felt slightly sick—his stomach was like a suitcase someone had packed too full of heavy clothes—he held tightly to the waxed bag the waitress had handed Denver. A day or two earlier, Denver might have said, "Let's share those doughnuts, Andy," or "You go ahead and eat them all, son. Plenty more where those came from." Now that game—which Denver never thought was a game—was over; and Denver did not touch David or smile at him as they drove east through the afternoon.

What Denver had provided was not love, or even caring, but it had masqueraded as both. With the disguise torn away, David felt crushed by the weight of Denver's indifference. An indigestible rock of knowledge was caught halfway between his throat and stomach. He knew that Denver didn't want Andy anymore, that Andy was . . . David's vocabulary had always been too good for his age. There was even one fifth grader at Sherwood Elementary who would yell, "Here comes Big Words" when David crossed the yard. David knew that Andy was disposable.

He would run. When they stopped to eat again, he would run to the waitress or to the people at the next table and hold on to them. Or maybe he could run into the bathroom and lock the door. Maybe he could grab a pencil and write his name. As they drove through the silent desert miles, David exhausted himself by running again and again in his mind and flinging himself against the soft body of some nameless woman.

Tucson, sprawled to the left of Interstate 10, has 3,800 hours of sunshine a year. Bathed in sunshine, David could not keep himself from dozing. This time, no superhero came to help him escape. He lay atop the upper boundary of sleep like someone forced down on a bed of nails, and his dreams were pricked by monsters. He jerked awake when the car slowed and circled off the interstate. The indicator on the gas gauge was barely above empty. Denver snorted with annoyance. At the end, Denver was always impatient. But not impatient enough to be careless. He bypassed the big gas stations with their freshly painted signs and triple rows of pumps. He had an instinct for decay and for faces with incurious eyes. The gas station at which he stopped was mounded with discarded tires, and the attendant sat slumped in a narrow glass cage behind shelves of candy bars, potato chips, disposable lighters, and cigarettes.

"Stay in the car," Denver said.

David put his hand in his pocket and touched one of the packets. Then he shifted back and forth in his seat and motioned toward the door of the men's bathroom just beyond the tire dump.

"Just sit 'til I get back," Denver said.

With his hand on the door handle, David watched Denver walk his cowboy walk toward the man in the kiosk. But there was no one to run to here and no place to run except the desert. And he knew that Denver could run faster. Maybe there would be a bolt on the bathroom door and he could lock Denver out and wait for someone to come and rescue him.

Denver left a twenty dollar bill in the tray in front of the attendant and filled the Honda's tank. Then he went back to the booth to pick up his change. When he opened the door of the car, he was carrying a sack of candy bars.

"Eat these if you're hungry," he said. "We won't be stopping anymore."

He pulled past the bathroom and on to the blacktop. A mile or two down the road, he turned into a gravel space where a few stunted trees and bushes fed by some sort of drainage ditch grew at the edge of the desert. "You can pee there," he said, and pushed open David's door.

Although the light was fading, the sand was still hot, and David could feel its warmth against his ankles. The trees were perhaps forty feet beyond the car. Half hidden by waist-high scrub, David unzipped his jeans and urinated into the soft, warm sand. A stream of tears flowed, too, down his cheeks and into the collar of his jacket.

When the boy came back to the car, he crawled into the backseat. Denver turned to watch but said nothing as David curled with his head on a balled-up towel and his face buried in the crevice next to the seat belts. The seat was a trash heap of rubber bands, Coke cans, candy wrappers, scraps of cardboard and cellophane, and piles of coarse crumbs. Crumbs stuck to David's wet cheek as Denver swung the car around and headed back to the interstate.

The borders between states are almost invisible. A new speed limit, a different-shaped sign with a different name, a beacon welcoming the traveler to California or Minnesota indicate that something has changed. But the scenery, the language, and the feel of the road remain the same. Yet David, still facedown and unable to see the New Mexico signs, knew from the excited slam of Denver's palm against the door that something was different, even before he heard Denver say "Silver City, here we come," with an anticipation in his voice that mimicked the buoyancy of his "I got anything to do with it, you'll be the best hitter in the league, Andy."

David kept his eyes closed and prayed that when he opened them the kind Denver who had played ball with him all that long afternoon would be here in the car. For an hour David had protected himself with all the magic he could remember. He had counted backward from five hundred by fives and held his breath for at least a minute and circled each of his fingers three times. He had made bargains. If he was allowed to go home, he would empty the dishwasher the first time his mother asked him and never again drop his wet towel on the bathroom floor. He promised even more. He would take down the NO BROTHERS ALLOWED sign on his bedroom door and let Kiley come into his room whenever he wanted.

When David opened his eyes and sat up, nothing but the scenery had changed. They were climbing now, and they had shed the desert as easily as a teenage girl discards a pair of no-longer fashionable jeans. As the road twisted upward, Denver guided the car with hands that seemed so eager to be going in this direction—home—that first one and then the other fell from the steering wheel and waited, trembling, for an instant in Denver's lap before they leaped up and caught hold of the wheel again. David moved to the right edge of the seat so that he could see Denver's face. Once again, the man was looking down the road at things David could not see.

"Soon," Denver said, but whether he was saying the word to David or to himself was unclear.

Soon it will . . . Soon he's going to . . . Soon no one can . . . David's brain started all the logical sentences. Something stronger and more self-protective than logic stopped the boy from completing them. He kept his brain empty and his body rigid as he lay down on the seat again so he could not see where they were going or how quickly they were getting there. As he lay down, his hand brushed the vinyl gym bag Denver had brought back to the motel room and given to David with the words *Like mine, partner.* Denver had put his own bag in the trunk of the Honda with whatever secret things he kept locked there.

It is almost impossible to keep from hoping. They would have to stop for gas again, David thought, and next time there would be somebody to run to—a nice lady in another car. And maybe he could drop his baseball cards out the window and leave a trail. Even if most of the cards blew away, maybe some of them would stay and someone would see them and follow. David transferred the remaining packets to the pockets of his jeans. Then he unzipped the gym bag and stuffed baseball cards into his jacket pockets. His hand touched the square edges of his pocket Scrabble, and at first he didn't know what it was. Since David had had the much too dangerous thought of writing "Help, David Greene" in magnetic letters, he had kept himself from opening the Scrabble or even thinking about the game. And, though Denver had taken David's flashlight and comic books and all his markers, the man had had no interest in the word game.

Lying on his side so that even if Denver looked back the man would not see what the boy was doing, David pulled the Scrabble open for the first time in two days. The three Clue cards sat on top of the alphabet soup of letters. In that last game, Colonel Mustard, carrying his riding crop and wearing his safari hat, had committed the murder with a coil of yellow rope in the billiard room. These unexpected bits of home, the edges of the cards dog-eared and the billiard room stained with grape jelly, made David start to cry, and the sobs came in whoops and gasps that rose and burst and began again.

"Shut up," said a voice from the front seat that didn't sound like Denver. "Your mother's not coming back. Not ever. Shut up, or I'll kill that damn dog she gave you."

David pressed his mouth into the dirty towel until the sobs grew shallow and trickled away. Then, in the growing dusk, he cupped the tiny letters in his hand. It was easy to find E and D and the N he needed, but he had to search a long time for a V. When he had written "Help David Greene" and put the game inside the waist of his jeans—it was too big to fit into his pocket—and zipped his jacket over it, David sat up again. He held the three Clue cards between his palms as tenderly as he had once held a baby chicken hatched in the school science lab. He felt the heartbeat of the cards as he had felt the thump of the bird's chest. The cards were a sign that everything would be all right; the cards were a sign that he was going home.

Somewhere between Lordsburg and Silver City, the engine began to sputter. Denver pushed down on the gas pedal as though he intended to force the car into smoothness, and for a moment the car seemed to respond. Then the Honda started to jerk again.

Denver reacted with the quick anger that had flared up so often during the first week and had burnt out equally quickly. David was almost comforted by the sizzle and spark of "Damn car!" It was better than the awful coldness in Denver's eyes.

"Damn car!" Denver floored the gas pedal again, but the car continued to shake and quiver. He took his boot off the pedal and coasted into the right lane. They had left the interstate at Lordsburg and were climbing out of the high desert plains full of yucca and prickly pear cactus into a landscape of pinion and juniper trees. Slowed to fifteen miles an hour, the car still labored and heaved like a horse given too heavy a burden.

They must have spent twenty minutes lurching down a road carved out of the forest, with ponderosa pines and dense spruce barely visible high above them, before they saw the truck stop off to the right. Pink neon spelled out FAT STAN above a fat boy outlined in blue neon and loaded down with green neon hamburgers and shakes. Fat Stan ran to the edge of the sign, faded, and began his neon run again. Denver drove under the sign and down the length of the one-story building and parked in the shadows beyond the two rows of square, well-lighted gas pumps with their *Pay inside* labels.

There were two eighteen-wheelers on the far side of the diesel pump with their lights off and their drivers sleeping in the cab. An assortment of Blazers, Broncos, and battered pick-up trucks was sprinkled in front of the coffee shop. The gray Honda, lost in the midst of dozens of similar cars in Los Angeles, was an interloper here.

David moved until his shoulder was touching the window; then he put his right hand on the door handle.

Watching from his hiding place in the shadows, Denver had found what he was looking for—a tin-roofed space at the edge of the building and a man in coveralls blocking the open hood of a car. He started the Honda's engine, and the car lurched toward the man.

The mechanic, fair-haired and no more than twenty years old with his cheeks still streaked by acne, listened without looking up. His coveralls seemed to have been made for someone thirty pounds heavier.

"Can you take a look?" Denver asked.

"Sure," the boy said and kept both hands in the steel belly of the car he was working on.

"Now." The demand in Denver's voice made David cringe. The mechanic paid no attention to the tone.

"Sounds like fouled-out spark plugs," he said cheerfully. "Could be a bad spark plug wire. Or maybe you got a blocked fuel filter. I'll take a look when I'm through changing some hoses here."

Denver had the sociopath's instinct for other people's weaknesses. He had flattered and wheedled his way to safety more than once. He could find rotten spots, bruised places, and push them in, but he could sense the lack of weakness, too.

"Hey, sure," Denver said, grinning at the boy. "Thanks a lot. Just eager to get home. I'm dog-tired right now."

"Go get a piece of grandma's apple pie." The boy pointed his wrench in the direction of the coffee shop. "It's something else. And a couple of cups of my dad's coffee. That'll wake you up." He neglected to mention that his mother was the cashier and book-keeper and that they made enough money in the summer to survive the winter.

For a few minutes, it seemed that Denver was not going to move, that he would wait in the car for however long it took until the car was repaired. But the boy kept looking at the Honda as though he were disturbed by this breach of the usual etiquette.

No one sat in a car in the dark when there was apple pie and peach and cherry and strong coffee and flourescent light inside.

"Guess we'll get some of that pie," Denver said at last. His grip on David's wrist was tight enough to hurt.

The building was long and low, made of cement blocks and divided into a coffee shop at one end and a small general store at the other. Tampons and crackers served the needs of the general traveler. No-Doz, disposable razors, and cases of motor oil provided for the truckers. Except for the cashier, there were no women in the place, and the mechanic's mother was as stringy as a hen that has been rejected for the stewing pot. The men were rough and booted and not different enough from Denver to be trusted.

Denver waited for a moment near the chalkboard listing meat loaf and chicken-fried steak as the dinner specials, but no one came to tell them where to sit. The cashier, who was also acting as waitress for this night shift, had other things to do. Denver maneuvered David to a table in the far corner that was as much in shadow as flourescent lights allowed. At the next table, two young men pushed at each other and argued over fishing line.

In his fantasies, David had run to the forgiving arms of his mother. He searched the restaurant and saw only men with dark stubble on their chins and no welcome in their eyes.

"The specials're gone." Her voice was mean, although meanness was not her intent. It had been a long day. Every day in the summer was a long day.

Denver glanced at the menu. "We'll take two pieces of that cherry pie," he said, making only a halfhearted effort to charm.

"Gone," she said.

"Apple pie then. And two of those Jolt colas."

As he had done in the Sherwood Galleria, Denver used his glass for protective coloration. David found that he was thirsty and drank his cola without taking the glass from his lips. Both pieces of pie sat on the table untouched.

They waited. Denver's wait was the simpler one. It would take a certain amount of time for the mechanic to get to the Honda and another chunk of time before the car was fixed. Perhaps an hour. Denver could afford to wait. What he had to do was always done past midnight and before dawn. There was plenty of time.

David played chess badly. His father had taught him, and mostly because Chuck wanted to, they played on the weekends they spent together. Left to himself, David preferred the wizards, warriors, and magic spells of Dungeons & Dragons. But he experienced this waiting as though he were part of a chess game—not the mover of pieces but Denver's pawn—and this restaurant the board on which he had been set down. In the car, David had thought that, freed from the car, he would simply run. Instead, he planned and discarded moves for himself. If he went to the men at the next table, Denver was too close and would pull him back before he could give them his Clue cards and the Scrabble. And they had not looked at him once. They would not care if Denver took him back.

None of the men in the restaurant had looked at him. None of them would care. If he went to the bathroom and locked the door and banged and kicked the door with his feet, maybe he could make them care. Would Denver let him go alone? Denver's fingers had been so tight around David's wrist that there was a blue mark where his thumb had pressed.

Opening up one line of attack, David put his fork in his pie and pretended hunger as the crust reached his mouth. He swallowed, put down his fork, and stood up.

"Where're you going?"

David pointed to the alcove beyond the counter with a woodburnt RESTROOMS sign on burled pine and a wooden hand signaling toward the right.

"Later," Denver said. "We'll piss when the car's ready."

David sat down and, because Denver was looking at him with a look that was not suspicious but seemed, around the edges, troubled, the boy tried to smile. He put his face closer to the pie and stuffed his mouth and tried to keep smiling as he chewed.

The woman who came in then was no more than twenty, and the soft-faced man with her was within a year of her age. A sleepy two year old lay against the woman's shoulder; he sucked at a strand of her long blonde hair. The toddler's feet bounced against his mother's rounded belly. She was already six months pregnant with the baby who would dislodge if not replace him.

David did not think or plan. He ran across the coffee shop to the safety of her arms, pulling the Scrabble game from his jeans and holding it out to her as he ran. He pushed it into the woman's hand and then circled her waist with his arms and wound his fingers into the loops of her jeans. The boy on her shoulder, startled awake, began to cry.

"What the hell," said the man.

"Open it, open it," David shouted, but the words were unintelligible. "Save me," he yelled, but all that came from his mouth was a high-pitched wail.

Sensing David's terror, or perhaps merely so full of the chemicals of approaching motherhood that she had tenderness to spare, the woman did not try to push the boy away. She was holding her son with one arm. She took her free hand and brushed it against David's hair.

"Come on, Andy."

Denver, as quick as the tigers he admired, had already reached David. Now he put his hands on David's shoulders as though to wrench him away. David held on more tightly and shoved his Clue cards into the back pocket of the woman's jeans. Puzzled, the woman did not relinquish the boy.

"What's wrong?" she asked. And David couldn't answer.

"He knows his momma's gonna be mad when we get home," Denver said, improvising. The words sounded flat and artificial. Always, before, Denver had spun his tales at the beginning. Always, before, the end game had an inexorable shape. "He ran out on his chores." Denver's tongue was loosening. "And sassed her, too. We're near home now, and I sure wouldn't want to be in his shoes. His momma's got a heavy hand when she's riled."

"No." David mouthed the word. "He's not my daddy."

"I don't know," the woman said hesitantly. She was still stroking David. "He seems awfully scared."

"Got a right to be." Denver turned to the man with a "We know women" grin. "But it'll blow over. By morning his momma'll be making him pancakes."

The man was tired—tired of driving, tired of his crying child and his wife who had unaccountably gotten pregnant again, tired of standing there. "Forget it, Kathy," he said. "Let the boy go with his daddy."

She let her hand drop to her side, and Denver reached around and pulled David's fingers from the waist of her jeans. Then he held the boy tightly under one arm, as though he were hugging him, and took the unopened Scrabble from the woman.

The young mechanic had already replaced the spark plug wire when Denver led David back to the car, opened the door, and pushed him inside. The boy did not hear Denver's whispered, "Keep quiet," but he felt the twist of his arm that accentuated the words. With his other hand, David reached for the steering wheel and pushed as hard as he could on the horn. The sound was as shrill as a scream, but no one came.

"Crazy kids," Denver said, and handed an extra five dollars to the mechanic. "Home's gonna seem real good tonight."

Denver put the Scrabble on the dashboard and drove along the shadowy edge of the parking lot and down the deserted road beyond. He parked and turned off his headlights but kept the motor running as he opened the game and read what David had written.

"Bad boys get punished," Denver said. "Andy's been a bad boy." Then he took the handcuffs and cuffed David's hands together and turned the car back to the highway. The desolation David had felt during those first days with Denver returned. It settled like fog inside his brain, and smothered his will.

An hour later, when she was getting undressed, the woman found the Clue cards in the pocket of her jeans. Her son, who was bouncing on her bed, grabbed at the cards. But he was only briefly intrigued by the pictures. When he dropped the cards, she picked them up and put them facedown on the dresser.

CHAPTER 31

They landed in Albuquerque a few minutes early. While Drew waited for Brisket to be unloaded, West checked the paperwork on the Jeep Cherokee Drew had rented over the phone. Unexpectedly, despite West's pretense of slowness and Drew's insistent drive, they fell into the same rhythms, much as they had done in David's bedroom the first day they met.

The dog licked Drew so furiously that she had to put up her hands to defend her face. She poured some water into a plastic cup she had taken from the plane. Brisket was a sloppy drinker, and by the time he had finished, the sleeve of Drew's sweater was drenched. She stood near the back wall of the baggage claim area guarding the dog and the flight bags and watching the other passengers stand three deep at the carousel while they waited to retrieve overstuffed, strapped-up pieces of their present. Amid such solidity, her own luggage—a toothbrush, another pair of jeans, a clean sweatshirt—seemed as insubstantial as her future. The other travelers were hunters home from the hill, come back to wives who had welcomed them and then left to get the car and to children who were now clinging to their thighs; but her life was tentative—present imperfect, future uncertain. She saw West lean toward the far edge of the carousel and pick up Brisket's bag and hold it effortlessly above his head as he turned and walked toward her. And she was surprised once again by the delicacy of his hands.

Without discussion, Drew and West moved toward the thicket of telephones in the lobby. Without discussion, they separated, protecting themselves by inserting their calling cards into phones that were far enough apart so that neither of them could hear what the other was saying. They would not let bad news strike from behind. If the news were bad, they would have a chance to read it in the other's eyes.

Drew had dialed home before the busy signal reminded her that Tiffani would be using the line to surf the Internet. She fished out the number of the cellular phone Chuck had borrowed and felt, for a stinging ten seconds, the humiliation of calling her own house and asking for Chuck's lover. Then she ignored the sting. There might be time in the future for shame and anger. Right now she would have taken off her clothes and stood naked in this airline terminal if it would have brought her one step closer to finding David. "But at my back, I always hear Time's winged chariot hurrying near . . ." Andrew Marvell's poem had been echoing in Drew's head all afternoon. "And yonder all before us lie Deserts of vast eternity."

"Nothing yet," Tiffani said. "I've posted messages on some news groups, and I've left E-mail a dozen places. And I've, you know, got more links to follow." In a year of avoiding Tiffani, Drew had never heard her say more than "Hello" on the telephone. Even distorted by wire, Tiffani's voice was more confident than Drew would have expected, with the slurred casualness of someone brought up on the other side of the foothills that separated Sherwood and Beverly Hills from Encino and Van Nuys. Tiffani was a valley girl, raised in the heat of valley Septembers and cooled by its malls.

"Thank you," Drew said. "Thank you, Tiffani. For everything."

Ruth was next on the phone.

"He's fine," Drew said. "Thirsty. And happy to see me."

"When are you coming home?" Kiley asked.

"Pretty soon," Drew said. "I hope soon."

West was finished before Drew, and by the time she could get Kiley off the phone, he was standing next to her with Brisket's bag in one hand and the dog's crate in the other. West shook his head even before Drew asked, "Have the police found them?"

"We'll talk in the car," West said. It was four hours from Albuquerque to Mogollon, Glenwood, Pleasanton—names on a map. His job and his isolation had let West stalk through the days as bluntly as he wished. At first, it had pleased him to take no notice of Drew's feelings. Then he had found himself trying not to hurt her.

"You're right," Drew said and even managed half a smile. "We shouldn't waste time." The broken record kept spinning. "And at my back I always hear Time's winged chariot hurrying near."

West drove. Drew navigated. The southwest quarter of New Mexico was crumpled on her lap—cruel, stark, and filled with lightning storms in June. Twenty-five million years ago volcanos had spat out the Mogollon plateau, and in the 1890s the prosperous town of Mogollon had separate red-light districts for Hispanics and Anglos. Now it was a ghost town; less than a dozen people lived there.

During the plane ride, Drew had read guidebooks. There were one million people and seventy-three mountain ranges in New Mexico, and the lowest place in the state was a thousand feet higher than the highest peak in the Missouri Ozarks. The books were guides to beds for the night and chuck wagon feeds and old silver mines which could be visited by tourists who were willing to pay for their history. The books were worthless. They could guide her toward nothing that mattered.

They didn't talk until Drew had directed them out of the airport traffic and onto I-25 which led south from Albuquerque to El Paso, Texas. She spread the map of New Mexico wider. "We'll turn off at Socorro—that's about seventy-five miles—and go west on Highway Sixty," Drew said.

The clerks at the three car rental agencies had been vague about getting to the southwest, so Drew had mapped her own course. A third of the people in New Mexico lived in or near Albuquerque. Most of the rest lived directly south, in the irrigated belt along the Rio Grande. Where Drew was going—the high mountains and arrid, treeless plains of the southwest—there were few people.

"There's a state road that starts at Datil," Drew said, "and beyond a place called Reserve, it hooks up with Highway One-eighty which is where we want to go. Taking that diagonal, we'll slice off a lot of miles." She looked from the big map to the smaller map—to the spiderweb of trails and creeks in the Mogollon Mountains where Alan Beckstein's skeleton had been found. "We'll save time."

"They'll find the man," West said at last. "There's a watch out for the car, and they've alerted the ranger stations at Glenwood and in the Gila Wilderness."

Drew knew that West was telling the truth but only half the truth, and she held her finger to the flame: "They won't find him soon enough?"

Once again West admired Drew's refusal to pretend. There would be an uproar, and the FBI would storm in, competing with the state police; and a hundred man-hours of checking records would identify the car and the man. But that would only come later—after the body of a child was found. "We'll do what we can," he had been told on the phone. The voice was skeptical. "But what you've told us is a pretty far reach."

West spoke carefully. "The man has called attention to himself this time. Whatever he did before was done in the shadows. I don't think anyone ever looked for him before. This time, people will have noticed him—in motels or restaurants or on the street. The police will get descriptions and make a sketch and show it around. I'd guess that he was raised near those mountains. At least he must have lived there for a while."

"And David?"

West was aware of how much it cost Drew to ask that question, and he answered it as gently as he could. "It's David who has pushed him into the light."

When they reached Socorro, West pulled off I-25 and into one of the fast food restaurants that line the highways of America and make New Mexico seem no more foreign than the nearby strip mall at home. He had his choice of Taco Bell, Denny's, Burger King, Pizza Hut, McDonald's, and Tastee-Freez.

"We don't have time," Drew said.

"We need to eat," West said as he left the car. "And to drink something. Whether we want to or not."

Drew gave Brisket water and walked him up and down a grassy strip. Five minutes wasted, Drew thought, although she knew it wasn't. She put Brisket back in the car and found a phone.

Tiffani was buoyant. She was young enough to be captured by this as a game and enough of a hacker to be exhilarated by her own skill. "Somebody saw them. This afternoon. I've been trading E-mail with a fifteen-year-old boy in Arizona. His mother's a waitress, and she brought home a story about this weird boy who ate like he was starving and left this weird packet of junk on his plate. She brought it home to show her son. He's asking everyone in his chat group to look out for the car."

West had bought them hamburgers, large-size Cokes, and two cartons of coffee apiece. He had finished his hamburger and was feeding the rest of his bun to Brisket when Drew ran back to the car. Then it was Drew's turn to eat while West took her notes and telephoned the state police. Drew's elation—David was alive and unhurt and what they had guessed was no longer a guess but a fact—was felt by Brisket. Hoping that Drew wanted to play, the dog whined and put his front paws on her shoulders. She fed him a chunk of her hamburger.

West did not even try to disguise his anger. It was, West said, too late for the police to do anything more tonight. The dispatcher had said it was hopeless to try to find anyone in the Gila Wilderness after dark. They would send patrols to Glenwood in the morning. It was unnecessary for Drew or West to say aloud what they knew—that the morning would, almost certainly, be too late.

They stopped twice more at roadside phones. The flatness of Tiffani's voice answered their questions even before they listened to her words. This part of New Mexico had been a battleground. Half a century of war against the Navajos, Apaches, and Comanches had been fought here. The vanished warriors were remembered in black print on the maps Drew held: Apache Creek, Apache Mountain, Apache National Forest. After a while, it rained briefly and violently, and the sky was split by flashes of lightning.

They had reached the difficult place, beyond Reserve, where one fork of a Y led to Highway 180. "Which way?" West asked.

Drew slumped in her seat, carried under by fear and exhaustion. She was like a patient whose fever breaks and allows her to see that the promises of her dreams were only hallucinations. She stared at the map without seeing it.

West shocked her with the cruelest words he could find. "David may die. He may already be dead. But if you give up now, you'll spend the next ten years wishing you were dead, too."

His words pounded like fists against Drew's face. She bent her head into the beam of the map light. "The left fork takes us to One-eighty," she said.

Ahead, to the south, the lightning had set fire to the manzanitas. In the Mogollon Mountains, June was the heaviest month for wildfires, but most of the fires burned out by themselves. In July, the monsoon rains would come, and the fire danger would be over.

They drove south another thirty miles while Drew's eyes moved from the big map to the small one and then to the clumps of brush that masked the edges of the road. Off of Highway 180, a dozen dirt roads led to the edge of the wilderness—to South Dugway Canyon, Red Colt Canyon, Deloche Canyon, Mineral

Creek, and Dripping Gold Spring. Nine miles of impossible road led up to Mogollon and, seven or eight miles above that, to the Sandy Point Trail. They had come to the Mogollon Mountains, but it would take them days to explore all the roads into the forest.

The Becksteins' detective had reported that the campers who found Alan's body had hiked in from Forest Road 146. It was a place to start. Despite the map on Drew's lap, they missed the narrow entrance to the road twice. Even in daylight, the roads were elusive. They drove the four steep miles up 146 to the trail at Sheridan Corral, but there was no place to hide a car until they were within a quarter mile of the trailhead. Then West stopped the Jeep and Drew pressed Brisket's nose against David's socks and let him out of the car to search the dirt for David's scent. But Brisket found no trace of the boy, and no car was hidden among the oak bushes and mesquite.

"Let's call once more," Drew said. It was long after midnight now and cold. They had followed two more forest roads, with Brisket searching the darkness behind each patch of junipers and Drew swinging the flashlight from one side of the road to the other, hoping for the glint of metal. They had found nothing. Drew put on her sweatshirt. "Maybe . . ."

Glenwood was a dot on the highway—trailers and propane tanks, a few houses with roses or hollyhocks in their front yards, three motels, a cafe, and a bar. There were no lights and no sounds, and they drove up and down the highway twice before they found a pay phone outside the general store.

"I got a hit," Tiffani said, wide awake and without preliminaries. "Some guy at the University of New Mexico wrote a paper. Five years ago, some bones—belonging to a child but too chewed up to be identified—were found. Killed by a cougar, they guessed. It seems, you know, like it was near where they found the other bones."

"How near?" Drew asked.

"Somewhere on Holt Mountain."

Drew picked up the map that Anne Beckstein had given her. She remembered, with utmost clarity, some bad World War II movie she had seen in a film class where the navigator breaks down and the copilot has to plot a course to the target and if the plane doesn't reach the target and destroy the German factory all will be forever lost. North of where they had been searching and south of Bear Wallow Mountain, there was a thin line—the thinest of unnamed lines—leading to a trailhead.

Drew put her finger on the line.

CHAPTER 32

They drove through Silver City around midnight, although David had no idea of the time or the place. After they turned north onto U.S. 180, Denver drove faster. It was sixty miles from Silver City to Glenwood.

Glenwood was sleeping. Glenwood was always asleep when Denver returned home and still asleep when he left again. In mountains full of ghost towns and ghost warriors, Denver was also a ghost. It is doubtful if anyone would have recognized him. He was only eleven when his father drove away from the mountains, shoving the boy's head out the window of the car and telling him to take a last look because he was never going to see the mountains again. But the people in Glenwood—those who were old enough—would have remembered that the man had cut the throat of the boy's dog before leaving.

Denver turned off his headlights and coasted toward Pleasanton. There was no moon, but even in the dark, he found his way to the forest road. Whatever his impatience, he drove slowly down the dirt road. In a rainstorm, it was impassable.

Tonight's storm had had more lightning than rain, and the road was still dry enough for Denver to park under the cover of juniper trees. Leaving David in the car, he walked to the back of the Honda and opened the trunk. David was right; Denver kept his secrets there. The knife was a Buck Frontiersman with a seven-inch bowie blade. It had a nickel bolster and a nickel guard and a hilt of silver and polished cherrywood. The blade, of course, was stainless steel. It was the knife Denver's father had used to punish a bad boy by killing his dog. The knife had cost fifty dollars when his daddy bought it, but a new Frontiersman costs a hundred twenty-five today.

Denver attached the knife, in its cordovan-colored leather sheath, to his belt. The switchblade knife was in his pocket. As good as he was with a switchblade, that skill had come later. He had gutted rabbits with the Frontiersman when his hands were barely big enough to hold the knife.

When Denver opened the passenger door, David threw himself across the seat and held as tightly as he could to the steering wheel. Denver dragged him out of the car. For a moment, David stood panting in the road like a horse that has been ridden too far too fast. Then he ran. In ten strides, Denver caught up with him.

Denver had never handcuffed a boy for the walk into the mountains. It had never been necessary. For an instant, he seemed uncertain what to do. Then he pushed David in front of him. This boy was different. This boy could not be trusted to know his part in the ritual. But the handcuffs could be—would have to be—taken off later when there was no place to run.

The trailhead was half a mile ahead, but Denver had his own trails. Pushing David in front of him, he moved into a trackless wilderness. And when they had disappeared into the trees, there was no path to mark their passing.

The hike should have taken less than an hour, but the hand-cuffed boy slowed Denver down. Whether deliberately or because he could not keep his balance, David walked unevenly, as though he were a toddler not yet steady on his feet. Ninety minutes later they were still in the woods. At a stream—unexpectedly full of water—Denver had to pick the boy up and carry him. He carried David for five minutes and then, suddenly angry, hit the boy and threw him down.

"It won't do you any good to cry," he said. "Andy has to be punished."

It was the only thing he had said to David since they left the car.

This time, Drew ran with Brisket, weaving from one side of the road to the other while West drove slowly behind. It was less a road than an old stream bed dotted with clumps of juniper. Steep hills, so dense with brush that cactus crowded against manzanitas and manzanitas against fire oak, rose on either side. Two-thirds of a mile up the road, Brisket sniffed the ground and pulled Drew toward a patch of three junipers. She raised her flashlight, and the beam shone on the fender of a car hidden behind the trees. Drew and West might never have stumbled on the car, just another gray shape in the grayness of the night.

"We've won," Drew thought as she shouted, "West! Here!" Then West's hand was over her mouth, and she realized that they hadn't won—not yet.

Brisket sniffed again and then leaned into his harness.

"Hold him back," West whispered.

"But . . ."

"I need a minute."

Drew held Brisket's harness. With her muscles aching to let the dog go, she trusted West and whispered, "Wait," into Brisket's ear. West spit into his hands and rubbed the dirt from the Honda's license plate and wrote the number down. The triumph Drew had felt a moment earlier ebbed away. "If . . ." Drew thought, and she might have been stabbed, the pain in her stomach was so sharp, ". . . if something went wrong, they could trace the man, find him. Even if he—she saw no face, only blankness where a face might be—even if he fled her down the nights and down the days and down the arches of the years, she would, like the Hound of Heaven, pursue him through eternity.

Then she wouldn't, couldn't, wait any longer. Even before West shoved paper and pen into his pocket, Drew held the yellow rabbit in front of Brisket's nose.

"Find David."

There were no paths into the forest here where Denver and David had entered, but, with his head low and his shoulders forward, Brisket picked his own path through the underbrush. They followed blindly twenty feet behind, dodging when they could the spiny cactus that rose out of the darkness as though newly created to block their way. Drew, pulled forward by the dog, had less chance to duck, and branches slapped against her face and cut her cheeks. Retribution, she thought, when the cactus quills pierced her legs and catclaw thorns raked her forehead. Deserved punishment for failing her son. She put up her arm to push the bush away, but the internal thorns dug deeper. If only she had been capable of offering David unconditional love.

Where Denver had picked David up and carried the struggling boy across a fallen tree and down into the stream bed, Brisket stopped abruptly. In the moonless silence, they listened and could hear nothing. Brisket circled the tree trunk once and then again.

Trying to remember what to do, Drew gathered up the lead and stood next to the dog. Brisket, bewildered by this breach of pattern, licked her hand. "If he loses the scent, don't call him off," Ruth had said. "Stay behind with a loose lead and tell him to find David." Drew pulled the rabbit from its plastic and pressed it to Brisket's nose. "Find David. Please find David."

Head up, Brisket made wider circles. But David had disappeared into darkness, leaving no scent behind.

"The other side of the stream," Drew whispered.

Since they entered the woods, West and Drew had said almost nothing to each other. What they were searching for might be miles away or just beyond the ridge. They might be alone and unheard or already marked as targets by this man they had never seen. West turned his flashlight on for just long enough to mark a place where the banks were climbable. Brisket leaped into the water and up the bank, but Drew slipped on the smooth, wet rocks and had to crawl.

For five minutes, Brisket worked the matted ground on the other side of the stream and found no vegetation crushed by David's feet and no footprint with the smell of the boy imprinted on the fallen leaves. Panic was as solid as concrete in Drew's throat, but she choked it down. "Find David."

Silent, West watched Brisket's dark shape make wider and wider circles. He could not afford to lose his silence, to let himself be drawn into the agony of this search. He could not afford anything that would make his eye less accurate and his aim less steady.

Denver had carried the boy deeper into the woods and then, impatient with his burden, had thrown the boy to the ground. Trackers call the places where a layer has fallen on the track body prints. The scent is stronger and stays a longer time. Plunging and pulling, Brisket filled his nose with the smell of David's body print and stood on soft leaves where the boy had sprawled on his back until Denver pulled him up again and pushed him up the hill. Shoulders forward, Brisket sank into his harness and began to lope.

Drew touched West on the shoulder and gestured, and he handed her the flashlight; she lit the ground ahead of her feet as Brisket went faster. The dog was forty feet ahead of them now, at the farthest reach of the longe lead. They had climbed more than a thousand feet. They were among the big trees, and the dog pulled Drew still higher into the spruce and ponderosa pine. There was no underbrush here, and their feet, sinking into a carpet of pine needles as thick as anything that could be bought in a store, made no sound. There was an almost imperceptible trail winding to the top of the ridge, and Brisket, his nose to the ground, ran up it.

The fire they had seen from the road hours earlier was far below them and miles away, but as they topped the ridge it flared up. In its light, they saw Denver and David in a bowl-shaped clearing perhaps a hundred feet away. The boy, his wrists still handcuffed, had been wedged into a crevice in a huge boulder. Nearly thirty years earlier, the fissure—carved by lightning during another summer storm—had been Denver's secret place.

Drew saw her son and, above him on the flat surface of the rock, a long knife of silver and polished cherrywood in a sheath the color of dried blood.

"David," she screamed, sending him her voice and her heart and then her body. Unconditionally.

She ran down the slope toward her son. As she ran, the patch of manzanitas on which the fire had fueled itself was consumed, and all was darkness. Running headlong, holding nothing back, Drew fell and dropped the flashlight and lost hold of Brisket's longue line. The dog, with forty feet of line flapping behind him, leaped on the boy, and—at the same moment—Denver slashed downward with his switchblade, catching the edge of the dog's head and running the knife from the top to the bottom of Brisket's ear. Screaming, Brisket shook his head to get rid of the pain, and the air rained blood. As a dog just come from a bath will violently shake the water off, Brisket splattered David and Denver with blood. The fire, fed by another copse of manzanitas, flared just as Denver—always most alive when he was pushed off balance—reached for the boy. West, standing in shadow beyond the reach of the firelight, raised the Beretta, but before he could fire, Denver, as gracefully as a dancer choosing his partner, had unsheathed the hunting knife and—a knife in each hand—whirled David in front of him as hostage and shield. As though they were participants in a pantomime, no one had said a word since Drew shouted David's name.

Drew stepped forward then, limping out of the shadow to stand in front of Denver, and made herself a target. Hands at her sides, she moved toward Denver's knives.

He saw her through a veil of time. "You shouldn't ever have left," he said.

At the same instant that Denver struck at her, Drew shouted, "Run, David. Away from me. Into the dark." Even as the knife sliced Drew's arm and shoulder, she put into those eight words all the tyrannical power that parents wield in the early years of the lifelong battle for control between children and those who created them.

"Out of the street." "Come here." "Get in the house." "Stop

that." "Right now." Those words were a parent's weapons. David was too old to obey blindly the command to run, but Drew's voice insisted.

And David ran—away from the firelight, into the darkness. Denver had thrust underhand, toward Drew's heart. Drew expected an even exchange—her life for David's. Yet, by instinct, she threw up her left arm, bent at the elbow, to defend herself. The knife, deflected, carved her arm between elbow and shoulder. There was no pain at first, only the sound of cloth ripping and a feeling of wetness as though warm water was being poured on her arm. Then came a sharp, stinging pain, and as she felt it, Drew could hear the sounds of David's footsteps fading.

Denver had struck with the switchblade. The hunting knife would have sliced Drew open, gutted her. But that ceremonial knife was consecrated to its purpose, and Denver was a second slow in realizing that he must coarsen it with unplanned blood. He raised the hunting knife then, its inch-and-a-half-wide stainless steel blade shining in the light of the distant fire; and Drew threw herself toward the shadows and was amazed to see, as her hands touched the ground, that the water flowing over her wrists was red.

Drew was not startled by the sound of the bullets. But it was only years afterward, when bits of what had happened worked their way through her dreams, much as shards of glass from some terrible automobile accident work their way out of the flesh to the surface of the skin, that she realized how deeply she had trusted West.

There was surprise on Denver's face, a child's surprise at the pain. "Don't, Daddy," he said, as he slipped to the ground. "Andy isn't bad." And he made sounds that might have been sobs.

The first bullet, striking just above the nipples, had punctured Denver's aorta. It was a textbook shot; the others were unnecessary. Denver let his head fall back against the rock as though it were too heavy for him to hold. The blood leaked into Denver's chest, filling it, making each breath more difficult. Drew stood there for a moment watching him drown in his own blood. She had never seen anything die before. When she was twelve, she had found her hamster already dead in its cage.

"You shouldn't have gone away," Denver said, and reached for Drew. "You shouldn't have left me behind." His fingers touched her ankle. He was sweating now, and pale, his limbs turning to porcelain. "Please. It hurts."

Drew stepped beyond her triumph to the most unexpected thought—that the dying man who had tried to destroy her world had once been someone's son. She knelt at his side. She did not touch him. But, as he struggled to look at her with glazing eyes, like a slaughtered deer trying to make sense of onrushing blackness, she said, "No, Andy isn't bad." And then she said softly, as she might to Kiley, "Go to sleep, Andy."

He did, his eyelids still half open. The gray-blue eyes that had been so similiar to David's were now staring sightlessly up at his secret place.

Then West was wrapping something around Drew's arm and pulling it tight, and she looked down to see that he had torn his shirt into strips and was bandaging her arm and shoulder with it. And she was aware how gentle those delicate hands could be. West held her a perceptible moment longer than neccesary and smiled. It was, Drew realized, the first time she had ever seen him smile.

The fire had died again, and there were only stars. "David," Drew called and got no answer. Whining, Brisket crawled toward them, the line so tangled around his legs that he was unable to walk. His right ear was shredded and his coat was matted with blood, but the bleeding had slowed to a trickle. West found the flashlight and, by its light, unbuckled Brisket's harness and set the dog free.

When Drew stood up, pain burned down her left side, an internal fire lit by the fuse of motion. She waited, rigid, until the pain began to recede. Then she took Brisket by the collar with her other hand and led him to the edge of the clearing. "Find David," she said for the last time.

West had bent over Denver and reached into his pockets. When he followed Drew, he was holding Denver's keys, including the key to the handcuffs.

They found David crouched at the base of a pine at the farthest end of a stand of trees. Brisket limped to the boy and lay with his muzzle on David's knee. Drew started to run to David—to hold him and keep him safe forever. But it was already too late for that. When the flashlight beam caught David's face, he wound his hands into Brisket's fur and shrank behind the dog. His ravaged face told them that David knew safety was an illusion and was aware how short forever was. This was not the boy who had slid from his bedroom window ten days earlier and left on the sill one oblong drop of blood. That boy would never come back. It was as though time had picked him up and carried him forward into some future for which he was not yet—and might never be—prepared.

Drew stopped a dozen feet away from her son.

"It's over now," she said.

David didn't move.

"You're safe now."

And still David didn't move.

"The man is dead. He can't hurt you."

David sat mute behind the barricade he had made of Brisket.

Drew wanted to say, "Nothing will hurt you. Not ever again." Because it was not true, she couldn't say it.

She moved a little closer and sat in front of David. Her face was at his level.

"It's time to go home, David," she said simply, and held out her hand.

He launched himself at her then, and she screamed with pain and joy as he ran into her open arms. Blood soaked through her bandage as he flung himself against her face and throat to prove to himself that she was real.

West handed Drew the key to the handcuffs, but she couldn't twist her arms to unlock them. So West knelt on the ground—kneeling, he was as tall as the boy—and said, "I'm a friend, David." He reached for David's hands, but the boy shook his head and backed away. There was no cruelty in West's silence now. Motionless, he held the key in his open palm until David was willing to be touched. Then he unlocked the cuffs with the same gentleness he had used to bandage Drew.

And David was free.

When they reached the clearing where Denver lay, Drew and West joined hands, with the boy between them, as though to rush him past the dead man whose half-open eyes stared once again at something David couldn't see. But the boy pulled away from his mother, and in the ugly grayness just before dawn he looked a long time at Denver. What he was looking for and what he saw there was a secret he never told.

It was daylight by the time they found the road. When they reached the Honda, David tried to open the door. West unlocked the car, and David leaned in and unzipped the gym bag. He took his baseball mitt and filled his pockets with his polished stones. When they had passed the car, David turned and picked up a dozen rocks and threw them, one after the other, at the windows. Neither Drew nor West tried to stop him. The glass filled with spiderweb cracks but did not shatter. Disturbed by the noise, Brisket whined and pressed himself against Drew. Then there was silence in the pale morning.

It was David who broke the silence. Like water forcing its way through a disused pipe, the words were rusty. At first, they seemed not to be English words at all. Drew bent and listened, and he said them again. "We're going home?"

"Yes," Drew said.

"We're going home?"

"Yes," Drew said again.

Then he raised his head and he was almost David, and the words were clear.

"I'm hungry. Can we stop for pizza?"

"Oh, yes," Drew said.